May Day

May Day
John Sommerfield

With an introduction by John King

LONDON BOOKS CLASSICS

LONDON BOOKS
PO Box 52849
London SW11 1SE

First published 1936
This edition published by London Books Ltd 2010
Copyright © Peter Sommerfield
Introduction © John King 2010

The publisher wishes to thank Peter Sommerfield,
Marc Glendening, Bob Crow, Alex Gordon and Brian Denny
for their assistance with this edition of *May Day*

A catalogue record for this book
is available from the British Library

ISBN 978-0-9551851-8-2

Printed and bound in Great Britain by
CPI Antony Rowe

Typeset by Octavo Smith Ltd in Plantin 10.5/13.5
www.octavosmith.com

London Books wishes to thank RMT
for its generous support in the
production of this book

'Men make history – but not as they please.'

CONTENTS

INTRODUCTION

Britain is in turmoil – the people are fed up with the excesses of big business; workers are told to increase production for less pay; the wealthy meet to plan how they can become even richer; the unions try to mobilise the power of the masses; links between government, arms manufacturers and the media are hinted at but never proven; disillusionment spreads; a march takes place; the police clash with demonstrators; a man is killed on the streets of London. This could be Britain today, but it is also a summary of some of the events driving *May Day*, a novel by John Sommerfield, first published in 1936.

Set over three days, some time during the 1930s, a snappy, italicised description of London sets the scene – '*The sky oozes soot and aeroplanes and burns by night with an electric glow. Railways writhe like worms under the clay, tangled with spider's webs and mazes of electric cables, drains and gaspipes. Then there are the eight or nine million people.*' *May Day* is about these people – their hopes, successes, mistakes, regrets, dreams, reality. Slogans show the way ahead – ALL OUT ON MAY DAY . . . WORKERS OF THE WORLD UNITE. The busmen are going to strike and everyone is talking about their union's plans for May 1st – the day of the workers. Change is in the air.

John Sommerfield was a politically active man who rejected the bullying aspects of capitalism and, for a period of his life, was an active member of the Communist Party. He marched and spoke at meetings and had his front teeth knocked out in a fight with either the police or Fascists. He fought in one of the International Brigades during the Spanish Civil War and, like many idealists at this time, held firm views on how society needed to improve. He was also open minded, a lifelong optimist, someone who believed in the worth of each individual, and it is these qualities that elevate *May Day* above much of the fiction dealing in social struggle.

This belief in the individual shows itself in the large number of characters who make up *May Day*. No single voice dominates, no central character is in control. The political is made very personal as a series of smaller sketches connect to form the bigger picture. Scenes shift and faces change, but the links are neat and effective – some complementary, others adding contrast and conflict – and they always push the novel forward. It is a complex, experimental approach, which could easily have failed, losing direction and focus, but Sommerfield pulls it off. The result is a fluent, highly imaginative piece of writing.

The author's own experiences, as well as his beliefs, back up the text. The first of the larger characters to appear is James Seton – Communist, seaman, Civil War veteran; like Sommerfield – who is on a ship anchored off Gravesend, waiting to return to London. The next scene shows his brother John and Martine, their child and dog, sleeping in a humble house near the Harrow Road. John is a carpenter at Langfier's Carbon Works, and while he is aware that trouble is brewing, he has been unemployed so Martine doesn't want him to strike, fearing he will lose his job. (Sommerfield had also worked as carpenter and spent periods unemployed).

The first day dawns, and the Thames is heaving with ships, the great dockyards of East London throbbing with activity, and soon we are inside the Carbon Works where 'two hundred and forty girls in ugly grey overalls and caps live, breathe and think, their fragile flesh confused with the greasy embraces of steel tentacles'. They are on piecework rather than proper pay, and the bosses are demanding a 'speed-up'. These young women are kept on until they are twenty-one and then let go, as their rate would have to be increased. The conditions are cramped and dangerous, and the girls are tired. Machines roar and hands are mangled. This is the world of Daisy Miller, Molly Davis and Ivy Cutford. The London Match-Girls Strike of 1888 hovers in the background.

From Langfier's Carbon Works the book spirals off into the wider city, dipping in and out of the lives of the Seton brothers and the bosses and a wide selection of connecting men and women, spreading out from East London into the West End and West London, crossing boundaries of sex and class, moving from terraced streets and factories to detached villas and parks. The book starts to build towards May Day.

Generally in literature, and the arts in general, then as now, the common people are stereotyped or belittled, or, if they are lucky, treated as curiosities before being dismissed to the margins, so when a novel is written from a more sympathetic position it is natural for the author to want to reverse the prejudice – but John Sommerfield resists this temptation. He remains even handed and rejects a more dogmatic approach, and by doing so opens the story right up, showing that maybe the bosses aren't benefitting as much as their power and wealth would suggest.

The best example of this is Sir Edwin Langfier, owner of the Carbon Works, who comes across as a decent man, but someone whose real power has been lost in a deal with Amalgamated Industrial Enterprises, a big organisation with a cynical approach to business. We see him in his chauffeur-driven Daimler, passing through Hyde Park, reaching Commercial Road, travelling along East India Dock Road, heading towards the shipyards, a rich man in one of the greatest cities on the planet, yet despite his position in society he is disillusioned and empty inside. His wife is the same, while their son Peter lacks any meaning to his life – walking in the park, attending a society dance, searching for love. Everyone is looking for love, whatever their backgrounds, but it is John and Martine who are happiest together – making do, Martine shopping in Portobello Road market while John grafts at the factory, appreciating what they have because it has been earned.

Towards the end of the book Sir Edwin tells Peter that he has let his son down, that because he has never had to work for anything he lacks direction. Against the odds, the reader feels sadness for the Langfier family, and by achieving this reaction Sommerfield strengthens the novel and shows that, on a deeper and more meaningful level, an exploitative system is no good for anyone – rich or poor.

Family connections are clearly important, a concentration of the larger family perhaps – John and James Seton; the powerful (and well-named) Sloane brothers; Sir Edwin and his son Peter. James is a loner in many ways, married to his politics, searching for his brother, but he doesn't find him until late in the novel, and not in the sort of circumstances either would have wanted. By chance James meets an old friend, Pat Morgan, and this other sort of brother is an interesting addition.

A sub-editor on a leading newspaper, Morgan is a Communist and former comrade of James Seton, from either seafaring days or the Spanish Civil War. Pat's workmate is Vernon – the name of John Sommerfield's father . . . a journalist – and through their work Morgan sees what the newspaper's owner is planning to write about the busmen and their May Day protest. He visits one of the printers, Jackson, an older Communist. We are left with impressions . . . possibilities.

When tragedy hits the Carbon Works, Ivy Cutford steps forward and finds her voice, mobilising the other girls in a doubly brave move given the position of working women at the time. Some of the most downtrodden members of the workforce stand up and fight back. The May Day march is passing . . . the factory gates are locked . . . mounted police fight the marchers . . . a truncheon is raised in the air. It is one of the most symbolic and dramatic passages in the book. The great propaganda posters of the period are unfurled in the reader's mind.

Writing nearly fifty years after the book was first published, in May 1984, in a Note to a new edition, Sommerfield said: 'When I wrote it I'd have probably said that *May Day* was socialist realism. Now I'd call it early '30s Communist romanticism. I'm not in any way apologising for the book's enthusiastic, simple-minded political idealism. Because it was a genuine idealism.'

He is being modest. There is plenty of social realism in *May Day*, and while there is also simple-minded idealism, that has to be better than cynicism – or apathy. His optimism is clear throughout the novel, but also in the Note, which is reproduced at the back of this edition. He romanticises Communism, but this wasn't unusual in the 1930s. Being a British Communist in 1936 was very different to being one in 1984, when the gulags and terrors were well documented. This was the time of the Miner's Strike, when the term was casually used to smear anyone who believed in workers' rights and the importance of a trade union.

Sommerfield also writes about the changes that had occurred in Britain since *May Day* was written, the better living conditions enjoyed by working people, and that only 'the truly rich and powerful' carried on regardless, as if nothing had changed except for 'electronic improvements in the means of selling goods and bending minds'. Twenty-six years since he wrote those words, and seventy-four years after *May Day* first appeared, the rich and powerful are still doing what they want, while the internet and digital technology mean the selling and bending have gone into overdrive.

Following his death in 1991, another wave of change has swamped us. The exploiters are the same, but come in different masks to 1984, never mind 1936. Cool Britannia, the For

Sale sticker stuck to every element of our infrastructure and culture, privatisation and globalisation and the expansion of the EU superstate, free-enterprise crusades and a nation in debt to mobile-phone companies, ultra-surveillance and a tightening of state control, the ever-increasing slaughter of the meat and dairy industries, a loss of national law-making and boundaries, the digital breakdown of life into dots on a computer screen, multinational threats to copyright laws – maybe even novels themselves.

Idealistic literature, whether naive or not, is more important than ever. Rather than a cut-price file to decorate yet another appliance, it can offer an honest and independent take on life that is beyond money. It stimulates free thought, promotes imagination, invites people to create their own imagery and stretch their minds rather than have them bent by big business. Books such as *May Day* matter. Conditions have obviously improved massively since it was written, but they did so because there were idealistic men and women willing to fight for change. Those who want to control and exploit others are still with us and will never go away, it is just their methods that have changed. Books from the past tell us about our lives today. Everything changes . . . nothing changes.

The 1930s produced a rich seam of London authors who captured the grittier side of society in their fiction – James Curtis, Gerald Kersh and Robert Westerby are some of the best – and John Sommerfield belongs in this company. He was a regular in The Fitzroy Tavern, just north of Soho, and knew at least Curtis and Kersh, who also drank there, along with the likes of George Orwell, Julian Maclaren-Ross and Dylan Thomas.

The so-called 'lowlife' novels of Curtis, Kersh and Westerby – *The Gilt Kid, Night And The City* and *Wide Boys Never Work* being examples – are set in the criminal alleyways of London life, and in particular the broader Soho area.

This was an exotic location that drifted into theatreland and the older areas of exoticism and sleaze around Piccadilly and the Strand. The West End was a world away from the factories and dockyards of East London, a place where classes and nationalities mixed, the daily grind of industrial labour remote and ignored, and yet the lives of the prostitutes and villains who fill these books were rooted in these communities.

Curtis, a dedicated socialist, a more 'difficult' man than Sommerfield but someone who lived and suffered for his principles, was interested in language, and his work captures the speech and slang of a range of working-class characters in a unique and vital way. Yet Curtis was also concerned with prejudice, and in particular the unfairness of the judicial system. He deals with miscarriages of justice, with the threat and reality of capital punishment. Interestingly, the hangman Pierrepoint was another regular in The Fitzroy Tavern. So too was Robert Fabian, aka Fabian Of The Yard.

In *Night And The City*, Kersh positions Harry Fabian – a cockney ponce and chancer, who tries to sell his girlfriend into slavery – against his honest, costermonger brother Bert. Fabian attempts to pass himself off as an American, mimicking the movies, but despite his charisma he is a desperate man doomed to failure. *Wide Boys Never Work*, meanwhile, sees Jim Bankley leave his job in a car factory and travel to London after witnessing a Soho razor-gang in action at his local racecourse. He is impressed by their flash motors and sharp suits and ends up joining the Franks mob, his hardworking father performing the same role as Bert. In these books the main characters are trying to escape the hard labour of their backgrounds through crime. They are dreamers.

In *May Day*, John Sommerfield has attempted something very different. His working-class heroes are interested in self-improvement, the struggle against exploitation and, in some cases, the removal of capitalism itself. This is the common people in their more everyday form. *May Day* deals in labourers and craftsmen and factory girls who would never dream of turning to prostitution – though Sommerfield does create the character Jenny Hardy to show the choices some women make, in this case one driven by want rather than need. AIE man Dartry has set up Jenny – a former Carbon Works girl – as his mistress. She has a flat in a nice part of London, with cash and jewellery and a secret boyfriend she hides from Dartry. She has rejected the factory floor, and in Jenny we see a clear recognition of the truths written about by Curtis, Kersh and Westerby.

The majority of Sommerfield's working-class characters are keen to take on their enemies rather than imitate their values. On the surface this might not seem as exciting as the 'lowlife' approach, but Sommerfield is a fine author whose writing overflows with energy and empathy. *May Day* and a similar novel from the period, Simon Blumenfeld's excellent *Jew Boy*, complement *The Gilt Kid*, *Night And The City* and *Wide Boys Never Work*. Together they present a broad picture of working-class London in the pre-war years and a reflection of the society in which we live today.

On its publication, *Left Review* called *May Day* 'the best collective novel that we have yet produced in England', and the prose never weakens. The text is loaded with philosophy and observation, glimpses of more and more lives, the endless tangle of those 'eight or nine million people' – the Langfier's maid Jean visits her grandfather in hospital . . . he has been moved from the workhouse and is dying of consumption . . . a surgeon operates to save the life of Mrs Riley . . . while her son Bolshie Bill fights for a fairer society . . . but the leader of the largest trade union is enjoying his power and wealth and craves arbitration . . . and all the time nature pushes at the bricks and mortar of the city . . . the trees blossom . . . spring scents the air . . . May arrives . . . a baby is born . . . nearby there is loneliness and fear . . . another mother kills her unwanted child . . . and a great yearning for love and meaning presses at the minds of the people. *Left Review* rightly added: 'Sommerfield gives us the true London – smelled, seen, understood.'

The book culminates in the May Day march, the clash of controllers and controlled, the people heading towards Marble Arch where General Fitzroy struts, passing along Fleet Street on the way, watched by Pat Morgan, a free spirit lurking inside the pre-Wapping machine. The General Strike of 1926 is referred to often as something to recall with pride, to emulate, a lesson from history. The message is clear – the struggle continues. The last line of *May Day* reads: 'Everyone has agreed on the need for a big change.' Again, those words could have been written today.

John King
London 2010

NOTE

The action of the story takes place between the morning of April 29th and the early afternoon of May 1st a few years hence. However, though the scene is laid in the near future, the author has no intention of making any historical forecast. It would be better to view the situations depicted as belonging to an *average* year between 1930–40 rather than to any definite date.

The author would like to acknowledge his thanks to his friend NJ for her invaluable help and advice.

PART ONE
APRIL 29TH

. . . Let us take factory chimneys, cannons trained at dingy skies, pointing at the sun and stars, and blinding their aim with their own exhalations: towering more than church spires, their long shadows leaning across lives more heavily than did the medieval darkness of the hand of God . . .

Then there are shining tarred roads, glistening shop windows, arc lamps nightly flowering into electric buds, geometries of telephone wires and tramlines, traffic-lights flinging continuous coloured fireworks into the air, a hundred thousand motorcars and buses.

There are even places where the earth bursts through the tar and concrete, exploding into parks and squares, sooty trees and green spearpoints of grass: flowers come up in the spring, rain threads the air, paints the roads into dark-glistening rivers mirroring the concertinaed images of a million artificial lights, and there is the River itself, bridged and tunnelled and filmed over with the oily wakes of ships, the river that bisects London and does not divide it . . .

As well as factories and offices and shops and banks and cinemas there are houses, boxes of brick complete with carpets, gas stoves, beds and secrets of soiled underlinen.

Twenty million squares and oblongs of glass windowpanes, conceal or make visible symptoms of humanity.

The sky oozes soot and aeroplanes and burns by night with an electric glow.

Railways writhe like worms under the clay, tangled with spider's webs and mazes of electric cables, drains and gaspipes.

Then there are eight or nine million people. It's rather hard to see where they come in, these quivering shreds of flesh amidst so much concrete and steel. *They weave patterns of movement in and out of the jaws and tentacles of machinery, running up and down scaffolds, sitting in offices, standing in shops, dawdling in drawing-rooms.*

The years of their lives waste away under the keys of type-writers, in the metal shavings from lathes, their youth burns up in the furnaces of boilers, melts in tears and sweat, dissolves away in the bubbling ferment which they have created and which creates them.

In this whirlpool of matter-in-motion forces are at work creating history. These fragile shreds of flesh are protagonists of a battle, a battle where lives are wasted, territories destroyed and populations enslaved.

Every true story of today is a story of this struggle.

MORNING

It was not yet light. The *Arundale* lay anchored off Gravesend, waiting for the tide. A faint, chill wind blew intermit-
tently, and the river water gurgled against the ship's sides.
Ashore, a few lights twinkled. The air bore a cold, lonely
silence of the hour before dawn. The complete darkness of
the ship's fo'c'sle stirred with the breath of the sleeping
sailors.

The obscurely glistening mud-reaches were beginning to
dwindle, and patches of scum and bubbles floated slowly
westward with the incoming tide. It was not yet light, but
the sky seemed faintly to undarken. The night was over.
Dim, greyish shapes loomed out of nothingness.

Two bells clanged suddenly on the bridge and were
echoed from away forward. The sound rang in James
Seton's ears and he half-awoke, sensed the warm fo'c'sle
darkness alive with the breathing rhythms of sleeping men.
Then he heard the lapping river water and felt the ship
straining at her anchor-cables in the rising tide. An image
floated into his drowsing mind, an image that had accompanied him to sleep, of a drifting constellation of lights seen
across dark waters.

What was it? Where had it been?

Then he remembered the river smell, the smell of wet
mud, and the lights of land, the roar of the anchor-chains
and the silence of the stopped engines, the shattering stillness that they aboard of the ship had not known for thirty-
six days. They had been away too long; they had been too
far.

The fo'c'sle was full of a cheerful buzz of talk as the men

turned out. 'Home today, boys,' they said, as they swung themselves over the sides of their bunks.

James shivered a little as he lowered himself on to the deck, and he looked around at the familiar faces, George and Bill and Harry, old Thompson and Peter Evans the Welshman . . . the familiar faces and the voices speaking accustomed accents. These had been his companions through the long days and nights, the men whose lives he had shared, with whom he had worked, suffered and been happy, eaten and drunk, played cards, sung songs, quarrelled and exchanged confidences. Today was the last day. They would come out of the shipping office with a little money in their pockets and walk away in different directions, to different destinations, with hopes and fears that were no longer bound together. This was the common way of the sea, the routine of James's life. But now (while he pulled on his dungarees, while he dipped his head into a bucket of water) he reflected on this coming break as if it were a new, strange thing.

Around him everyone talked and laughed. In a few hours they would walk the familiar streets, see the familiar faces of home. Then, when the welcomes were over, when the few little luxuries had been enjoyed, they would take up the struggle again, the cruel land struggle of looking for work until even the memories of this long voyage and exile would come to seem sweet.

James quickly dried himself, rolled another cigarette and went on deck.

Home today were the words that rang in his ears; he had been so glad at the thought that he had not stopped to consider what it really meant to him, who had no real home. But London was his birthplace: it was always to London that he returned. Here lived his brother John, here were the scenes of his childhood, streets with memories, a park where he had played . . . He had no real friends, no family, no place of his own; he could only look forward to the possibility of seeing

John, and now, thinking of him, remembering his hazel eyes, clear forehead and thick brown hair, his rather slow, pondering voice, it seemed to James as if that kind, honest solidity of his brother was a thing of which he had been long in need, a balm for that disquietude which he had suffered since he had left Spain, a fugitive from a revolt drowned in blood.

And James, still preoccupied, went with his mates to get the deck-gear ready for docking. But later, when they stopped and swilled down a cup of strong, sweet tea by the galley door, he joined in with their talk and his thoughts began to go with the words. With the tea still hot in their bellies they got up anchor.

Now, really, we are at our journey's end, James told himself. And either we will sail away again, or there will be the hungry, idle days, hoping before the grimy doors of shipping offices. He remembered the New York dockside last summer, men starving on the grimy pavements in bright sunlight . . .

Captain Ginnery stood on the bridge, silent, beside the pilot, his parchment face wrinkled as a walnut, pondering impassively. This was his last ship, his last voyage. He saw tall, white, ghostly factory chimneys standing up against dark skies, and white, sulphurous smokes drifting against dark clouds, and they threw land shadows across his mind, shadows overcasting his declining years that would be spent in empty land-idleness. He thought of his wife with a tender irritation: his children were scattered and gone from him; he had nothing to look forward to now, only memories of voyages and the masts of sailing-ships.

The sky lightened, the riverbanks evenly slid by. The ship glided so silently, so smoothly, through the grey, formless, early-morning scene that she seemed to go of her own accord, drawn by some huge magnet.

James looked at the three white chimneys that breathed

great rolling smokes against the dark horizon. Now these shadows are falling across our lives again, he thought.

But also scenes, half-remembered, half-anticipated, moved in his mind, of London in spring, the April air sighing down the channels of dingy streets, budding trees in squares, barrel-organ tunes breaking through the traffic song . . . memories and dreams that were about to become realities again for him. Somewhere, in a certain street, there is a door upon which he can knock and find his brother John.

* * * * *

Behind the blistered door, up four flights of dark, broken-down stairs, through zones of smells – stale cooking and wet washing, cats, old clothes, sweat and urine, the odoriferous motifs in the symphony of poverty – John and Martine lie sleeping. A shaft of early-morning sun sloping through the skylight slices the room into two twilit halves and spills over on to the bare floor.

Four breathing rhythms dwell in the air – John and Martine, the baby and Mick the dog. In a moment the alarm clock will ring, in a moment the four of them will open their eyes to a new day. Under the low, sloping roof the bare white room waits . . .

The room is long, made narrow by the slant ceiling; the long, bare boards extend their narrow perspectives like the planks of a ship's deck. Alone and high up at the top of the house, the room seems to John and Martine to bear them under the sliding clouds like a ship.

Now that John has got a job they are able to move to somewhere more convenient and less smelly. Yet they are attached to this room, that has borne them through their long months of poverty and unemployment. And Martine will not contemplate getting another place until they have paid their debts and have some money put by. (She comes from French peasant people, she clings to security.)

The alarm clock explodes into a shrilly startled clamour. Mick raises his shaggy head and thumps his long, mongrel tail on the floor; Martine half-sits up (holding the sheet over one plump shoulder) and reaches out to extinguish the clock. The angry noise stops, and Mick's tail thumping on the floor sounds loud. Martine closes her eyes and sinks back for a last five minutes.

John is dimly aware of the clock and turns over, clinging sensuously to the last delicious moments of sleep. Only the baby has not wakened, and he still dreams his wild, shapeless foetus dreams, drowning behind closed eyes in the darkness of the womb. (Each time he awakes he is reborn, into a new, strange, confusing world. His dark eyes cling to night.)

A hundred small domestic thoughts strive to pierce Martine's drowsiness as she burrows back into the warm depression made by her body during the night.

The ray of sunshine striking down through the skylight, the whitewashed walls, the sloping ceiling, pieced themselves together in John's opening eyes; he was dimly aware of Mick's tail thumping on the floor. Then Martine's warm mouth pressed itself to his, her blonde hair tickled his forehead. 'Wake up,' she said, 'it's Monday.' She had a 'small' voice, and she still retained her French accent. Now she laughed: the sight of John rubbing the sleep from his tousled head always filled her with a tender amusement.

They had been married eighteen months now, but still when they woke in the morning they looked at each other full of a surprised gratitude that they should be together, in the same bed . . . The rays from their eyes darted into each other's pupils, signalling, for all to see, that they loved one another truly.

Martine stuck one leg out of the bed and leaned over to

kiss John again and tell him to get up. The sunray slid across her smooth, firm back and round breasts as she slipped on an old overcoat. Then she ran out to the landing and put a kettle on. John, still sleep heavy, washed in a tin basin on an apple-barrel and then began to shave, a Woodbine stuck in one corner of his mouth. The faint warmth of the sun on his left side made him smile unconsciously at the thought of the spring and the coming summer. He dawdled over his shaving . . .

Martine, coming in with the milk, watched him for a moment, smiling too in sympathy. Then she made a sudden movement and said, 'Hurry, you've no time to waste now.' And they were silent and a little downcast, both thinking of the job, the blessed slavery that had come to rescue them.

He thought of those long, miserable months of unemployment and how sometimes he would wake in the middle of the night, in the spinning silence of the night, and hear Martine breathing and the breathing of the dog, and then perhaps the baby would make a whimpering sound in his sleep. He would be quite wide awake, oppressed by the thought of their room sailing under the sky with its cargo of living souls, alone, alone . . . He seemed to drown in an immense ocean of loneliness upon which he had to sustain these breathing, helpless souls. In the world outside there was nothing but poverty and hunger for them. Society presented to them the shut faces of policemen, the impassivity of charitable institutions and terrorized them with the unspoken threats of paupers' hospitals, workhouses and gaols . . .

Then not even the breathing warmth of Martine by his side could comfort him. He was too conscious of their four suspirating rhythms dwelling in the air. Through the skylight he could see the dim, moving shapes of clouds, the baby whimpered in his cradle, and he was alone, alone and in despair.

That was finished. Now he worked, he had the blessed

liberty that was delivered to him in a pay envelope every Friday evening.

John was a carpenter; he had got a good job at Langfier's Carbon Works. But his worries were not over; there was talk of striking at the factory, where a lot of accidents had been happening. The workers said that they were speeded up too much and they had to take risks if they were to get a living wage. These grievances did not touch him, but he had seen the weary faces of the girls as they came off their shifts, he had seen their tired hands mangled in the machines, he had felt the invisible whiplash that drove the hurrying limbs. The speed-up did not directly touch him, but the sense of strain and the frayed nerves affected all the workers in the factory. He was for striking, but Martine held him back, the memories of those moments disarmed him.

As she was pouring out his tea he said, tentatively, 'Another girl was hurt at the factory yesterday,' and a dumb, miserable look came over her face immediately. They understood each other so well, it was just as if he had said to her, 'There will probably be a strike and I can't help joining it . . .'

So he talked about something else, but she answered dispiritedly and when he had kissed her goodbye and patted Mick and taken his bicycle to carry downstairs he had an unhappy, self-reproaching feeling for not having been able to comfort her.

Down the dark, ricketty steps he went, awkwardly burdened with the bicycle, and as each remembered sour nasty smell penetrated his nostrils he reproached himself for saddening Martine and not being able to help it and for not being able to lift her life from this poverty and discomfort. She was so gay and plump and pretty, so tender and easy to wound, that sometimes suddenly to think of her when he was working and away from her would give him a kind of ache inside, an unplaceable, fragile pain that almost brought tears to his eyes. Her dreams and ambitions were so small, so very modest and reasonable and yet so utterly unrealizable because she was married to him, in whose life was no security.

He opened the front door and wheeled his bicycle out. The sunlit air eclipsed the smelly darkness; the faint, delicious warmth drove away his gloomy thoughts. A smiling sensation welled up inside him to greet the morning air.

As he rode off, his head was full of country thoughts, of flint-dusty lanes with budding hedges, field-footpaths bordering orchards and sprouting wheatfields under a milk-blue sky in which floated large, indefinite clouds. The sootblackened boughs of trees in the squares were tipped with buds like greenish points of flame, the drying puddles in the gutters told of April showers, the April-soft air blowing past his face gladdened him with country memories of a happy spring and summer spent on a farm during the war, when he was a boy.

In the little gardens the last late cherry blossoms spangled the air like coral chips: pink, delicate and lovely.

He pedalled slowly. He could not make himself hurry. He thought of a day he had spent in the country with Martine, remembering country smells and fresh air, a milk-blue sky and the sound of distant sheep bleating. It would be a long time before they would be able to spend another day like that.

In front of a big house he saw the behind, the ankles and the half-raised skirts of a maid bending to scrub the lordly doorsteps. It was thus and upon such a morning he had first seen Martine. And he rode on, lost in memories of the first days of their courtship, those moments, those long silences spent in each other's arms standing in the obscurity of a friendly tree shadow . . .

* * * * *

Jean, the bending maid, straightened herself and ran down into the area with her pail, and then she came up and went in by the open front door. In the dark, plush-heavy hall gleamed the white bust of a Roman emperor, an opera hat cocked over its head. 'That's Mr Peter,' she said to herself when she caught sight of it. And she smiled, an indulgent sort of smile that she always gave at the recollection of Peter Langfier, his sturdy figure and thick black hair, his drawling voice and easy manner . . .

Now she paused and rubbed her eyes, stretched and felt waves of sleepiness running down the muscles of her back and legs. She was filled with a yearning to return to bed, to burrow back into the drowsy-warm sheets and know that there was no more sweeping to do, no more dirty dishes to wash and greasy saucepans to clean.

She stood in the middle of the hall, her grey eyes soft, her red mouth a little smiling, chained to stillness by the sleepy, dragging sensations at the back of her legs and down her spine, the sensuous langours of a young girl in spring; and as she yawned again she thought of last night's kisses and how she had run back to the house, how she had thrown off her clothes and lain on the bed in the kind darkness (Dora breathed heavily, Millicent snored a refined note), her eyes wide open, her whole body tingling with the recollection of those kisses that made her feel weak behind the knees, weak and drowsy, like she felt now.

'Jean,' she heard the cook calling. 'Where are you, Jean . . . ?' And the persecuted, nagging voice filled her with a sharp pang of loathing for the kitchen-world, the world from which she could not escape. (She was young and lovely. She saw herself at the cinema, always triumphant, young and lovely, undergoing a thousand miseries and misunderstandings but always winning the rich young man in the end and fading out in a misty, haloed kiss and the wedding music playing. But when she came out into the open air afterwards she knew very well that the world was not so, that rich and hand-some young men might look kindly on her but the embraces proffered in their eyes would bring her no triumph. She dreamed, but also she knew . . .) 'Where are you, Jean . . . ?' wailed the cook in a voice of despairing irritation. 'Coming,' she called back sulkily and went downstairs.

* * * * *

Two flights above, Peter Langfier lay dreaming to waltz time. The crystal glitter of chandeliers flashed in the scattered prisms of pendant jewelled earrings, waltz time music rippled in gay curls through the warm and odorous air. Dreaming he sought a face through a flashing spray of music and could not come upon it. He woke tasting a delicious ache of this impalpable longing; he woke, still dreaming, the waltz music still sounding within his inner ear, a warm and drowsy mist pervading his sensations. He was in bed, in a moment his eyes would open to behold a familiar scene, but still last night's waltz time echoed in his head, his actual memories confused with the memories of dreams, the trivial dance tunes charged with romantic meaning and association.

His opening eyes beheld the sunlight straggling through the curtain-folds. A fine morning, he said to himself, a fine day, a day for riding in the Row, for a drive out into the country. But it was too early to wake, too early even to drowse and plan the day. He heard the faint stir of the awak-ening house, breakfasts cooking and stairs being swept; he dimly caught the muffled overtones of Jean calling back to the cook and turned over to sleep again, to sleep and dream . . .

And as he closed his eyes his father, Sir Edwin Langfier, was being wakened with a cup of tea. Wearily he ran his hand through his thinning hair, reached for the cup, while distastefully regarding his sleeping wife and listening for a change in the regularity of her breathing which would show that she had been disturbed.

Nothing of that rhythm altered, and he sighed with relief as he sipped his weak tea. He shut his eyes, tightly, as if by excluding light from his senses he could make his mind an unsleeping blank. But it was useless, it always was useless, even for a moment. The noise of his running bathwater roused a hundred weary thoughts of yesterday's burdens and today's tasks.

He slipped out of bed very quietly. The task of getting up without waking his wife was the first of the day's irritations. Her good-natured morning platitudes and solicitudes quite shattered his slightest peace of mind. At night, struggling to empty his brain of worries and to sleep, this anticipation grew into another spectre of insomnia. Trivialities threw monstrous shadows across his mind. It would have been possible for him to arrange to sleep alone, but it would have meant a struggle, yet another struggle, so he went on, as nowadays he went on with all the activities of his life, carrying on quite meaninglessly with things in which he no longer had any real interest or belief, just going on like a flywheel continuing to run after its motive power had ceased.

He slipped a plum-coloured silk dressing-gown over his long, bony body and went into the bathroom. When the door was shut and he was quite alone in the steamy jade-and-white room he felt easier in his mind. He lowered himself into the bath, lay back and relaxed exhaustedly, as if it was the end of a long day instead of its beginning. His bony knees, the skeleton ridges of his ribs showing through the sallow skin, his greying, pointed beard made him resemble, as he lay stretched out in the water, a painting of the corpse of Don Quixote.

In the breakfast room a newly lit fire burned sullenly, its flames dull and smoky in the sunlight that streamed through the big window and splashed gleaming over the tablecloth and china.

Langfier breakfasted on weak tea, grapefruit and cereal. Eating was not very important to him, but he heartily disliked the diet that was imposed upon him by a spoiled digestion.

When he had finished he lit a Burmah cheroot and looked vaguely through the papers. Today was the start of the great round-the-world air race; there was little else in the news. He turned to the financial pages, glanced at the New York quotations of some of the AIE companies and noticed that nitrates were still rising.

Then the dark blue Daimler drew up outside, and he took up his portfolio and went out. 'Fine morning, sir,' said Henry McGinnis, the chauffeur, in his cold, hard, uninterested voice, and drove off smartly. Langfier opened his portfolio and took out a pile of papers, began to look through them and then dropped them on the seat beside him and lay back.

The long shadows of the factory chimneys darkened his thoughts. He hated going down to the works . . . Faces of the directors swam in his mind: the pink, well-fed face of Sir William Gilray, Amalgamated Industrial Enterprises chairman, and then more faces, hundreds of vague, living, white smears, the faces of the straggling, hurrying procession of men and girls that drifted in and out of his factory gates . . . From each pair of eyes looked an enemy, every brow hid a mind against which he had to struggle.

Now the car glided through Hyde Park, where trees budded, where grass grew and moved in a gentle wind that cleared the morning haze. But Langfier noticed nothing of this. Still, in the background of his thoughts, yet dominating them, dwelt that ghostly procession of factory workers, their half-visioned faces pale, dumb and resentful, hating him for their hard work and little wages, seeing his imagined greed in every accident, the cause of every one of those factory-maimed and broken lives. They worked under an invisible whiplash and thought him the giver of their pain.

And the car went on, through the unawakened West End, past the City. (He glimpsed hurrying business girls, young faces, breasts shadowed under fabrics and trotting silk ankles. The ghosts of old desires stirred in him.) Then there was the wide, characterless sordidness of the Commercial Road, down whose indefinitely lengthening perspectives the car slid noiselessly.

They passed a Labour Exchange with a crowd queueing up outside. And a meeting was going on: Langfier saw for a moment a mass of caps, a speaker projecting head and shoulders above them, one arm held out in mid-gesture, and in the background, the impassivity of police helmets . . . and then it was gone, the picture in his mind the same as hundreds of others, a scene that fascinates him and yet one that he half-fears – the workers in a mass, held together by a silent, unspoken force . . . the crowds that pass through the factory gates, the crowds at meetings. They are (he knows) people: they have homes, wives, children, also they love, hate, have hobbies, go to the pictures . . . They share the same flesh, appetites and passions as he does, yet there is a subtle difference, an antagonism between him and them. They are people who call him 'sir', who are sometimes timid before him, sometimes defiant but who always face him with an unspoken, half-acknowledged anger and resentment of the power that he has over their lives. But when they are together, in a mass, they exhale a sense of their own power that deeply disturbs him.

Now the car negotiated the noisy confusion of the East India Dock Road. Langfier's eyes snatched at cranes and masts projecting above house silhouettes, glimpsed ships and patches of dock and river water. He saw a rusty smokestack glide across a strip of sky. The *Arundale* was docking. The faint tinkle of the engine-room telegraph ringing 'Dead Slow' sounded amongst the land noises.

* * * * *

James, on the fo'c'sle-head, his hand on the regulator of a hissing, impatient winch, glimpsed, near at hand and tangible, the life of the streets, the shabby virility of London. For an instant the life of the sea and the land life were almost touching one another, going on side by side, then a rope was thrown and a hawser linked the ship with land. A narrowing strip of dirty water swirled between the *Arundale*'s ocean-worn sides and the edge of the dock. The noise of trams and buses, the cries of the streets, were music in the sailors' ears. 'Soon we'll be ashore,' they whispered to themselves, as if it was a precious secret.

The engines sighed as they stopped: cranks, cams and pistons arrested in mid-gesture, steam hissing as if it was the last dying breath of the stilled machines. The firemen lit cigarettes, their grimy fingers making dark smudges on the white paper. In the hot stokehold gloom, below the water-line, their imaginations saw and heard and smelled the scene outside as vividly as did the men on deck.

* * * * *

Down the river came a tug, towing a couple of big lighters. Two men wearing dungarees, dark-blue sweaters and black caps, were standing in the tug's well-deck, leaning over the side. One of them, an oldish chap with a big moustache and a ruddy, toil-creased face, spat and said, 'There's the old *Arundale* docking. Ain't seen 'er for years . . .' 'She's a Nelson boat, isn't she?' said the other, a young fellow with a big nose and large green eyes, who spoke with a Scotch accent. 'No,' said his mate weightily. 'They've been bought up – Amalgamated Industrial Shipping Lines.'

'The buggers damn' near run everything,' said the young man bitterly. 'My sister used to work in one o' their big factories up North . . .' His voice trailed off. He thought of Mary, his young sister, her face gone all sallow, her hands stained with chemicals, and always coughing; she used to be so gay and pretty . . .

'Swine,' muttered Jock, half to himself. And his mate said, 'It's the Capitalist System, that's how things are . . .' He knew what he meant, though he mightn't have been able to explain those words that he always thought of with capital letters.

'You're right mate,' said the Scotchman. 'It's the bloody capitalist system. When I think of my sister wearing herself out in that blasted factory I wonder we don't all join the Communists . . . there's a big change needed, and we'll make it some day.' He stopped suddenly. He had never spoken to the mate like that before. He looked sideways at him to see how he was taking it. But just then the tug altered her course for the north shore and the two men had to set to work.

They were making for the wharf at Langfier's Works. Behind it was the factory with two big chimneys and a new-looking small one. The wharf was directly in front of a long, high concrete building with LANGFIER'S CARBON WORKS painted right across the top in plain black letters.

A man in the cabin of one of the overhead cranes waved to the tug, pulled over a lever, and the crane swiftly and easily hauled up a half-ton iron hopper filled with graphite from the hold of a barge below. Then the crane ran around the curve of its track and disappeared into the building.

Inside, the track went right around and out again through another door. The huge long room was bare and empty. A muffled roar of machines working beneath was the only indication of activity.

The crane stopped above a hatch in the greasy floor and discharged its load into the bunker below. A few men working in the barges and someone in the crane-cabin were all that were needed to carry out the unloading and storage of tons of raw material.

At the other side of the building was a great yard, where stood a dozen furnaces sighing to themselves. Behind them were the offices, housed in a grimy, ugly, old-fashioned red-brick building.

At the moment a meeting was going on there, in the works manager's room, where the heads of departments and their assistants and a dozen or so young technicians – engineers and works chemists – were gathered. Joseph Meek, the works manager, a tall, cadaverous, middle-aged man with a petulant mouth and weak grey eyes, was giving them an uplift talk on the subject of accidents in the factory.

He said that there were far too many accidents taking place. 'Not only does this lead to inefficiency, lost time and expense generally, but a bad feeling is being engendered amongst the workers,' he said.

Mr Meek continued with scholarly quotations from the Factory Acts and from a recent court case to prove that these accidents were not the legal responsibility of the management, but of the gentlemen there assembled. All they had to do, he told them, was to see that the machines were properly protected. In cases where they considered protection inadequate or where dangerous conditions existed, it was their duty to rectify them and requisition the necessary guards and structural alterations.

With a few last words about everyone 'pulling together', Mr Meek dismissed them. People drifted back to work in little groups. Vicat, one of the junior engineers, was muttering angrily to himself, 'Bloody fool, bloody fool . . .' 'What's up,' asked the ingenuous Johnson. 'You're new to this,' said Vicat. 'We've heard it all before. But the accidents go on increasing.' 'Well,' replied Johnson in a reasoning tone of voice. 'It's up to us, isn't it.'

'My dear, good Johnson,' said Vicat. 'You try applying for

proper guards for the belting in your department and see what happens . . . nothing, it never does. But when an accident occurs the management have their alibi. You were told . . .' Johnson was about to chip in, but he went on, 'Anyway, you know what really causes accidents – speed-up and cramped working conditions. If the machine rooms were rebuilt and the girls put on a wage basis that didn't drive them to death there'd soon be an end to all the bloody accidents. As long as the girls know they won't get enough to live on unless they go all out at their jobs they're bound not to take enough precautions and be "careless".'

'Really, Vicat, you talk as if our employers are a lot of bloodthirsty ruffians.' (That was pretty good for Mr Vicat, he thought. The man talked like a street-corner orator.)

'So they bloody are,' said Vicat morosely. 'So they bloody are.' And he wandered off.

He saw John going by with a length of three-by-one over his shoulder.

'Hullo,' he said. 'Old Meek's just abolished accidents in the factory.'

'That's good news,' said John, smiling slowly. 'How's he managed to do that?' John had been on a job in Vicat's office for some days last week, and they had grown to like each other.

'Told us they're all our fault and we must be good boys and see they don't happen again.'

'Well I never,' said John in mock surprise. ''S about time they were stopped anyway. Fair getting on my nerves this speed-up is. I'd go off my nut if I had one of them girl's jobs.'

'Our respected chief engineer, Mr Langton,' said Vicat in a cutting voice, 'says "It's extraordinary how the girls don't find their work monotonous, as you or I would."' John thought of saying something about the strike but didn't. After all, he thought, going on his way, Vicat seems all right, but you never know . . .

'Wotcher, John, me old pal,' shouted Jock as he came into the carpenter's shop. Jock was a cheerful soul with a large nose, laughing eyes and a lecherous expression. He was John's workmate and enlivened their time with quite impossible stories of his amorous adventures. John, Jock and an old man called Peter Lamont did the odd carpentering jobs around the factory. Their workshop was a fair-sized wooden hut with a tin roof, situated on one side of the furnace-yard.

John liked the work. And he liked being under old Peter Lamont, who was a fine craftsman and glad to teach him things. The three of them got on very well. Most of the factory workers were on shifts, but their time was from eight to five, with an hour off at twelve.

The industrious peace of the workshop, with its smells of glue and wood, was a delight to John after his long spell of enforced idleness. He had worked ever since he was fourteen. Free days without money were no use to him.

''Ve you got my working drawing?' he asked Jock.

'Yes. He said it was all right.'

John was going to make a set of drawers for the stores department. He went over to the wood-rack and got down some lengths of six-inch plank. 'They'll do,' he said. 'I'd 'ave rather used twelve-inch, though . . . There's not enough left.'

'Didn't see you down the branch, Friday,' said Jock.

'No. I went to the pictures with my missus.'

(They were both members of the same branch of the Amalgamated Society of Woodworkers.)

'Anything come up?' said John, trying to sound casual. He had wanted to go, but Martine had begged him to take her out, and though he half-suspected that she did it in order to prevent him going to his meeting, he took her all the same. But to admit the truth of this, even to himself, was something he did not want to do. He didn't tell Jock that he had wanted to come because that would have been disloyal to Martine, and he tried to sound as if he didn't care, but that went against the grain too.

'I brought up about there being a strike likely here and what should we do,' said Jock. 'Old Kitteridge said something about referring it to District. "Damn that," says I. "If the others come out, we should too."'

'That's what I feel,' said John. 'But my wife's dead against it, 'specially as I've been out of work so long.'

'It's the wives that break many a strike.'

'She says my conditions are all right and what the others do is their affair.'

'That's the worst with women – no offence meant to your wife, mate, but they're all of a piece. You can't make them see we've all got to stand together. The girls here see it all right, 'cos it's *their* rotten condition more'n anyone's.'

Outside the factory gates were the whitewashed slogans ALL OUT ON MAY DAY. And they had seen it written on walls, on roads and the blank sides of warehouses, and now the words were echoed in their minds. 'The busmen are coming out Thursday,' said Jock in a meditative way. 'So they are at Hopper's,' replied John slowly. 'And the taximen.'

Old Lamont had come in, a little withered man with a long, drooping moustache stained with tobacco on one side. 'Well, lads,' he said. 'I've had me own one-day strike on May Day for thirty-five years, and as long as I can walk you'll see me in the park on the first of May.'

'There was some talk about it at our branch,' said Jock. 'Lot of them said they'd be coming out.'

'Bet that bothered Kitteridge,' said John.

'He didn't know which way to look. "We're marching on Sunday," he said, awkward like. "May Day's the first of May," says some chap, "and that's good enough for us." He was proper flummoxed.'

'I know 'em,' said Lamont bitterly. 'I know 'em. May Day on *Sunday* . . .' He was an old Labour Party member who

45

had left in disgust after the General Strike, and now he would have nothing to do with politics beyond his trade union.

'Seems we're a right lot of Reds here,' said John, half laughingly, as he began to mark out his wood.

'Pity there's not a lot more like us,' said Jock. 'There's a change needed.'

John pondered. The idea of strikes and demonstrations was beginning to have a real meaning for him these days. Before he had been out of work he had accepted things as they were, but the bitter experiences of those days had altered his outlook.

'That's a rotten bit of deal you've got there,' said Lamont, peering over his shoulder. He picked it up and looked accusingly at it, stroked it with his fingers and dropped it on the floor. 'It'll warp before the glue's dry on it. I'd use another bit if I was you.' 'We're short on flooring,' said John. 'I'll get some in,' replied Lamont. 'I was going to make up the stock list, anyway.'

They were silent. Jock was sawing, Lamont writing on a greasy bit of paper with a flat, carpenter's pencil. In the brief silences when Jock stopped sawing one could hear the hissing of the glue pot and the faint scratch of John's pencil across the grain of the wood. In the background was the confused murmur of machinery.

John pondered on social phenomena, his mind working slowly and heavily. He was beginning vaguely to sense the direction that his conclusions were taking. But there was something else in his mind too, a feeling that always accompanied these thoughts and opposed them, a kind of inner ache of disloyalty to Martine. He knew what she wanted from life and could sympathize with her little ambitions for a nice home with bright curtains and new furniture; he knew her passion for security and how heavily the fear of poverty bore upon her. To think her husband was a 'Red' would fill her life with a perpetual sense of danger.

Whenever he thought of her like this he imagined her drawing in her lower lip with an expression of repressed, dumb pain, an expression that was the faint shadow of the awful patient agony that had been on her face when her labour pains began, upon that early dawn on Friday when they hadn't had a penny in the house, and she had set out with him to walk to the hospital. It was then, in the empty cheerless streets, walking beside her, feeling her arm pressed tight to his, that he first really understood how he loved her, and also it was then he really saw the true bitterness of their lot, it was then that he cast from him the idea that poverty and unemployment were 'misfortunes' coming from the sky like thunderbolts. It's because we work for capitalists, he thought, and then they can't sell enough. If we made them for our own class it would be different. Martine had had to parade her labour pains upon cold pavements because there were two classes in the world. But it's not quite as simple as that, he thought, knitting his eyebrows together.

'Them drawers would be better with slots in the top instead of knobs,' said Lamont, suddenly breaking upon his thoughts, and as he spoke, John's mind was brought up with a sudden jerk as he visualized the job finished, up the big storeroom, with people coming and going, sliding the drawers in and out, slipping their hands in through the slots at the top, and he felt the palms closing around the edges of the wood and saw how it would become worn and rounded with use.

'You're right,' he said. 'I'll do it.'

'Better ask the storekeeper and make sure. Once it's done it's done, and 'e loves to kick up a dust about things not being made like what he asked for.'

'I'll take a walk over and ask him, eh . . . ?'

'Be back next week,' Jock called after him.

In the yard he was encompassed by sighing furnaces. The

pale-blue sky above was smeared with the breath of the towering chimneys. An ever-present, faintly choking, sulphuric smell contaminated the air. But still there was a softness, a blowing softness that brought April buds to mind and growing things. Even in the towns it becomes spring, even in the shadow of the factory chimneys, amidst the hurrying machine songs, the young men's and girls' thoughts wandered amorously, and their blood was sluggish with tender dreams.

Now John stopped at the entrance of one of the big machine shops. A tall, vivid, red-haired girl bounded through the door, smiling, half at him and half at nothing at all.

As the door swung open and shut a pandemonium of noise swelled out and receded.

John went in. It was a tremendous room, shivering with the loud, undeviating music of machines, the air loaded with their oily breath.

The floor is slippery with oil and graphite, as with some horrible blood. After a while the noise comes to seem a fearful, shattering silence.

Here, two hundred and forty girls in ugly grey overalls and caps live, breathe and think, their fragile flesh confused with the greasy embraces of steel tentacles. Each has a simple set of movements to perform for eight hours. The machines, Langfier and the AIE do the rest. Everything moves meaninglessly, repetitively – wheels, axles, shaftings, belts and drills spinning and hurrying, rods, pistons and punches shuttling a savagely exact rhythm, while arms, fingers and bodies, rigid with urgency, perform a terrible mechanical ballet. Unfortunately these girls are not power-driven automata; they also go home in the evening, have lives of their own, preoccupations with love and hate, with laughter and amusement, which cannot be integrated with the machines. They have minds that strive to carry on with their private functionings while spinning with the wheels, dancing with the pistons and humming tensely with the electric motors.

So there are also machines which work themselves, each of them capable of carrying out half a dozen different operations far more quickly and accurately than could half a dozen girls tending half a dozen lathes. They form a whole side chapel in the cathedral. Sweating oil and weeping streams of soapy water they clash insatiable metallic jaws with a machine-gun rattle that drowns their motors' electric whining and slavering. The bright metal peels away in delicate helices, a golden rain of dust drowns in greenish oil. The chucks come around and around in turn with eager exactness, with the same monotonous inevitability of movement as the girls' hands, only faster, ever so much faster. There is no weariness to spoil their work, no fallible mind to guide them. And they never bleed. One man can look after a lot of them. All he has to do is to see that they get a regular diet of metal rod and strip. And he could be eliminated if it was cheaper.

Here one reflects on mortality, seeing the days and weeks of the girls' lives wasting away in metal peelings, in the golden rain of bronze filings. When they are twenty-one the factory sees them no more. They would have to be paid an uneconomic wage, so they are replaced by a fresh batch of schoolgirls. Out they go through the factory gates for the last time, worn-out, broken-down jades whose only saleable talent on the labour market consists of being able to drill four holes in a carbon block almost as accurately and nearly a tenth as quickly as an automatic lathe.

Blondes and brunettes, beauties and uglies, good girls and bad girls, virgins and tarts, so much flesh, so many thoughts and feelings, so many drab, cheerless destinies, so many who might have been born at some other time in some other place to live the lives of human beings. At least once the moment will come in each of these lives when they will stop and think, 'What have we been born for, why do we live as we do, toiling only to eat, eating only to toil . . .'

49

This moment may come and be forgotten in an instant, or it may be a sudden revelation altering the whole course of a life.

These silly girls with their synthetic Hollywood dreams, their pathetic silk stockings and lipsticks, their foolish strivings to escape from the cramped monotony of their lives, are the raw material of history. When their moment of deep discontent comes to them in a mass, taking form in the words of their class leaders, then there are revolutions. What happens to the revolutions depends upon other factors – automatic lathes for instance.

Amongst these two hundred and forty there is a Communist. Her name is Ivy Cutford. She's not very much to look at, tall and thin, with blondish hair, blue-grey eyes, ordinary nose, wide mouth, rather diffident and shy manner. She works a polishing machine. All day she stacks rows of carbon blocks into slides and shoves them into a slot; her foot depresses a treadle, and to the accompaniment of agonizing mechanical howls they are ground flat, true to a thousandth of an inch. She has to do several thousand a day. If she falls behind her quota she can't pay her rent. If by a superhuman effort she manages to do more she is able to pay off some of the back rent owing.

She is a Communist, one amongst two hundred and forty. She can't do much perhaps, but circumstances do a lot for her. The girls are beginning to take a good deal of notice of what she says because they like her. She can tell them a lot about Langfier and Meek, and she knows about Mr Dartry, AIE's representative on the board of directors, chemical engineering expert, director of Langfier's, of three chemical factories, of a soda mine in South America that takes considerable ingenuity to work at a slight loss, an OBE, ex-Conservative MP, a man of some weight in the affairs of the country. But Ivy understands a lot that would surprise him, including the scandal of the soda mine and the government concessions (as detailed in the *Daily Worker*).

And while she is finishing off her first five hundred carbon blocks, Mr Dartry is having a conference with Langfier in a tastefully furnished office. Technically the building and furniture are owned by Langfier, but what Dartry says goes, he speaks with the voice of AIE's ninety-seven millions. Langfier doesn't count. He objects to all the machine shops being put on piecework, but it doesn't matter. He says there will be a strike. Dartry says let there be a strike; it will be smashed.

And, what is more, after the present rush orders are executed, after about ten days, a strike will be positively beneficial in saving overhead costs. Don't let Sir Edwin imagine that Mr Dartry is not aware of what's going on in the works. Mr Dartry has his confidential men in all the important departments. Mr Dartry's men are prepared, are willing, to take a leading part in a strike if it is to the financial advantage of AIE.

'Mr Dartry,' said Langfier icily. 'Perhaps the factory is a more profitable and efficient undertaking than it was when I had the sole voice in its affairs. I have seen in many of your published speeches that you advocate the community of interest between workers and employers. I believe in this too, but I do not believe that such a community of interests is best served by the employment of agents provocateurs amongst my workpeople.'

He walked out and shut the door forcibly behind him. He was white and quivering with rage. Dartry contemplated the shut door and spluttered for a while. But it took more than that to pierce the hide of his complacence. Langfier didn't understand modern business ideas. But he was a nuisance: it was a good thing that 'they' would soon be getting rid of him altogether. Dartry's self-esteem did not come from a consciousness of his own strength but from the strength of the interests he represented.

Langfier checked himself outside the door, not wishing to parade his rage through the office. He exerted his whole strength of will to restrain the quivering fury within him; unconsciously he clenched his fists, set his jaw tightly and achieved a rigid calm. He was able to smile 'Good morning' to a typist who was walking down the corridors importantly carrying a sheaf of papers; he presented a shut face to the office entrance and said 'Hotel Riviera' to the chauffeur in an impassive voice.

But as he sank back into the car he was quivering all over. The knowledge of his anger's impotence inflamed it all the more. He was a servant of AIE, a glorified factory manager with responsibility and little authority, and this was continually and bitterly being brought home to him. Daily he was forced to repress his rage and irritation, which fed upon itself and grew. And what irked him most of all was that this long, bitter struggle (whose predestined end he knew) was no longer of any real interest to him. He no longer desired the illusion of power.

He had understood what was happening when AIE first began to penetrate his firm, he had understood their manoeuvres and had guessed what would be the final result. Yet it would have been impossible for him to have done without their money, their markets and their privileges.

All the time he had fought a power whose victory he knew to be inevitable. And now he knew he was almost at the end of the struggle and he realized that he no longer cared. He was worn out. All he wanted was peace. He was going now to see Gilray, AIE chairman. They would probably be glad to buy him out. His family could have most of the money. As for himself . . . he could not yet visualize the future of his private life.

* * * * *

Now the car was retracing its earlier route along the East India Dock Road, past where the *Arundale* lay.

Her hatches were open, her decks invaded by strangers. Cranes roared above her and delved into her hatches, while the long-lit stokehold fires smouldered into quietude.

Some of the crew were going ashore. James, in a double-breasted blue suit, white shirt and black tie, with a black cap on one side of his head, was walking down the gangplank, a kitbag over his shoulder.

The earth was hard, was strangely solid beneath his feet. A confusedly vivid multitude of colours, noises, shapes and smells beat upon his senses. For a moment he was completely dazed, unable to catch hold of any certainty in the mass of sensations.

He stood, hesitating on the kerb, while people passed, while traffic thundered by. A moving wave of air displaced by the smooth passage of Langfier's Daimler cooled his brow . . . All this activity, all these multitudes of people went on living and functioning, taking no account of him. This had been the same while he was in Spain: this endless stream of traffic and humanity had flowed while his long, empty sea-days had gone by; these windows had reflected the same shifting, continual procession of shadows while he had sat gloomily drinking in Valparaiso. All these faces had been and were shut from him: he was a stranger who did not exist for them.

But this moment of confusion passed. He caught sight of a remembered bus number and, jumping aboard, he climbed to the top.

He took a penny ticket to the Sailors' Home. People half-smiled at him: he was so obviously a sailor just come ashore, with a reddish, sunburned face and sailor's eyes, china-blue and rather piercing, a figure haloed in their minds with a false romance of foreign ports and foreign girls.

He looked out of the window at the confused and crowded

street. These scenes that were strangers to his eyes and yet so familiar, appeared glamorously to him now. When he saw the May Day slogans his heart beat faster. This too had been going on apart from him, yet something to which he was no stranger, a movement in which soon he would be taking his place again. Those rough chalked letters moved him strongly: they were the first visible signs of the revolutionary movement that he had encountered for so long. And these, and the London street scenes, gladdened him. A flood of memories rose in his mind, of long-lost friends, of long-forgotten girls . . . of his mother and his brother John and the stuffy little house off the Harrow Road where they had grown up.

But now these streets breathed to him the air of a battle-field. Here, in the shadows of the factory chimneys, amidst the pulsating rhythms of millions of lives, once more he felt clear-headed, potent and full of purpose.

He was impatient to take up working-class political activity, eager to find John, and somewhere in the back of his mind was the dim, unformulated hope of a girl, a laughing girl with whom he would be able to make love. He had enough money for a good few weeks ashore, and this gave him the notion of most sailors in like circumstances – that this time he might really try to settle down on land for good, get a job and a home. As he laughed at himself for imagining this, he also half-believed it.

The bus stopped opposite the Sailors' Home, and he got off. The newsbills of the evening papers met his eye. THOMPSON OVER RUSSIA and AIR RACE – THOMPSON LEADING he read uncomprehendingly. To one long from home the newspaper headlines speak a foreign language. But a million looks glanced upon these words understandingly, with varying thoughts, no two quite the same yet no two altogether different.

* * * * *

To Peter Langfier, riding in the park, those brief captions had been a spur to the imagination. He thought of a misty flying-field at dawn, the roar of aeroplane engines and their first soaring flight, and then the earth, a geographical globe girdled with cotton-wool clouds, turning in space, and the planes, like little black specks, like crawling flies, slowly moving around, above cold grey seas, above fields and towns and mountains, lonely in their flight, yet companioned by a million thoughts. This was a splendid vision to him, the romance of modernity, the heroics of technology. The world is changing, he thought, men and machines are altering the face of the earth and their own lives. In the cold light of laboratories men are moulding vast forces to change the world.

His pleasant, sensual, weakish mouth had tightened while he was thinking this. And then it drooped into rather a petulant expression to which his face was becoming accustomed. He loved to dream of men's feats, of endurance and bravery, great discoveries, artistic achievements. Then he was always oppressed by a sense of the futility of his own life.

Now he rode his fine chestnut horse; he sat easily on it, strong and young and healthy, in good clothes, a favoured member of a ruling caste, of a ruling class of a ruling nation. He had but to will it to realize possibilities that were beyond the hopes and most difficult ambitions of ordinary people. He saw that the potentialities of his life were to be envied. There were so many that he could decide upon nothing, and in the meantime he tried to amuse himself expensively.

Now, as he rode, his thoughts became more cheerful. The sun irradiated him with a smiling sensation; the earth was so rich and brown, the grass so green, the air so charged with the breath of spring, that he was filled with a wordless song of physical wellbeing. He leaned forward, smacked his horse's neck and set him to gallop.

His eyes were on the racing earth below. His glance slid

forward a little; ahead were pounding horse's hooves, scattering clods behind them. He felt with the thrusting muscles under the silk-smooth skin of the slender, galloping legs.

As he overtook the horse ahead he looked up to see the rider. It was a girl, a slim girl in breeches and a sweater. She wore no hat, and her short flax-blonde hair scattered itself in the wind. She looks nice, thought Peter, and slackened his horse's pace.

They were riding almost side by side now, and he turned to look at her. She had wide, pale-blue eyes and a small, humorous nose; her upper lip was very short, and her mouth was of the type often found in conjunction with that characteristic – rather oversensitive, generous, the lips full and sensual and of a particular flower-petal texture. She smiled to herself, and her face was intent, flushed and happy. An English miss, thought Peter, lovely and rather inbred. He half-turned and looked again. There was something puzzlingly familiar about her. He had a sense that she was connected with a host of elusive, fading memories, as if he had wakened from a dream with one vivid picture in his mind with which he could not connect any other impressions.

He was almost past her now, going just a little faster than she. A nice girl, he thought. I wish I could remember . . . And he was about to put her out of his mind, when suddenly he recollected the dream from which he had woken this morning, the flashing music and the warmth and light and the girl for whom he had vainly sought. This was she and now (for the first time) he knew her. He had seen her last night, at the dance, standing with a group of girls, gravely smiling and a little apart from them, and then his partner had looked up and laughed, and he had forgotten.

He turned again, and as she caught his glance he smiled in recognition, quite unselfconsciously, and checked his horse a little.

'I remember you,' he said, his voice as if continuing a conversation rather than beginning one. 'I remember you, I saw you last night at the dance, and I dreamed about you, and then I forgot your face.'

She blushed suddenly, a warm pink. Her mouth trembled undecidedly a moment, and then smiled back. 'I didn't see you,' she said, with an unconsciously coquettish intonation.

Both slowed their horses to a walk.

Now that Peter saw her close and heard her voice – it was soft, slightly throaty, just the intonation he had imagined for it – he was delighted by her. She exhaled a breath of lovely innocence; she seemed a country girl, from some fine country house whose chimneys always smoked with the fires of fat cooking meals, a girl from a rich sleepy countryside, who often dreamed and was filled with uncomprehending pity, like a Galsworthy heroine: a girl good with dogs and horses, unsophisticated and ignorant, yet with capable instincts.

(Such a girl, he thought, was bound to meet a simple, naive young man who would love her with an inarticulate fervour, that she would return, becoming suddenly aware of it and her own unawakened passion, perhaps in some great garden upon a flower-scented summer night.)

Such a story Peter quickly fashioned for himself and became its hero. His sophisticated manner was forgotten; he held himself back from attempting clever remarks, and drew in his lower lip, which accentuated his ingenuous expression.

They chatted unremarkably, their conversation mostly questions and answers about each other. She was twenty. Her name was Pamela Allin, the daughter of the Earl of Dunbourne. 'My father knows him well,' said Peter, and mentally dropping his new role added parenthetically to himself 'and hates his guts.'

It was unlikely that they should have met: their circles did not really touch. She, as he had imagined, lived mostly in the country and, when she came to town, moved in a more staid section of 'society' than that in which Peter disported himself.

The crocuses were late, and they yet glimmered in the grass; the may was early and now budding. All Peter's repressed romanticism was roused. Thus, to go slowly riding, the soft air flowing by him, the air soft and laden with promise of summer delights of lakes and lawns, with a young and lovely girl by his side whom he had just met, this was his unacknowledged idea. For now he saw himself a simple, pleasant young man about to fall in love, on the verge of delicious pangs, of romantic heart-rendings, of sufferings that would be painfully delightful to undergo. He would meet other, ravishingly lovely women, a little older than him maybe and very worldly, and they would look kindly on him, but they would be nothing to him: he would just treat them with a courteous aloofness, and they would understand . . .

The rest of the story was rather vague. He could not, in his furthest flights of imagination, see such a young woman becoming his mistress, while marriage was something he had never contemplated. The best would be, perhaps, a tragic misunderstanding, when they would part with broken hearts and noble sentiments. Ten years later they might meet. She would be married and have delightful children, and he would gravely smile saying, with a world of meaning in his voice, 'I am still a bachelor.'

Past the budding trees, under the faintly misty milk-blue sky, trotted the horses. An unemployed (George Eversden, gas fitter, 47) gloomily leaning against the railings of Rotten Row, passing the time, saw them go. The horses' skins, so smooth and glossy, mocked his shabbiness; the youth and lightheartedness of the riders mocked the dull pangs of his hungry misery; the ease and assurance of their voices laughed at his uneasy leisure. Yet he did not see the mockery nor resent his unease. Their lives, their thoughts and laughter were too remote from him, whose laughter had palled, whose thoughts moved uneasily in the narrow orbit of his life. They were a different race, a different species. In heat and cold, in want and woe, in different scenes, pondering in different languages, millions of his fellows hoped and despaired, passing time away as did he, who shared and suffered in all their want and woe. They were his fellow men, and in each country too, were others who went in silk and fine linen easily laughing. There are two races in the world, and they live in all countries.

The horses' hooves padded away, and he turned and watched them ride out of the park with a musing eye. On his poverty and their riches he did not muse but accepted it as part of the sad, unbitter order of established things.

Out of the park rode Peter and Pamela, their horses' hooves suddenly ringing hard upon the shiny tar skin of the Bayswater Road, which ran straight and smooth, east and west, a river between the fenced-in budding trees and the stucco façades of the rich houses.

From Lancaster Gate tube station floated the warm, dusky smell of underground air. The newsbills lolling on the pavement proclaimed THOMPSON HAS FORCED LANDING. CAPTAIN COE'S FINALS. BAYSWATER MAN FALLS TO DEATH.

'Thompson down,' said Peter.

'What a shame,' said Pamela.

'He's got such a clear lead,' said Peter, 'he may pick up yet.'

* * * * *

KENSINGTON MAN FALLS TO DEATH, read Martine. THOMPSON FORCED LANDING IN SIBERIA. Thompson down, she said to herself. What a shame. He's a nice man, she thought, remembering a picture of him that she had seen in the Sunday paper. And she forgot, looking at her shopping-list. 'Marg, lard, sugar, cheese,' she read, looking down at the parcels in the foot of the pram and checking them off. Now vegetables . . . And she intently surveyed tomatoes, onions, cabbages and potatoes, piled in splendid profusion on the barrows.

Alluringly the costermongers bellowed the litany of their wares, but she looked meditatively and unblandished. Tomatoes here were fourpence, there fourpence-halfpenny. This man's cabbages were splendid, that man's not so fresh but a penny cheaper.

In the pram, David, the baby, lay on his back and gurgled cheerfully to himself. Shapes, sounds and colours swam into being around him with the surprising inconsequence of aquarium fish. Also there were smells, there were contacts. But they came and went and nothing stayed in his mind beyond fading, lingering impressions, like dying echoes.

Beside the pram gaily lolloped Mick, keeping one wicked, glittering eye on Martine. The morning's Portobello Road shopping expedition was the flower of his day, his torment and his delight. There was so much responsibility for him, to watch and guard Martine and David amongst such a con-stellation of smells, to cling to his mistress's heels while other dogs disported themselves and ran and sniffed and piddled. He was always straying, stopping a second to baptize a lamp-post with four negligent drops, becoming involved with some rude mongrel who would not retreat when growled at. He would be lost in these circumstances until, with a start, he would realize that his cortege had passed on. His nose would go down to the ground in a panic, frantically trying to resolve Martine's smell from a thousand distracting and delighting others. Then he would hear her calling, and he would bound joyously forward until he saw her, then he would forget and remember again: he had been lost; he had been bad. His tail drooped, his walk became a procession of guilt. Then for a while he would trot beside her very soberly, until an orange-box or a sack of potatoes on the ground attracted his attention. Gaily he would cock his leg, to be interrupted by a menacing shout from above, threatening kicks and blows.

Mick was a fair-sized shaggy, curly, bluey-grey with bits of white, sort of small sheepdog, only with a long, gay tail. John and Martine had bought him at the Dogs' Home for five shillings when they were first married, and they both loved him very much. But for all his charm he had a devil in him and was always having to be beaten for fighting or getting lost or stealing or becoming overfamiliar with a policeman's trousers.

Martine deposited a pound of onions at David's feet and smiled at him. David gurgled back amiably. She hummed a little French tune. All around her was cheerful noise and confusion, costermongers shouting, people shoving and pushing, dogs barking. Fruit and vegetables loaded the air with smells and colours. And there were baskets of spring flowers, for which she yearned. Everywhere was sunshine and the promise of a new summer. Martine was happy. John had a job, the baby was growing, and soon they would be able to move. She was full of the gaily expectant lightheartedness that she had felt in the days when she and John had been first married, the feeling that tomorrows were full of exciting surprises. Those days were only a little more than eighteen months ago, but they seemed far away, separated from now by so much poverty and suffering.

She mused over this for a little, until she came to the butcher's where she always got her meat. She stood looking at the window, and the men inside recognized her and smiled. This was the climax of the morning's shopping, and contemplating a nice bit of stewing mutton she let her mind run on ahead to the preparation of the stew. First David would have to be bathed and fed when she got in, and then the water would be boiled, the vegetables and meat prepared with Mick hungrily yearning up at the table. When the stew was on, she would have some bread and cheese and a cup of tea. Then there was washing to do all the afternoon. The time would go by so quickly until it came to those last moments of pleasurable suspense while she waited for John to come in. This was the time she loved, when the stewpot was gently bubbling out delicate smells and the table ready, and there was nothing for her to do but sit listening for the sound of John's footsteps on the stairs.

After she had bought the meat she turned to go home, out of the noise of the market, through quiet, shabby streets, slums of houses that have come down in the world.

In front of her, painted in white on a long blank wall, was ALL OUT ON MAY DAY, MARCH FROM RAG FAIR AT 12.30 in huge letters. This somehow threw a shadow across her light-heartedness, the shadow of a world she feared and could not comprehend.

* * * * *

To others these words were an ugly, irrelevant scrawl. The Earl of Dunbourne, peeping out of the back of his long Rolls Royce irritatedly read the slogans again and again, along the Great West Road, in Hammersmith, written large across the road in Chelsea. He had a really sincere *Morning Post* attitude to the working-class movement. Every one of the crude whitewashed hammers and sickles were insults to him. He couldn't stop himself bobbing up in his seat to look at them.

He was a little gnome-like man. Looking at him it was hard to believe he was one of the richest and most powerful men in the country. As Augustus John Templeton Allin, fourteenth Earl, he inherited lands, great houses, slums and old masters. But also he was a financial genius, a man filled with a single purpose, a devouring spirit with the tremendous rapacious vitality of Balzac's characters of the rising middle class. Always he reached out for ever-greater and more unresplendent power. He was a director of the National Bank, of half the railways in South America, chairman of brewery-holding companies and nickel mines, owner of vast blocks of shares in armaments, motorcars, finance corporations and shipping lines. And he was of the elect of AIE, a ruler amongst rulers. Factory chimneys blackened the air of towns whose names were unfamiliar to him, and their fires stoked up wealth for him.

Beneath him purred the lovely engines of his car, which slid smoothly eastwards. Eastwards ran the tar-smooth road, past the glittering shop windows, past the shops whose glass doors opened and shut like turnstiles marking the flow of money. Then there were the grave, tall trees in the park, brown earth and cantering horses. The huge blue-and-grey pseudo-modernistic façade of the Riviera Hotel loomed through the misty boughs of trees. Then earth and grass were eclipsed; the car swung into Park Lane, into the hotel forecourt where laundered palms grew from synthetic soil in coloured tubs.

Large men in blue uniforms opened doors and made smooth the way of the noble earl. Steel and glass, soft fabrics and coloured woods encompassed him; the interior air was warm, discreet, hushed with the cathedral sanctity of wealth. If an elephant had appeared into this twilight hotel world they would have managed to make him seemly and unobtrusive.

Silently a door slid open, and from the amber-lit coffin of the lift stepped Sir Edwin Langfier, walking aloofly, moving on the soft honey-coloured carpet as inaudibly as a ghost.

Dunbourne saw him. Their glances coldly pierced into each other's eyes, they bowed and passed. Langfier's glance turned inward upon himself again. Doors were opened for him by men who moved as if they were trying to be invisible. Then there were no walls or roof. He stood outside, hesitating on the steps. From somewhere his car materialized and the chauffeur stood at his elbow, rigidly expectant. 'No,' said Langfier. 'Take it home. I'm going to walk.' The chauffeur was not there; the car vanished.

Then he was in the park, staring at trees. There was a feeling in his head as if his mind had run down, like an over-wound clockwork motor that had been buzzing furiously for a long time. The trees poured upwards from the earth in fountains of metamorphosized soil, the grass reappearing in green leaf buds. A child bowled a hoop and fell over. Dogs ran about gaily barking.

Then he looked up and through the fountain spray of budding boughs he saw the hotel, leaning upwards like a cliff, and his mind started to work again. The windows glittered coldly, like hundreds of staring eyes. A little while ago he had been up there. The arrow-line of his sight splintered upon the glass pane of the window behind which he had stood, a room of Sir William Gilray's private suite.

* * * * *

The big window looked over the tree tops. The room was light and airy, pleasantly furnished with luxurious unobtrusiveness.

Gilray stood in front of the fireplace chatting to the Earl of Dunbourne.

Half a dozen other men stood around talking casually. All diffused an atmosphere of expensive subfusc fabrics, of brilliantine and clean shavenness. They were past middle age, but all well preserved, with immaculate false teeth, soft hands clean and plump as those of babies. They lived well-fed, well-ordered lives. Everything they did was made effortless by servants, chauffeurs, shopkeepers, hoteliers and secretaries.

Gilray himself was stout, grey haired, with a small white

moustache, exhaling false geniality. Beside him Dunbourne looked more gnome-like than ever. Arthur Sloane, MP, newspaper owner and of fertilizer and explosives fame, was taller than the others, rather more dandified with a monocle and a stock. There was Danvers with pouches under his eyes, rather debauched.

A bluish haze of cigar smoke drifted in the room. Beneath the current of talk, beneath the smooth and well-tended scalps, minds worked alone and calculating. These gentlemen represented the power, the unresplendent glory of what is rather tactfully named the Capitalist System. Directors of banks, newspapers, mines, armaments, railways, shipping, insurance, housing trusts, employers of governments, at the moment they were acting in their capacity of being the Amalgamated Industrial Enterprises. But they were to be found where and whenever men gather together in the name of the largest financial undertakings.

Now they are met to plan restrictions: they are scheming to close down factories and speed up others, to consume their lesser rivals. They are making their class an ever-smaller and more exclusive society: control of production passes into the hands of an ever-shrinking group.

They sit around the table, scribbling on notepads (Dunbourne draws imaginary graphs; Danvers impossible houris) and listening to the careful toneless sentences of Georg Eichner.

He speaks as if he were giving a lecture. He is short, fattish and sallow, a brilliant economist, doctor of trusts and combines, who suspects their diseases are in the long run incurable. But they can be prolonged. He is a doctor whose life is bound up with his patients'. To his audience his income is a flea-bite, but he lives very well and wishes to continue in his way of life.

He speaks of falling rates of profit, long-term factors of expansion and decline, of labour unrest . . . the economic crisis is now permanent, the absolute volume of world production continually shrinks. But there are rises in this downward curve. A little boom is now on. Eichner says it is soon going to break. AIE can consolidate itself at the expense of less highly organized capital provided they do thus and thus . . .

The cigar smoke hazes the sunlit air. It is twelve. The sirens of factories now being doomed are bounding. The top hats seethe around the Stock Exchange. The little boom is at its height and a new little crisis around the corner. This meeting, whose decisions will result in preserving AIE through the slump, also serves to precipitate it.

The cigars are burned away; the spit-damp ends moulder in ashtrays. The meeting is over, noses are blown, throats cleared, and everyone stands and stretches their legs. Some chat in little groups; some prepare to go.

Dunbourne and Gilray lean against the mantelpiece. Says Dunbourne, 'I met Langfier coming out of here. What did he want?'

'Wants to sell out. Doesn't like the way we run his factory.'

'Why see you about it?'

'Oh, he's old-fashioned, you know . . .'

They both smile not very tolerantly: realists, strong men.

'We're going to hang on to it,' says Dunbourne suddenly, in an assuring voice.

'Certainly. But without him. Only it would be madness to buy him out. I'm afraid he'll have to get out of his own accord.'

Dunbourne made a grimace that expressed nothing. He had seen so many men ruined. They simply became removed from his mental sphere.

'I'm sorry,' Gilray went on. 'He's a good fellow, but there's no place for people like him today. You can't help respecting him, but his ideas . . .' He shrugged his shoulders.

He too had ruined many men, but he always had a kind word for them.

He walked over to the window, thinking about an appointment with his tailor and the new suit that was being made for him.

* * * * *

Below, in Park Lane, crawled a monotonous procession of buses and cars. In the artificial-leather interiors of the Radio Taxis, clear, slow-dropping notes of a Mozart sonata issued from the loudspeakers. The music bubbled like crystal fountains, like awakening birds trilled the flutes. These, thought some, these pure, rapturous sounds are the true notes for living. Thoughts, feelings, passions, should flow thus, with the effortless clarity of running brooks. These clear, icy, uncontaminated ecstasies were the realities.

Suddenly the music stopped, in the middle of a phrase. For a moment there was a surprising silence in which trembled the faint hum of distant dynamos. Then into this sudden pool of quiet splintered an alien voice, a hoarse shout of, 'Workers, all out on May Day. Demonstrate for a free Soviet Britain!'

* * * * *

This rang in a million ears. Eyes remembered the chalked slogans on walls and pavements. The slogans, the rain of leaflets, the shouts and songs of demonstrators echoed in a million minds.

* * * * *

In the sub-editors' room of the *Evening Mail* two men were leaning against a tape machine, reading about the air race. Then the machine stopped, stuttered and restarted.

COMMUNISTS CRASH MICROPHONE AGAIN it haltingly spelled out. The men nodded to each other, smiled a gratified smile. 'He's got away with it,' said one. 'Good work,' said the other, a tall young man called Pat Morgan. 'Will you handle it? I've got to go out.' And he walked away, thinking of that proletarian voice ringing out from the loudspeakers. It's grand, he thought, remembering the slogans and the rain of leaflets, the Communist voices raised everywhere where there are workers, speaking low in factories amidst the songs of machines, hammering home the May Day slogans until their clangour sounded everywhere, until even the radio and the newspapers, the loudest instruments in the orchestra of suppression were forced to echo the undertone of a working-class motif. This year, he thought, this year will be the finest May Day ever in London, and his memory leaned back to others. He had been in the Communist Party two years now, two years in which his vague miseries and discontent with the life he led and the life he saw around him had crystallized into a clear understanding and belief, from a despair that rendered him inert and impotent to a hope that could be expressed in action. Two years . . . he thought. The year before last had been his first May Day demonstration.

His long legs carried him lazily along the crowded Fleet Street pavements. He put his hands in his pockets and whistled a soundless tune. Even here the air was warm, was soft with spring. Soon it will be summer, he thought, and there will be the long dusty days, the breathless nights, and how we will long for the country, for the dreaming afternoons on lawns listening to bird-songs and smelling country air. Here we will hear only the songs of machines, smell only dust and petrol. Remembering this, one longs to escape, to live quietly in country scenes. This is the contradiction; in each of us there are these longings for irreconcilable themes, for ways of living and acting that mutually exclude one another. To seek for compromise is to admit defeat . . .

Now he climbed the dank and prison-gloomy stairs that led up to Holborn Viaduct. In a dark corner a man sat on the steps, comfortably settled. Beside him was an uncorked penny ink-bottle; a pad of lined, pale-mauve paper was on his knees, and he was writing fast in large block letters. Several sheets already covered lay by his side. He took his ease, was wrapped in library seclusion. A large, greenish, age-lichened bowler hat balanced over his hunched shoulders. Pat observed minutely his projecting teeth and the days of unshaving on his chin, the tin-rimmed spectacles that magnified the cold blue stare of his protuberant knobbly eyes. His suit was dark, a little frayed and glossy. Between the ends of his trousers and his enormous dull boots showed grey, very woollen socks. He wore a celluloid collar, no tie but a worn, shiny brass stud. Somehow he was very clean and well kept. And there he sat, not composing possible masterpieces, certainly mute and inglorious, but no undiscovered Milton, full of suffering and unselfcompassionating, perfectly complacent, absorbed and at ease.

'*He wrote on a pad, sitting on the steps leading up to Holborn,*' Pat said to himself, seeing the words in italics, significant, the heading for a poem, the title of a drama . . . His eyes had been a little mad, the eyes of a religious fanatic perhaps, or of a kindly, respectable family man who also violated little girls and dismembered them. Pat longed most passionately to know his life and what he had been so absorbedly writing in those fluent block letters. This was a human being, accurately observed, utterly remote and unknown, never before seen and never to be seen again. Pat was a journalist, a very good one: he saw, noted, wondered but could not make the imaginative synthesis that goes beyond the facts and discovers the truth.

He stood pondering until a 7 bus came along and he

jumped aboard of it. 'Penny,' he said to the conductor, and as he fumbled in his pocket noticed a red-and-white sticker fixed to the back of one of the seats. 'All Out On May Day,' he read and smiled to the conductor, pointing it out with his eyes. 'You chaps will be there, eh . . .' 'You bet,' said the conductor. 'There'll be lots walking on Wednesday who won't be doing it because they want to either.'

In front of Pat was a blue-serge back, a closely cut section of sandy reddish hair and a black cap. The head turned, a face appeared, a sunburned reddish face with sailor's eyes, china-blue and piercing. The eyes stared into his, the mouth suddenly broke into a smile.

'Jimmy Seton!' exclaimed Pat. 'Well I never . . .'

'What a bloomin' coincidence,' said James, 'and me just ashore too.' They grinned at each other with warm, inarticulate pleasure.

'You old bastard,' said Pat, 'it's grand to see you.'

'You should've stayed by the old *Euphrosyne*,' said James. 'There was a regular revolution soon after we left New York.'

'I've joined the Party now,' said Pat. 'That's something you've got yourself to blame for.'

'I thought you would in the end.'

'You're just ashore, eh . . . What ship?'

'*Arundale*. A lousy tub . . . It's good to be home. Haven't been in London for years. 'Re you working?'

'Sure. My old job, on the *Evening Mail*.'

'It's bloody fine seeing you. We must go round the pubs.'

'We certainly must . . .' Pat looked anxiously out of the window. 'Look here,' he said, 'I've got to get out here. Are you free 'sevening?'

'Yes.'

'Well, let's get together. Give me a ring at the *Mail* – ask for the sub-editors' room.'

'Sure I will,' said James. And Pat was gone, jumping off

the bus, his feet running of their own accord under him while he gave James the Red Front salute.

James sat, still smiling, the warm, pleased feeling of surprise still bubbling in him. It was fine to meet a friend, and Pat of all people. And now he was in the Party, and they would meet this evening and talk together, their friendship closer than ever now . . .

Now, now, now . . . went the tune of his thoughts, so urgent with happy anticipation.

Also, meeting Pat set him to memorizing, while the bus retraced a track for him in space and time back towards the geography of his childhood's memories. His thoughts ran back on double roads, a dual rambling course, back to the times with Pat aboard the *Euphrosyne* and ashore, back to other voyages, other watersides, and also he began to live again the memory-changed scenes of childhood, from whose actuality his memory had travelled so long a journey that he recollected them half-uncomprehendingly, half with an adult stranger's sight.

The bus had navigated the dangerous river of Oxford Street. Now came the whirlpool around the island of Marble Arch. For a moment James glimpsed the green shores of Hyde Park, as they swiftly circled the traffic vortex and plunged from its periphery to safety in the broad stream of Edgware Road. Then those green lands receded and vanished, as he had seen many a shore drown beneath relentless horizons.

Away, away down Edgware Road they went, but the green park grass and the fountain spray of leafing trees stayed in James's mind, which began to ponder in a sweet, elegiac mood, mourning for memories only because they were forever past and not for their own sweetness's sake, for half their mournful charm lay only in that they were no more.

There had been a warm summer evening when he was a

little boy, and his mother had taken John and him into Kensington Gardens. They had lain upon the grass, their senses leaning with a drowsy interfusion of sight and smell towards the heavy coral blossoms of may, the white which shone so ghostly bright, the pink that glimmered so duskily. And his mother gave him an orange. 'Share it with John,' she had said, and he did, amicably for once. Her worn face creased peacefully. This was the scene he now remembered, sweet with the overtones of remoteness, loaded with the rich harmonics of past time. The heavy blossom-scent and the evening's islanded quiet affected him now, not as if it was an image of a scene through which he had lived but the memory of some picture seen long ago.

The tawdry impersonality of the street began to change to a shabbier cheerfulness. Ahead was the corner of the Harrow Road, where the tramlines began. Fried-fish shops flourished here (he remembered), and their smell mixed with the iron clangour of the trams expressed to him the shabby virility of the working-class town, the London that was real to James, the background of his thoughts, in which memories of parks, squares, rich houses and quiet, seemly streets, were recollections of scenery rather than environment, scenery with all manner of associations yet without that special dear and hateful familiarity of kitchen smells, of a ticking clock and a door that creaked.

And here by the trams, before the corner of the Harrow Road, he got off. (The bus turned wearily down Praed Street, to thread a wilderness of pornographic bookshops and contraceptive stores.)

He turned to walk by the canal, by the little houses with gardens, whose last late almond blossoms still flourished, and he remembered here, in these streets, the first time he had seen the almond blossoms and known that they were beautiful, in the pale and still wintry gardens, after strange days of March sunshine, and he had seen the petals against the slate sky, the twigs and petals against the dun hides of houses, like snow petals, like jewels and stars and coral chips, so that there was suddenly a new feeling born in him, and he knew that this was beautiful, that the word which he had read in books and registered unmeaningly in his mind, had a real application for his life, was about something that he could feel as vividly and strongly as hunger or pain.

Quickened with memories, his mind also woke to an acute perception of the present: he was aware of, and able to delight in, the movements of walking, the smooth-functioning muscles and the living breath that fed his heart; the sunlight was a warm and lovely liquid that bathed him, and the air that sighed down the channel of the street caressed him.

Into this serenity penetrated a clattering uproar with a loud and cheerful song in its midst. Along the road came a great shaggy carthorse at half a gallop, trundling an empty coalcart behind him. And, standing up, flourishing the reins like a chariot driver, stood the coalman, young, handsome, his cap at a terrific angle over his close-curling reddish hair, singing at the top of his voice. His chest was broad, splendidly bared by a wide-gaping, collarless shirt, his laughing head balanced on a magnificent neck, and he stood with his legs apart, easily swaying, rejoicing in his body. The cart rattled and jangled, the great hooves echoed, and in the midst of this cheerful clatter sounded the coalman's jolly song.

People in the street smiled; the girls sighed and laughed at the amorousness of their thoughts.

Down the quiet street passed the cart, like a wind, a wind that ruffled the complacency of the little bourgeois houses, and a few more blossom petals fell to the ground as tenderly as snow, the snow-petals of which James had dreamed when, slum-living, he had dreamed of beauty, had longed for grace in ugly, shabby little rooms. Adolescent, in ugly, shabby clothes, he had watched the falling blossoms with a fretful nostalgia for loveliness beyond his reach. Even in the slums there had been trees that could put forth green leaves and blossoms, even in the towns it had become spring, and there were squares where the night air was may-drenched, was summer-soft, and the blossoms hung out flags of a foreign country. Beauty, the token of his exile, flowered from bricks and pavements. The undertone of the may blossoms had sung to him in the jangling air. (Now he turned from the trim streets, now he walked by rows of decaying houses that had been slums for a hundred years.) Here the spring had engendered country thoughts on him, thoughts that cried *away to summer scenes, to country scenes*. For bird-songs and country air and the drowsing afternoons on lawns he had longed, to escape from his prison town and embrace lakes, woods, meadows and clear skies, spring burnished and summer promising. The undreamed-of April gift, the daffodil rain, had not been for him. The spring had mocked his hungry mouth with splendour, had mocked the soiled parade of the pavements with delight. In the cramped torments of ignorant and poverty-stricken adolescence, he dammed the may-drenched air, the damned summer-soft air, the dusty leaves languishing in the day of arc lamps, the flowers drooping in little sooty gardens. The thoughts that sang *away to summer scenes* taught him of his prison towns and stirred up a dreaming bitterness. In the squares, the decorous squares, the flaunting chestnut blossoms teased him like the smells of food from the rich houses. He observed, inhaled and cursed the dust of cars fleeing to country scenes. These were the rich who prisoned him in towns, the spring-thieves and sun-stealers.

And James had become a Communist. The Aprils of meadows and green things were not for him, who had been prisoned in the arid summers of towns, the summers without harvest. The trees had hung out flags of a foreign country to him, and he had got himself a new flag, the banner of a different spring, whose harvest would be plentiful – the spring of revolution.

So now the almond blossoms fell, and he did not repine. He was not disarmed by nostalgic remembrances of past things: delight in clear skies and growing things, in everything in the world that was good and joyful, strengthened his resolve to help to win them for his class.

Here was the corner of Brickling Street, the last address of John that he knew. And also, in this street was the house where they had been born, where he had grown up and suffered and been happy. It appeared to him with the surprising, shrunken and diminished shabbiness of all familiar childhood's scenes when revisited. The little house was the last in the row, and its outer wall was bulged and cracked. He remembered the long cracks in the plaster indoors that his imagination had made into rivers and railway lines on maps; he remembered the gaps by the edges of the doorposts through which blew draughts, cold little winds that worried his mother in a way he didn't understand. And now she was dead. He had been in Santos when his mother died. The large, wobbling handwriting of Albert Seton was framed in the white space of quarter-inch mourning-edged notepaper. 'She said she would have liked to see you, Jimmy, before she died.' The letter was waiting for him at San Francisco. Tears hotly prickled behind his eyelids, and the orange sunset blurred behind a lattice of ship's masts.

On the side of the house where the wall bulged, an iron cross had been bolted. This was new. He wondered who lived there now . . . A car went by, a long, low Bentley bearing a young man and a blonde girl who smiled. The sight of their rich, easy, indifferent elegance rounded off his thoughts for him. For all he knew the two of them might be thoroughly decent people, but in order to preserve them, who seemed so secure in ease, removed from toil and hardship, the factory chimneys smoked and leaned their darkness across the lives of millions, and working-class women died, made old before their time.

The car went by, with Peter Langfier and Pamela, whom he had persuaded to come out for a drive with him. And bypassing the beginning of the Harrow Road they came this way, fleeing to country scenes.

Pamela leaned back, her hair liquidly rippling in the wind. She no longer smiled, looked a little grave.

'These streets are terrible,' she said, her voice low and concerned.

'I know,' said Peter. 'They don't bear thinking about.'

But one must think about them, she said to herself. When you read about these places it can move you like the tears of a film heroine. But when you see them and know that millions of people live and die in them, you've got to think about them . . .

And Peter, seeing with her eyes, trembling with her pity, easily forgot his own opinions to strengthen hers.

'There's never been so many people living in want like this before, and the world has never been so rich before . . .'

'But what can one do . . .' she murmured, with real unhappiness in her voice. 'I used to think that charities and all that were some good, but they don't really *change* things a bit. My father is terribly rich, but if I had all his money and gave it away, the world would be just the same in the long run.'

Peter wasn't really interested. He didn't like having to think about such things; his mind skated over them. But in his absorption with Pamela's thoughts and feelings he strained to understand and formulate contradictions that he dimly knew to exist.

The car swept by a wall with a hammer and sickle painted on it and the slogan: FORWARD TO SOVIET BRITAIN. Peter didn't notice it, but she did. That's one answer, she thought, for there to be no more rich or poor. But it means hatred and class war, and it's not right. But people see us and see how we live . . .

it's natural that they should cling to anything that promises them a way out.

The car swept on, past slums and factories and slums, fleeing to country scenes. The ugly red-brick rectangles of the Albert Hospital cast shadows across the road and did not bar them.

* * * * *

It was visiting day at the hospital, and a little crowd was gathered by the main entrance, waiting for three o'clock, the time when they would be let in. Jean, the Langfier's between-maid, stood halfway up the steps, leaning on the stone balustrade, dazzling herself with the sun-glint through the bars of her eyelashes. It was her afternoon off, and she had come to see her grandfather, who was dying of consumption.

There was so much she could have done this fine afternoon, but she didn't grudge the time; she was sorry for the poor old man, who, though her grandfather, was almost a stranger to her.

He lay quiet on his bed, in a dark little ward by himself, waiting with the dumb patience of the aged and humble for Jean to come. He was all bones and parchment skin: his face had become very yellow and his long, bushy whiskers drooped. He knew vaguely that he would die soon, but he did not care very much. What really worried him was that he had nothing to smoke. He still kept his old blackened clay pipe in the cupboard by the bed, and he often took it out and fingered it wistfully, or sucked at it gently to get a whiff of air scented with the ghosts of old smokes. He was too tired to read and the nurses had to hurry all the time, so there was no one for him to speak to. He simply lay and existed in a stream of time; even food was no longer of much interest to him. And he couldn't sleep much. He missed the company of the workhouse people, though he hadn't liked them very much.

When Jean came to see him he would talk to her in a whisper, of the country and the towns he had known and the men with whom he had worked; he would tell her of battles, and he would always take out and show her his greasy, tattered army discharge papers.

He never thought of being bitter or resentful. Life was like this for him and his people. It always had been and probably always would be. Only he did wish he could get some tobacco. He was an old soldier, and it wasn't fair . . .

And all around the busy hospital life went on, the dying and the recovering, the routine of sheets and bedpans and thermometers, of medicines and dressings. In the operating theatre at the moment a certain Dr Marshall was removing duodenal ulcers from the inside of Mrs Clara Riley, aged forty-seven. He delved into her interior with an easy grace, watched by a cluster of admiring students. The patient lay, corpse-white but horribly and unmistakably alive, under the flood of lights. She breathed noisily, her displayed entrails slightly bubbled. 'Ah!' exclaimed Marshall, holding up the first detached ulcer and gazing raptly at it with cold, green eyes. 'A perfect horseshoe. Most remarkable. I've never had one like that before.' He was delighted. The students giggled. 'You exhibit a distressing lack of aesthetic sensibility, gentlemen,' he said severely and went on with the job.

Not very long afterwards Mrs Riley lay in her bed again, in the ward, neatly stitched up and recovering consciousness, the pain mixed up with the agony of chloroform dreams and the sound of her moaning that seemed to come from far away to her drowsing ears. 'Bill, Bill,' she moaned, calling for her son, of whom she had so frightfully dreamed. The world swam into being around her, charged with nausea and tears and pain. 'Oh, Bill . . .' she sobbed.

* * * * *

But Bill Riley was miles away, across the other side of London, tamping down powdered graphite and retort carbon into the slot of a hydraulic press at Langfier's. And he and his mother hadn't met or written to each other these five years now, since they had quarrelled.

The hydraulic-press room was long, low, almost windowless, full of a hot, oily gloom. It was a semi-basement at the bottom of the main factory building. You could feel the weight of the machines and labour up above pressing downwards into the gloom, and the noise that filtered down was dull and menacing, a background for the hissing of the presses. The work here was slow, and they had to do a twelve-hour day, but all the time they were aware of the hurrying machines above waiting for the carbon rods and blocks. The work was slow and irritating to the men's minds so that their thoughts were always running ahead to the next job and always thinking of how much had to be done that day . . .

But Bill Riley was the least affected by this. He was a fine chap, large and strong, good looking, with a wide, good-natured grin. He was called Bolshie Bill by his mates, which he took as a compliment, being treasurer of the factory Communist cell. You couldn't help liking him; when you saw his broad, honest grin you couldn't help smiling too. He was noted for the slowness of his thinking. When he grinned particularly hard, the chaps said he was seeing the point of a joke he'd heard yesterday. But Bill was no fool, just slow and solid. He always wore a black cap and a white scarf knotted around his neck, which somehow he managed to keep clean amidst the carbon dust and oil and muck. His shirt-sleeves were rolled up to show naked ladies tattooed in red and blue on large, muscular arms, and he kept up his trousers with a wide leather belt with a Church Lads Brigade buckle on it.

He was whistling the 'International' as he was tamping down the powdered carbon. 'Chuck it, Bill,' said Alf Millman, his mate who worked the machine next to him. 'Old Langton is snooping around somewhere.'

'OK,' said Bill, and he whistled 'Forward You Workers'. 'The old sod won't know that tune,' he said to Alf. Alf's press gave a long hissing sigh. Alf sighed too.

'Not four o'clock yet,' he said. 'Roll on seven.' He was a young, very serious, very alert-looking chap with a squint, neat and terribly energetic and efficient. Bill rather looked up to him. He was the factory cell leader. They both worked big hydraulic presses which squeezed the graphite and retort carbon 'mix' into hard square blocks of 'green' carbon. There were a dozen of these machines and then a lot of slug presses, which extruded a kind of long, soft worm of hot carbon that rapidly hardened into rods.

Most of the men were working in a rather sour silence. They all felt fed up.

Langton, the chief engineer, had been prowling around, not saying anything but just watching them. They were fed up: it was a lousy job and they got lousy pay and they worked a twelve-hour day. They did their work all right, and the bosses knew it, so why the hell did they come snooping around getting on people's nerves.

'That bastard fair gets on my tit,' said someone.

'He's not so bad as some of 'em.'

'He's too soppy, that's all.'

'Wot's 'e want to come 'anging round anyway?'

'Can't tell if we are doing the work right.'

'Like to see 'im working a press.'

'Lot of bastards.'

'Gets on my tit it does.'

'Fifteen quid a week 'e gets and wot for . . . muckin' about and 'anging around.'

'Maybe he is a silly bleeder,' (this from Alf) 'maybe he does get fifteen quid a week. But 'sno good grumbling about *him*. He's just a fool; 'snot his bleeding factory. What we want is a bit of satisfaction from Langfier and Gilray . . . *and* AIE. If we had a works committee . . .'

'You and your works committee . . .'

'Why not. 'E's right. If we 'ad a works committee we could get things a bit better . . .'

'Works committee! Wot about the bleedin' girls.'

'Wot about 'em, eh. Let me tell you, they're gettin' fed up, bloody fed up.'

'I 'eard 'em talk about a strike . . .'

'. . . no bloody union – no bloody strike pay.'

'. . . works committee c'd help to get a union branch going . . .'

'. . . never get them all together . . .'

'. . . electricians are in the union all right. No bleeding twelve-hour day for them.'

'Jock tole me the carpenters was union men too.'

'All bloody three of 'em . . . hundred per cent. Where does that get *us*.'

'What'll get us somewhere is getting a union branch our bloody selves and seeing the leaders do as we want – like the busmen.'

'They're the boys; they've got a bit of guts.'

'What about when you've got to walk to work Wednesday.'

'If we did what they're doing we'd be with the others in the park Wednesday and not slaving down here in this rat-pit . . .'

'Pipe down. Here's Langton again.'

They bent their heads over their work. The presses hissed, the hot rods came oozing out like nasty worms, and above the machines throbbed their endless note. Langton walked by abstractedly, not noticing the men's rigid silence. He wore a brownish suit and a moustache of the same indeterminate colour; he walked with a shamble, peering about in a short-sighted way, like some kind of large and rather stupid rodent. The men didn't mind him much as a rule, but he was detested by the girls.

He was worried. The machines were having the guts knocked out of them, being worked day and night, overloaded, not being overhauled enough. It gave him a sense of strain at the back of his neck when he thought of their bearings. No good saying anything to Meek. He wouldn't listen. No good seeing Gilray. 'Your job, Mr Langton, is seeing they work properly, ours is to see we're getting enough output from them.' The percentage of rejects was going up. They didn't care, not now. When they'd got a two hundred per cent increased output, a five per cent increase of rejects didn't worry them. But it would go up. The machines couldn't stand the pace. There'd be more rejects, more breakdowns. He'd get the sack. No good saying he'd told them . . . He'd get the sack just the same. Phillips would have the job – for less pay . . . He'd seen it happen before . . . He worried about his drinking too . . .

Langton used to do his job efficiently and forget it the moment he was away from the factory. He lived in a villa at Blackheath with his wife and daughter, a pair of suety British matrons whom he didn't even feel strongly enough about to dislike. At home, he spent his time pottering about in the 'study'. This was his nearest approach to happiness, the fire and the comfortable warmth of a drop of whisky in his stomach and perhaps a broken clock or something to tinker with.

But now it was different. He came home worrying about his job, worrying about the machines and the rejects. His family got on his nerves, and he'd sit in his study and feel depressed, taking nips of whisky until he felt the worry go away into a kind of muzzy mist.

Last night when he got to bed he realized that he was really drunk, and he started to reckon up nips and glasses and bottles . . . and this was another worry. He felt miserable about it on vague moral grounds.

He went through the boiler room on a short cut back to his office, going through corridors and locker rooms, past rows of clocking-in machines and cutting across the factory's business entrance, a hall with museum glass cases of samples. A few travellers were sitting about morosely or leering with rimy eyes at the ankles and jogging breasts of office girls who trotted by carrying papers and trying to look important. He heard the telephone operator saying, 'No, madam. He left this morning and hasn't been back since.'

* * * * *

'Well, I really don't know what can have happened to him,' sighed Lady Langfier in her irritatingly placid voice as she put down the 'phone. And she turned to Henry McGinnis, the chauffeur. 'Well, Henry, I don't suppose he will be wanting the car when he does come back. Will you take me to Lady Brackenhurst's.' She was always charming to her servants and gave them orders as if she was asking them favours. But somehow they never really liked her and got a kind of mean, rather perverse, sense of pleasure when they took advantage of her easygoingness.

'Can I have my coat, please, Mary,' she said, putting her head a little to one side in the manner that had been so charming twenty years ago.

And then she went out and sat in the car, vaguely wondering what could have delayed her husband, while she fidgeted with a split finger in her glove. She dressed expensively and plainly, but there was always something, a split glove or a laddered stocking, that was not quite right. And when Langfier remonstrated with her she would agree and call herself silly or careless with an utterly stupid imperturbability that had come profoundly to annoy him.

She was a Jewess who had been a singularly lovely girl, possessed of a dusky, mysterious beauty. Then, her cheerful placidity had been delightful, her unresponsive silences alluring. Of course, she had no sense of humour whatever, but somehow that had been charming: she would say such silly things and then join in people's laughter without knowing what had caused it. Now her figure was still slender and attractive; that dusky skin had become only a trifle sallow and yellowish, and her eyes retained their dark lustrousness, though with a slightly protruding stare of possible exophthalmic goitre, and her girlish manner, that mild and harmless coquettishness, she still exercised to a degree that set her family's teeth on edge.

The drive was short; the car quickly drew up in front of a very high-class mansion with a chromium-and-black door and a flunkey attached.

'Dear Lady Brackenhurst,' said Lady Langfier, 'I *do* hope I'm not late.'

'Of course you're late, my dear,' said her hostess in a hearty voice. She was a very tiaraboomdeay-looking personage. 'So is *everyone*!'

For some reason or other this was construed to be frightfully witty. Lady Langfier giggled girlishly. Lady Brackenhurst neighed until her bosom quivered. ('*Bust*, my dears,' one of her son's nancy friends had remarked. 'It's not a bust, it's a positive explosion.')

This was a bridge party, twelve more or less noble ladies, three card tables and some hundreds of cards. Also there were dozens of really wonderful little cakes and sandwiches, but they were for later. The room was a pale and misty grey, furnished with exquisite and unostentatious simplicity. It would have looked nicer empty.

And the ladies began their game, contract bridge, to be exact. These, not quite the noblest in the land but getting on for it, grappled with the following gargantuan intellectual problem – given fifty-two cards and you know where twenty-six of them are, find the rest. They had been wondering about this for years and had never really satisfactorily cleared the matter up. They played for rather a lot of money, but they didn't worry about that. The real sweat lay in controlling the temper. Of course, most of them took the game quite seriously: they had so much money and so little to do that they had to fall back upon intellectual diversions. Taxes, death duties, servants, these were worries from which they had to distract themselves at times. Being rich is hardly worth it you know. Their husbands were in the government or something with responsibilities. And all were devoted to charity.

The minds worked, the cards turned over, the hands moved and the hearts beat. From the world outside came no sound, no breath. Only anonymous servants ventured into this cloistered calm, treading with ghost-feet upon the silent mist-grey carpet, pushing their little rubber-tyred truckloads of cakes and sandwiches. (I forgot to mention – the whistle had blown for tea; the girls were taking a breather.)

Into the secret, pampered guts slid the warm tea (not the strong and cheerful drink of common people, but a pale, an ethereal Chinese distillation at six bob the pound).

The women's talk ran evenly, on trivialities . . .

* * * * *

But time passes, the earth turns, the sun declines and the clock on the mantelpiece struck, a gentle ringing note repeated, and hearing it the players were brought to mind of time's flight and the turning earth, and in their minds began to expend perspectives of appointments to be kept, of dinners and theatres, the hands of other clocks in other rooms inexorably moving towards appointed moments.

It was not long before the games were finished and the

players rose, smoothing their skirts, and already the after-noon was over. There was a rustling of coats, a picking-up of bags and gloves; farewells and thanks were spoken, invitations given and received. The cars and taxis drew up at the black-and-chromium door and drove away again, dispersing in the flowing tide of traffic, the tide that now ran swiftly with homeward-hurrying workers. Under the clay, the crowded trains burrowed their wormy courses, and far from sight and sound of natural things, in a steel-cased electric day that burned precariously in the dank and fearful subterranean darkness, thousands of living human beings sat thinking their lonely thoughts or reading 'Bayswater Man Falls To Death', and the results of the last race. And the scarlet buses roared through the streets, pouring east and west, north and south, packing together in a blocked, slow-moving mass, like jostling tree trunks floating down a narrow river.

The bridge party was dispersed, its separate entity now broken up, parcelled out in the thoughts of its scattered members, living a changed and fragmentary life that whirled swiftly through quiet streets or in the plush twilight of limousines caught in throbbing traffic jams.

From factories and offices, in buses, trams or on bicycles, began to march the dispersed and scattered army of the day's work. To the west rode John, dazzled by the lowering sun. His head down, he pedalled in the roaring traffic stream, choked by its spray of dust and petrol vapours. He darted between cars, hung on to the backs of lorries waiting for traffic-lights, dodged pedestrians scurrying across the road. This homeward trip was like a long journey across perilous mountains and through forests full of ravening wild beasts, a journey in which his life depended on his nerve and muscle, on his quickness of eye and alertness for lurking dangers.

The trip took him the best part of an hour, but it was quicker than any other way, and it saved money. However, its cost in nervous energy was immense; he was cutting down the years of his old age. Unconsciously, his brow contracted itself, his eyes slid from side to side, and his mouth made itself a hard-closed narrow slit. But also his private thoughts went on behind the mask of concentration, pursuing their own, their isolated course, homeward bound to Martine and the baby, to the remembering anticipation of a warm kiss awaiting him and the patter of Mick's welcoming dance of delight.

The newspaper vans sped westwards, ahead of John, leaving a trail of newsbills, whose words his sight irritatedly registered again and again: WORLD FLIERS BEAT RECORDS. DEATH OF PEER. SCHULTZ CRASHES IN SIBERIA. DEATH OF PEER. AREA SUICIDE REVELATIONS.

The earth was being girdled, a peer had died, a German aeroplane smouldered into a heap of blackened ruins, lost in the flowery wastes of the tundra. On page four a woman had quadruplets in Paraguay; a peer had died and there had been a revolt in a Nazi concentration camp. Eastward, eastward went the planes, the pilots' tired gaze leaning forward to the invisible horizon of the Pacific.

From these reached out a spider's web of cables whose wires quivered with electric messages. Through tape machines and telephones news poured inwards upon the nerve endings of sub-editors. A peer was dead, someone had quadruplets in Paraguay . . . it was all one to them. The cigarettes dangled from their mouths, the typewriters clattered, the tape machines spat and stuttered their halting stories.

The last edition of the *Evening Mail* was going to press. A cigarette hung from the corner of Pat Morgan's mouth, its neglected smoke slowly curling upwards. His blue pencil did figure-skating across proof-sheets. The quadruplets in Paraguay were deleted, they were no longer news; the dead peer's obsequies were performed on another page. Schultz was dead, Fernandez was out of the race. But Thompson was off again.

THOMPSON FLIES ON streamed across the top of page one. And Faulkner had crossed the Yenesi River, leading the others by two hundred miles. Eastward roared the propellers, eastward across the map of Socialist Siberia. And in smudgy photographs the pilots' wives and sweethearts languished for their lovers' fates. The world is being girdled; the world is being changed; it grows smaller, it grows larger; men change the world, and the world makes men to change it.

Pat's cigarette burned down, the great presses roared below, the advertising staff washed their hands and put on their hats, the secretaries folded up their typewriters.

The mahogany wilderness of the editor's room was deserted, left to cigarette ends and stale smoke. The paper's policy that helped to mould men's thoughts had been decided here by the thoughts of men. The magic words 'rationalization of industry' had been spoken and taken new wings again. Redundant factories must be closed down. Prosperity is here, and we must go poor to keep it. Thus, already a widening ripple of events spread outwards from this morning's AIE meeting to take shape in men's thoughts and actions. Thus was the power of these big men in this panelled room. This is possible because of AIE, because of banks and railways and factories, the world of profit which they control and which controls them. We are free to have six toes or seven eyes, this is the freedom of the press, thinks Pat, and his glance leans across to the strong lean face of Vernon, the leader of the Fleet Street Communist group. 'The freedom of the press,' he murmurs, and Vernon smiles, his face breaking up into lines and creases like the suddenly disturbed surface of a smooth pool. 'We'll be free of it in five minutes,' he says. 'There's nothing in tonight about the busmen,' says Pat. 'It's a pity . . .'

In five minutes they will be done. And there will be a 'phone call for Pat and he will hear the ghost of James's voice sounding in the receiver, and a meeting will be arranged, a meal somewhere, and then they will go back to the flat, perhaps with a bottle of whisky, and the words will flow between them, talk and memories of days at sea; also they will speak of revolution, of the changing world whose conscious task it is theirs to change.

He crossed the room and stood waiting by the window, looking down on to the channel of Fleet Street through which the traffic poured. Like ants the people scurried, like rabbits from out of warrens, pouring into the streets, into buses and trains, homeward bound to private lives.

For each now a day is over, he thinks; for each a new day begins. There are so many of them, so many blinded ants swarming and struggling to live and to beget life and knowing nothing of what they do beyond the narrow orbit of their own immediate scurryings. And what makes this orbit is Sloane, the banks, the financiers, the armaments firms and the steel trusts, the masters of the world whose world is crumbling around them. Thus these little orbits change, the even tenour of these little lives is broken; ideas, created by things, are shattered by material decay, and they react in turn to refashion things.

The 'phone bells rang in his ears, and one call was for him; he turned from the street below as William Dartry's car drove by, a long green Renault.

* * * * *

Dartry's fleshy, complacent face was very red; he chewed the ends of his little reddish moustache and bit his nails. Whenever the car stopped he unconsciously leaned forward, straining in his mind to urge it on. He was angry at being delayed at the factory, at the slow-moving traffic. All the day's irritations bubbled in his mind, the row with Langfier, the reports of accidents and discontent in the factory, the fear of a strike, of something happening to delay this big rush order. There was Meek and Langton and the others, coming to him, complaining, making excuses, only thinking of themselves, only thinking if they could make it all right with him it would be all right, as if he was some independent godalmighty, not seeing AIE behind him saying 'do this, do that', as if there was nothing beyond giving an order to get things done.

And the traffic jammed, the car crawled and stopped and jerked forward and crawled again. These wasted moments were precious moments, stolen from those brief and precious hours of delight in the warm, the naked sensual charms of Jenny Hardy, his mistress. The anger of his impatience for those lost and wasted moments was fused with his impatience to behold and enjoy his Jenny. Remembering and anticipating, his thoughts dwelt upon the warm, rosy seclusion of her flat, the warm soft rosiness of her lovely naked flesh.

This man of affairs, this man masked with power, was vanquished by his lusts, which melted him to sentimentality, which quite disarmed him, until in the arms of a woman he became a child seeking his mother's breast.

The car progressed in brief dashes, halting and darting forward and halting again, past the two islanded churches, into the Strand, until it reached the Savoy and swung up the little drive and stopped at the hotel entrance.

Dartry got out. 'Don't trouble to fetch me,' he said to the chauffeur. 'I don't know when I'll be finished.'

'Thank you, sir,' he said, full of pleasure at the thought of a free evening, an evening in which to do as he willed, without the nagging thoughts of predetermined time to cut short his pleasure.

Dartry stood and watched the car drive away. Then he hailed a taxi. When he stepped into it he was free, he stepped from one life to another, to his secret, sensual life of women and soft lights, away from the struggles and responsibilities of a man masked with power.

The hotel lights slid blurred across the window glass as the taxi wheeled. Then it turned down quieter streets. At a certain and unremarkable door it stopped. Dartry rang and was let in by a chubby, white-haired servant. 'Good evening, sir,' she said in a country voice, smiling welcomingly as she took his hat and gloves.

They went upstairs, into a little hall dimly lit with an amber glow. His feet made no sound on the soft carpet. It was warm and quiet. A door opened, and Jenny stood in the entrance, a lithe and strong girl with bronzy hair, wide-set topaz eyes, a firm chin and a splendid mouth: warm, generous, sensual, yet firm. She wore an oyster-coloured satin evening dress, simply cut, that showed off her strong round breasts and rather large hips. As she stood there for a moment, framed in light, lovely and luxurious, his mind jumped back to remember her as he had first seen her in the factory, wearing the ugly grey overalls, looking ruefully at a cut finger. The bright blood flowed, she had bared strong teeth and licked the cut and laughed. His eyes had dwelt on her, undressing her, and he was deeply shaken by a sudden spasm of lust. She looked into his eyes, and she had known.

Jenny had not grown too old for her job, nor had she been displaced by new machinery. She was warm-hearted, sentimental, but she knew clearly what life had to offer her, and without questioning she took her chance. Now she had a flat, a bank account, a car and also a lover. Once or twice a week Dartry visited her. Gravely, unthinkingly, she submitted to his embraces, a little grateful to this stranger who had changed her life, who had taken her virginity, yet who remained a man outside her life. She drew her money from the bank and saved most of it; she never asked for gifts or jewels but was grateful when he gave them. A day would come when she would be quite free; this life would be over and forgotten.

Now she kissed him, took his arm and led him in. 'I've

got a lovely dinner for you,' she said. He sighed, sank into an armchair, and she sat on his knee without anything being said between them, yet as if he had invited her.

How quiet, how peaceful am I now, thinks Dartry. Here in this domain of naked desire I am at ease, a man, instead of a figure behind a desk masked with power and feared or hated, or a husband whose home is no home, whose wife and children are strangers.

How strange is the quality of his middle age, thinks Jenny. Look at the thick neck, the pouched eyes, the sagging belly beneath the waistcoat. He is a man, yet how strangely different is his body to the strong and ardent flesh of Jack, my lover.

She pressed his hand to her left breast (he likes me to do that, she thinks) and kissed the top of his head. 'Are you glad to see me?' she said caressingly.

'Am I glad . . . ? You're free of the factory now, but you know how you felt in the evening when you were through with your work . . .'

'You hate it too. It's funny. We never thought of you like that.'

'Little bitches . . .' he smiled. And she began to talk of the factory girls as he liked her to, of their amours, their desires and adventures, using their frank, coarse words . . .

Outside the taxis wheeled, the newsboys cried through the streets. Life went to another pulse, of evening, and a gayer rhythm informed the air.

EVENING

Now light fades from the air, the rosy dusk is threaded with the glowing beads of a necklace of streetlamps. A mist of light and darkness interfused ascends from the river and gathers in the lost perspectives at the ends of streets.

In the powerhouses the dynamos are switched over to a fuller load, louder and faster goes their tune. It is evening and life moves to another pulse, a different rhythm, and our story must go with it too, with a swifter rhythm and a wider range, the different currents of its lives flowing together in one stream, a stream that flows a winding route but always moving forward, even when it seems to turn back on itself. (The currents strive to run all ways, confusedly, each trying to follow its own separate course . . . they are lines that make patterns of confusion, the invisible spider's webs that lead, through a million routes, to the factory chimneys.)

Take Dunbourne, Sloane, Redesdale, Gilray . . . the men masked with power. Now they are scattered, their masks laid aside. Lights burn for them to illuminate the bare shoulders of silken women, waiters' shirt-fronts, crystal and cutlery, singing mouths and kicking chorus legs. They move in the narrow orbits of their world of pleasure. The night is their day.

And for others too, the night is a day. At street corners the platforms are set up, the Communists speak, the Communist voices are sounding now, in the trade-union meetings, in the night shifts of factories, in pubs and upon doorsteps. And there are echoes in laboratories and libraries, in college rooms and in quiet corners at middle-class parties. The day after tomorrow is May Day, and there is a new mood amongst the workers.

These are the conscious protagonists of the struggle that extends throughout society; a struggle that is both of minds and things, both between and within classes and individuals. This struggle of men's lives controls the orbits in which they move.

* * * * *

Now Langfier is returned, and he sits in an armchair thinking bitter thoughts, while upstairs his wife dresses for dinner; and Peter too is at home and making himself ready for the evening's pleasure, his thoughts still drugged with memories of his afternoon in the country with Pamela. Now James and Pat both sit in buses going towards their meeting place, their minds ahead of them and already meeting. Now John and Martine are eating stew and smiling at each other while Mick sits at John's feet and yearns upwards at the food smells. Now Dartry and his mistress wait to dine, while in the factory a night shift works. Now old Peter Lamont sits in a stuffy little backroom reading an astronomical textbook, while Jock drinks a pint of mild and bitter at the Kings Arms before the great darts match begins. Now Riley, Millman and Ivy Cutford are walking down an ill-lit, drab street, going to the factory cell meeting. In a Rowton House the man who had sat writing on the steps leading up to Holborn fries a kipper on the communal stove, and he watches it sharply with eager eyes: once he had turned his back for a moment on a bit of bacon (five years ago it was) and someone had pinched it. He would never be caught that way again. Now the factory girls are home from work, making themselves up and putting on their best clothes to sally forth to cinemas, to dates with boyfriends. It is evening, it is spring, life goes with a lifting pulse to a different rhythm.

* * * * *

The Langfier factory cell usually met in Alf Millman's front parlour, a small room with too much furniture and too many china souvenirs of fairs and holidays. Some pretty vile pictures on the walls added to the general oppression of the atmosphere. Everyone would have felt more comfortable in the back room, but Mrs Millman was a stickler for the proprieties.

The room was very full of six people. Richardson was coming down from the Sub-District Secretariat to attend their meeting, and they were waiting for him. Bill Riley was usefully employing the time by stamping the comrades' cards.

The sound of the machines still echoed in Ivy Cutford's ears as she discussed the situation of the girls in her shift with Millman. There was a picture in her mind, of the word STRIKE in jagged red letters and the machines stopping with a stunning silence. She jumped nervously when the bell rang. Her nerves were getting into a bad state.

Millman answered the door and let Richardson in. He was a rather ugly young chap, with straight brown hair and a long straight nose. He wore a dark-blue double-breasted suit and looked very clean. 'Evening, comrades,' he said, looking around at them and trying to size them up quickly. Millman he knew, and Ivy Cutford, both fine comrades, though Alf was too impatient and inclined to be over-optimistic. Then there was Bill Riley, a good type, he thought, but looks as if he needs leadership. Next to him was a small, rather depressed man in glasses, an electrician and an obvious trade-union man. There were two other middle-aged chaps wearing mufflers, steady, quiet-looking fellows whom he rather liked.

''S everyone here?' he asked.

'There's two on night shift who can't come,' said Bill Riley.

'D'you mind leaving over the cell business till I've gone,' said Richardson. 'I've got to get to two other meetings tonight . . .'

'Sure,' they said.

'Well, comrades,' he went on, 'I want to give a short report of the situation as regards May Day first, and then we can discuss what lead is to be given in the factory . . .' He tried hard to visualize his own words, to spur up his own enthusiasm. He had given this report seven times already this week. It was so difficult not to make it mechanical. It was no good giving leads, however correct, unless they were given so as really to convince the comrades of the burning necessity of carrying them out correctly.

Then it came to discussion of the position at Langfier's. It needed very careful handling. The main body of the workers were unorganized; strong grievances of every sort existed, and there was a rising militant temper. The Communists were trying to get a representative works committee formed; they were all agreed that this could be done quite soon: the Party had a considerable amount of prestige in some of the departments, and individual comrades were very much liked. But it was very difficult to give a correct lead on the May Day question. There was no existing organization or committee with the authority to call the workers out on strike even on economic issues; also the majority of the workers did not yet see the connection between fighting against their immediate grievances and the political issues of the demonstration.

'You see, comrades,' said Richardson, replying to Millman, 'we mustn't put forward our immediate demands as things in themselves; they must be linked up with the fight for Soviet power, with the need for building a mass party. Now we hope to get these girls in the union. If we haven't given them the correct lead beforehand they'll either be led up the garden or just see that the union leadership is no good and get fed up with the whole business . . . But what about this leaflet . . . let's get it drafted out now, and someone can come up to Sub-District with it tonight, and we'll give it the OK and get it printed.'

'Can you get someone to hold a dinner-hour meeting outside the factory tomorrow?'

'I'll see . . . I can't promise.'

'And we can advertise the meeting in the leaflet.'

'How about calling for a ten-minute stoppage of work on May Day . . .'

'I don't think we can call for any *action* for May Day whatever. Most of the workers may feel ready to take some action, but they don't know what the others feel. They've got no certainty . . . and they won't have any till we get the works committee going . . .'

Richardson's attention was darting about the room like a little quivering ray of light; there were questions to be asked; answers had to be interpreted in conjunction with what he could make of the speaker's character. His mind struggled to get a clear picture of this factory and what the workers were thinking and talking about. Everywhere were tremendous possibilities. The temper of the workers was rising: everywhere the slogan of Soviet power must be put forward. The Communists had tremendous tasks now, tremendous responsibilities; they were the men of the future, the men destined by history to change the world. There was a picture in his mind now, of hundreds of little rooms like this, hundreds of little groups all over the world, meeting and talking together and organizing all with one common end . . . Where there were hundreds now, a few years ago there were tens. A few years hence there must be thousands.

* * * * *

But also curtains were going up on the first acts; fathers of families switched on the radio and lay back in their armchairs digesting with pipe smoke; the warm darknesses of picture palaces quivered with humanity; in the newspaper offices the blue pencils still did their figure-skating. A vast world existed unconscious of the ferment that worked within it. The lovers walked in the parks too and laughed or were sad. And in area dustbins, searching for fishbones amidst ashes and dead, withered daffodils, cats began their evening promenade. But Tibbles, the Langfiers' kitchen tabby, a fat eunuch, lay drowsing by the kitchen stove, indifferent, deaf to the call of romance. The smells of a cooking dinner irradiated his heat-drowsed senses, and he purred gently. 'Master Peter's in to dinner,' said cook to Dora. 'And *don't* offer 'im soup again. It's a thing 'e can't abide.'

And the front door slammed as Lady Langfier in a grey shimmering evening cloak descended to the car.

Sir Edwin, sitting in the brown leather armchair by the fireplace in the library, heard it with a sigh of relief. The faint rustle of her dress still dwelt in the air with the little fading cloud of her perfume; an echo of her goodbye still lingered in his ears. But the front door slammed, and she drove away. A useless fire flicked in the hearth with a rotting sound. The irritation of her presence faded from his mind, and he was back again with his lonely, bitter thoughts.

Tibbles arched his back and stretched when the dinner gong sounded, and Langfier went downstairs automatically, hearing with habit-deafened ears the brass still quietly booming to itself as he passed it in the hall.

And in the dining-room, warming his behind in front of an empty fireplace, stood Peter in full evening dress, pink and sleek from his bath.

'Hullo,' he said. 'I've not seen you for a long time.' Peter and his father were friendly strangers now: the period of their conflict was over. They were a little pleased, a little embarrassed with each other's company. In Peter this was masked by a bantering manner.

'How's trade,' he said.

'Bad,' said Langfier.

'You should grind the faces of the poor a bit more then.'

'That's what I'm having to do,' said Langfier, and there was such an expression of concern on his face that Peter changed the subject and said, 'I'm hungry. Been out in the country this afternoon. It was lovely.' And as he spoke he blushed a little, for what he had not said, for his tender thoughts of Pamela. How lovely it had been, going fast against the wind's onrush, his senses taut to the car's controls, yet also strongly aware of her by his side, her hair flickering in the wind, her face cool, reposed and lovely. And then they had stopped, and it was suddenly quiet, the silence of the countryside rushing down on them . . . How lovely the country must be now, thought Langfier, his mind reaching back to long-forgotten memories of lanes and woods, clear skies and quiet scenes.

Then Dora brought the soup in. 'None for you, sir,' she said proudly to Peter. 'Cook's done you a nice bit of toasted cheese.'

They sat at the end of the long table, lonely Robinson Crusoes in an island of light whose shores were sombre walls and gloomy pictures. This was a depressing room for two people to dine in: it only assumed its proper proportions at large and rather formal dinner parties. They were chilled to silence: both minds registered the fact that Lady Langfier was not there. On the few occasions when the family dined by themselves at home she kept the conversation going with cheerful platitudes that demanded no replies. Now their two minds were so preoccupied, so concerned with thoughts whose courses flowed far apart, that it was forced and unreal for their conversation to be a joint stream. There was no one to whom Langfier could tell his troubles, there was no one to whom Peter could speak of those impalpable delights, those elusive and unrecapturable pleasures whose fading recollections he held so carefully in the fragile vessel of his mind.

'Where are you going tonight?' his father asked him.

'To the Hawthorne's dance.'

'They're rather out of the run of your usual amusements, aren't they? What's the attraction?'

'I didn't say there was one.'

'Oh . . . but there must be.'

'As a matter of fact there is . . .' he replied, thinking of how Pamela had said she might be there if her mother went. 'Ve-ry nice,' he said, in rather an affected voice, half-despising himself for the silly, oblique reference, half-delighted at being able to refer to her in any way at all.

'Nice of cook to remember that I like toasted cheese,' he said, eating it with pleasure.

'Dora is a one, isn't she . . . I do like having cheerful maids.'

'As you put it so happily – she is a one.'

'Mother stands for her pretty well.'

And they thought of Lady Langfier again, not noticing how much more her personality was impressing itself on them in her absence than when she was there.

* * * * *

Open the big walnut wardrobe in the bedroom, and there are rows of her dresses gravely hanging; there is something of her in each of them, and in the impalpable smell that the wardrobe itself breathes out.

In her desk lie pieces of paper marked with her round, unformed handwriting; there may be a crumpled handkerchief somewhere, and a few combings of her hair in the dustbin. She is gone, she is out of the house, but her presence lingers in material objects. Is it in the place itself or the heads of its inhabitants? The house may creak at times, have its own smells and moods, be ageing and changing in its own way. But still, it's only a shell, a box for humans, dead without them. Langfier has an idea that it's *his* house, that the bricks and planks and slates, the chimneys and the plaster, even the cracked area paving-stones, *belong* to him, just as his tooth-brush or his watch does. '*How* is it yours?' you may ask him, and honestly it's difficult for him to say. Go down the street, knock at all the dignified doors, and who will be able to tell you why such and such a brick in a certain wall is theirs? And the poor deflowered earth upon which the houses are reared, that *belongs* – to the Ecclesiastical Commissioners to be exact. Something happened in 1473, and now this earth, stretched like a corpse under a winding sheet of tar and brick, belongs ... to what? A parcel of old gentlemen? Dig a hole in Langfier's garden and find a nice big bit of flint and take it along to the old fellows. Say 'I've found a stone belonging to one of you gents. I'd like to hand it over. Whose is it?' Really, sir, they won't have the slightest idea. It's something to do with something that happened in the year 1473.

But when you've gone down to the end of the street and walked for five minutes east or west, you find quite different sorts of houses with different sorts of people in them, brick-layers and carpenters, for instance. Nothing that happened in 1473 did them any good. They don't have any peculiar ideas about land and bricks belonging to them. They have it all on hire from a gentleman in a top hat whom they've never seen. How do they know it's really his? That's a difficult question ...

Fried-fish shops and pubs abound here, and children play in the road. Only a few dim streetlamps support the dark canopy of the night that presses so heavily downwards. Several people in several places happen to look up and notice a little ice-green star. It's the only one appearing tonight. This happens while the Langfiers, father and son, are eating a nice bit of roast mutton. The factory windows make oblong holes in the night through which streams the yellow radiance of another day, while Jock stands in the public bar of the Kings Arms playing darts.

This isn't just any casual darts game. Jock, Ginger and

Nosey Parsons were the pick of the Dog And Duck darts-club team, and they were here tonight playing a game of 3,001 against the undefeated champions of the Kings Arms. Even the most casual drinker leered over the rim of his glass at the scoreboard tonight.

Dog And Duck, 1,094; Kings Arms, 1,113 – stood the reckoning. 'A ve-ry close game,' muttered Nosey Parsons. 'Go it, Jock.' And Jock stepped up to the brass line and threw a 20, a triple-20 and a bull. There was a hoarse mutter of applause. 'Good ole Jock,' said Ginger, as Jock walked back to his stance by the door, swaggering slightly, his pleasure added to by the fact that he was wearing his best suit and a rather dashing shirt.

The landlord of the Kings Arms threw next and scored 57. A good night for trade, he thought, as the door kept on swinging open and letting in customers. And once they were in and leaning up against something they stayed and watched. The air was a smoke-dim warmth of yellow light, swirling with voices. The darts thudded on the board, the scorer's chalk scratched, while the beer-engines gushed merrily.

But when the door swung open the noises of the outside world filtered in, a distant barrel organ, dogs barking and children playing, and the voice of a street-corner speaker. Jock, standing beside the door, could see him when it opened. He stood under the streetlamp, his hand sawing the air, a red flag hanging behind him and a dark sea of caps surrounding the platform. And the door swung to again, cutting off the words 'Soviet power'. All through the game this was happening, and he heard snatches of words, of the Communist voices, the phrases that took shape from a conflict that was changing the world. Jock was playing splendidly tonight, and he was filled with a glow of pleasure, the warm glow of his mates' admiration; but also the speaker's voice was pricking at him so that his mind divided itself between two atmospheres, between the smoke-dim warmth and the cheerful hum of talk within, and that other and known atmosphere, of the silent crowd and the speaker's voice, whose words were uttered like hammer-blows. And somehow he felt ashamed for taking his ease and being so pleased with himself when he should be out there. The Communist words had grown into his mind, and now he began to feel that he should be taking his part helping to turn the words to action. When a young chap in a khaki shirt and red tie stuck his head around the door and shouted out, 'Anyone want the *Daily Worker*?' Jock bought one and gave him threepence for it, and this made him feel a bit better. I'll take it along and show it to old John tomorrow, he said to himself, remembering their talk of this morning.

* * * * *

And John was remembering it too now, but differently, as he sat with Martine in the ninepennies at the Blue Hall Cinema.

As he watched the romance of chorus girls and big businessmen, various rather complicated things were going on in his mind. Right at the bottom of the pool of consciousness the screen images of breasts and thighs stirred up the dreaming thoughts of lust; at the same time he silently enunciated within him certain words spoken that morning, and a whole collection of sensory images accompanied the remembered sounds – ghosts of the smells of wood-shavings and glue, images of Jock's large nose and Peter Lamont's tobacco-stained moustache. And other memories of other associated thoughts clung to those images. But this was not all. He recollected ideas that those words had called up this morning, and they conflicted and interacted with present thoughts on the same lines. Also he watched the screen and registered what was happening there, heard sounds, was warm, was aware of his behind pressing on the seat. And in the same depths where those lust dreams moved and coiled was an obscure bodily awareness of Martine by his side, an awareness of a current flowing between his flesh and hers.

But the world is *not* so, was the burden of his thoughts. It was not all love and breasts and the romance of big business. For me the factory is the world, the house we live in, the May Day demonstration, David's messing his napkin, Langfier's car, the price of tobacco and food, pain and fatigue and going to the lavatory. Life is a struggle for us, life is a battle under the long shadows of the factory chimneys.

* * * * *

We say that life is this, we say it is that . . . thinks Peter Langfier. We exist and we invent a word called 'life' to give a reason for existence. Now the music curves and ripples in the air like the music of my dream; around and around the dancers go, their bodies leaning towards each other, their faces grave or gay, their lips dumb or speaking; life is for love and dancing, they think, life is for hunting and shooting, for sitting in offices, for wearing clothes, for flirting, for ambition, for pleasure, for service, for being served . . . around and around they go while the dowagers and the fat old duchesses sit against the walls, fan themselves and talk to the old men. But is life just this, is it just for this . . . ? I have believed it is for something. I have had intimations that I do not exist solely in order to pass time away . . . But Pamela is not here; my gaze has gone around with the dancers, has leaned against the walls with the old men and women, has quivered in doorways and slid down corridors, flickering on faces, on arms and legs and hips, and has not glanced upon *that* face, has missed those arms and legs and hips. That Pamela has not come is only a minor tragedy, but on its account life is meaningless. I have stopped to think, I have stopped to reckon up the days that go so swiftly, the hours that dwindle away so smoothly, and I have stopped to think what is in them . . . We go on because of an unspoken, unacknowledged hope that tomorrows will be different, that the pleasures which we have not experienced hold a secret to be revealed in the future. We live in tomorrows . . . and when we no longer believe in them we might as well be dead. We have not wasted time because there is nothing to do with it other than that which we have done . . .

The big chandelier is lapped in waves of music; around and around go the dancers. 'Do you hunt?' asks Lieutenant Bullock of Miss Clara Foskett.

'. . . but it's so *cruel*,' she breathes, while her brother Tony, slowly revolving in the middle of the room with the Hon. Miss Petersham, presses her close to him, smiles into her eyes and says, 'I shall have to take you out and kiss you in a minute.' And Brigadier-General Melton-Brewer leans over Miss Petersham's mother, twirls his whiskers and murmurs in a worn-out rattling voice of the glories of pre-war Vienna. *Vienna, Vienna* . . . echoes the orchestra. 'I prefer to live in the country,' says Miss Foskett. 'Give me London any old time, except for huntin',' declares the Lieutenant with a fatuous expression on his face. A nice piece of goods, he thinks, a charming bit. Around and around we go, she thinks, and it seems this dance will never end. James, James, my lover, come and take my hand, come and put your arms around me, and let us dance as if we were alone, as if these hot-faced, fox-hunting young men were not in the world at all . . .

There goes that simpering Clara Foskett, thinks Peter Langfier; there she goes, dreaming of love in the arms of her beefy cavalier. Around and around they go . . . Now she catches my eye, now she smiles, and I have to smile back, a sickly grin . . .

There's Peter Langfier, thinks Clara. Look how he stands against the wall, melancholy and alone. He wears a sad, a disillusioned air. Now I catch his eye, now I smile at him, a sympathetic smile that tells him I understand, that I too have leaned against a wall, forlorn and melancholy, waiting for someone who does not come.

I have given up hoping that she will come, thinks Peter. But the door keeps opening with a premonitory rustle of women's clothes, and every time my heart beats faster for the little space of time it takes to prove that it is not she. A girl does not come to a dance, and life is meaningless . . .

'My dear General,' exclaims Lady Petersham, 'how can you stand there talking of pre-war Vienna as if nothing had happened, when my girl has disappeared with that *notorious* young Tony Foskett.'

Vienna, Vienna . . . echoes the fading music as it sobs and subsides and the tune finishes. The pairs become ones, the twirling figures have scattered to their peripheries and now cling to the four walls, mingling with the generals and the duchesses. But the wicked Tony Foskett is kissing Miss Petersham in the library; his arms around her, their mouths are mingled, the thoughts of their flesh stream together like the smoke of two fires mingling.

The dance is over. Peter Langfier has leaned away from the wall, has straightened himself and strolled with dejected mien across to the buffet, where he gets a glass of brandy. She will not come, he thinks. Maybe I'll go home. And he imagines the dark, the plush-heavy hall with the Roman emperor's gleaming white bust; he sees himself spending the rest of the evening at home, watching the minutes burn away in the library fire . . . Life is meaningless, and he gulps down his brandy as Miss Foskett comes fluttering up to him.

'Have you seen James Dampier?' she asks breathlessly.

'I didn't know he was here,' answers Peter, reaching for more brandy. 'Have a drink,' he says. And these ones, forlorn for their beloveds' absence, draw close to commingle their self-pity.

But Tony Foskett is kissing the trembling eyelids of Miss Petersham. If only this moment could last, she thinks, if only I could hold it in my head so that I could wake with it in the morning and bear it through the day like an unborn child. I have kissed her eyelids, thinks Tony Foskett. She trembles in my arms, and I cannot turn back. Once again my feet are set upon the path of a love affair that I have not sought. Life is meaningless, thinks Peter Langfier, because Pamela has not come. If James does not come into the room and take me by the hand, thinks Clara Foskett, I shall wish I had never been born.

Now the band strikes up again, a different tune, a tune that outrages the Brigadier's pre-war phantasies. Blue, blue, silver-blue sliding into pits of deepest cobalt are the notes of the saxophone. The sounds no longer swirl about the room like the effortless curves of figure-skaters, of eddying autumn leaves. The music throbs and moans, it is a pulse beating in blue darkness, a sound of swamps crying of life in the cities, of life that is meaningless without love. *My head is aching*, cry the muted trumpets, *My heart is breaking*, sob the saxophones. With aching heads, with breaking hearts dance these mayflies of history, born too late into a brief day of cold, weak sunshine. *My heart is breaking. Without your caress Life is meaningless* they hum to the sound of dark swamps, to the sound of exiles moaning for a life that is meaningless . . .

The saxophone notes fade into the air, fade and spread outwards in faint waves, in tiny ripples dispersing into the night outside, the spring night.

Across the square, where the trees are budding in the day of arc lamps, goes the spreading, dwindling ghost of a cry that is meaningless, sighing silently and invisibly through the lacework of branches, through the soft air, down the dingy channels of streets, dying and losing itself in the exhalations of other sounds that seep through windows, under the cracks of doors and out of chimneys – the faint, diminished cries of life vanishing into the air like little puffs of smoke, the sounds of quarrels, the noise of kisses and tears, the mumble of newspapers being read aloud, the scratching of teeth being brushed, the gurgle of hot tea descending into gullets, the faint whispers of private lives that rise like a fog over London, an invisible fog murmurous and alive with the grasshopper whir and rustle of speeding thoughts.

* * * * *

And in the Kings Arms the darts match is over. The Dog And Duck has won, Jock has thrown the winning double and been acclaimed, and now they all sit in the bar drinking pints of mild and talking cheerfully. Nosey Parsons is telling them about his famous constipation. 'I've tried everything,' he says. 'No good . . .' And he squints gloomily through his boss-eyed tin-rimmed spectacles, down his long nose to the dark-gleaming beer at the bottom of his mug. 'Wot you should do,' said Alfie Roberts didactically, 'is to take two tablespoonsful of Epsom salts in a pint of 'ot stout. That'll do the trick.'

'I've tried everything,' mutters Nosey with gloomy pride. 'No good.'

'There was a chap in our works,' says Alfie, 'who was *worse* than you. 'E 'adn't done nothing for three weeks. "George," I says to 'im, "George, you take two tablespoonsful of Epsom salts in a pint of 'ot stout. That'll do the trick." And in the end 'e did. 'E was in the lavatory for near 'arf hour and 'e comes out pale as a sheet. But 'e never 'ad no more trouble wiv 'is bowels.'

'That's nothing,' says Jock dramatically. 'Wot about my grandfather's pet goat. There *is* a case for you . . .'

From the meeting outside comes a sudden burst of cheering and songs. 'Wot's the row about?' says Jock and goes to the door. The meeting had been swollen by a contingent of marchers, who now stood grouped around a banner. 'Wot's up?' says Jock to one of them who has slipped over the road for a quick pint. 'We're all marching over to a big meeting at Brickling Street,' he replies. 'Hi, Jock,' cries Nosey Parsons. 'Come and tell us about your ole grandpa's pet goat.' But the Communist words were sounding in Jock's mind now. *Forward you workers, Freedom awaits you*, they were singing outside, a marching song, a song for them to tramp the dark streets with. How can I go and leave Nosey and the crowd? thinks Jock. But how can I stay knowing they are marching down the dark streets singing *Forward you workers . . . ?* It won't half look bad if I go, he thinks. But to stay is like running away.

'Come over and 'ave a listen to the meeting,' he says to them in an awkward voice.

'I don't want to listen to no bloody meetings,' says Nosey.

'Meetings is all very well,' says Ginger. 'Mind you, I 'old with what they say, but we've got our beer to drink.'

'They're going to march off,' says Jock. 'I've a mind to go with them.'

'That don't get you nowhere but in jug,' says Nosey.

'You stay and drink wiv us,' says Ginger.

The bar-room door swung open, and a burst of singing flooded in. 'They're forming up to march,' says someone.

'I'm going,' says Jock. 'I'm going to march with them.' It's hard to go and leave your mates, he thinks. It's hard to leave them thinking you don't want to drink with them.

And the door swung to behind him; night air surrounded him; he breathed the stuffy pub atmosphere out of his lungs. And now they were marching off, behind the banner with the hammer and sickle on it. NORTH KENSINGTON COMMUNIST

PARTY. FORWARD TO SOVIET BRITAIN, he read on it. *Forward, you workers*, they sang, and Jock slipped into the ranks, his feet keeping time of their own accord to the swing of the marching song. 'Forward to Soviet Britain,' they shouted to the beat of the marching feet. And Jock shouted with them. Ginger and Nosey and the others could think what they liked of him, sitting over their beer and gossiping, but he was glad he had come, he was glad to march through the dark streets feeling all the voices and bodies moving together, feeling the strength of them, all united with a common purpose.

The tramp of feet, the sound of the marchers' songs and slogans lapped upon the sides of houses like the waves of a rising tide, shot up in a spray of sound and rattled on the windowpanes, beat upon eardrums and echoed in minds that remembered the rain of leaflets, the slogans on the walls, the rough voices forcing their way through the microphones . . .

DEMONSTRATE ON MAY DAY FOR SOVIET POWER proclaim the chalked slogans, the words and letters that make walls and pavements shout defiance, that can linger in minds and work like a ferment . . .

* * * * *

Now the chalking squads were busy in dark streets, little squads with chalk and whitewash and posters and paste. Under the big painted slogans they write up the times and places of local contingents' departures. Also they decorate lampposts, pillar-boxes, hoardings and telephone booths with stickers and flyposters. Cyclists on look-out patrol up and down marking policemen's beats.

* * * * *

Ivy Cutford, coming away from the cell meeting, ran into a squad at work. 'Hullo, comrades,' she said. 'Hullo,' they replied. 'We're doing fine.'

'It's going to be a grand turn-out Wednesday.'

'I wish we were coming out,' she said.

'Where do you work?'

'Langfier's.'

'That sweatshop! You bloody well ought to be turning out.'

'I wish we were,' she said again in a wistful voice. I wish we were, she repeated to herself as she went on her way.

The chap who had spoken to her had been handsome, redheaded with a very pale complexion and clear green eyes. He had looked at her with the cool, friendly glance that told her he thought she was a good sort, the look that she often got and that often warmed her heart; but also, on such a night as this when she makes her lonely way back to her cold little room, it could pierce her to the heart with its cool indifference. She had seen those eyes, those cool and friendly eyes, lean their glances towards other girls and melt into something else, to the look that says, 'You have a different flesh from mine, a delicious flesh that I yearn to embrace.'

Now, walking through the soft April air that stirred with amorous thoughts, going back to her lonely bus ride, to her lonely little room, the memory of those glances aroused in her an intolerable longing for a lover, a longing to be desired for once instead of liked, to be followed by amorous looks through the soft night. She was so often the confidant of the other girls' stories of their love affairs, their pick-ups, their little exciting adventures . . . she laughed with them, commiserated with them. Nothing like that happened to her. It was not love she ached for now, it was not lust; companionship she had, but she wanted to be of dear importance in some man's life, and she feared she never would.

Here was the main road, alive with light and movement; here was her bus. Before her stretched the twopenny ride, a walk down two dark streets, a shabby front door, two shabby flights of stairs and another door that would open to disclose the little wallpaper-lined box in which she lived. This was her home, the vessel that bore her through the nights.

There was a sagging bed, a chipped white washstand, wallpaper strewn with faded roses, two large pictures of ladies standing in Tennysonian postures with streaming hair falling over large semi-disclosed bosoms, one picture of some stags blowing into a brook, also a *Daily Worker* calendar and a framed photograph of Lenin. Then there was a chest of drawers, also white and chipped, and a tin trunk with a pile of old *Daily Workers* on it. On the mantelpiece stood a row of pamphlets and paperbacked Communist books, leaning up against some sixpenny detective stories. An alarm clock ticked stridently, the gas meter sighed a little; the gas would be lit and faintly roaring; on the landing a cistern gushed and gurgled. In other rooms people quarrelled, played gramophones, hummed, walked up and down, creaked furniture, sneezed, coughed, belched, farted, blew their noses, whistled and read aloud. A smell hung about the landing and the stairs, an old, stale, musty, miserable, untraceable smell . . .

This was the house, this the room in which she lived: this was her home. And behind ten million squares and oblongs of window glass existed other rooms, other homes. Nearly everyone must have a place in which they can sleep, everyone must be able to remember and anticipate a door that opens to disclose a bed with whose softnesses and hardnesses, with whose lumps and bumps and creakings and yieldings their bodies are familiar.

There must be about two and a half million of these brick boxes in London, complete with floors, ceilings, sinks, doorknobs and secrets of soiled underlinen. At one time or another seven or eight million people lie in the beds, look out of the windows, open the doors and sit at the tables.

In every room the walls and floors and ceilings are soaked with the exhalations of thoughts, so that the brick and wood and plaster breathes out a transformed and diffused personality. There is soil beneath too, and under the pavements and tar and woodblocks lies dead earth, soaked with blood and sweat and tears and cloyed with the minute dust of two thousand years of life.

And through the worm-burrowing drains and sewers swirl the excreta, the dirty water and the old tea leaves of millions of homes. Everything ends in Barking Creek.

* * * * *

Everything ends in Barking Creek, said Pat to himself as he pulled the plug and heard the rushing lavatory waters. 'Everything ends in Barking Creek,' he said and laughed as he came into the room. James was sitting on the divan drinking Irish whiskey. 'What a stink of tobacco,' said Pat. 'You pull the plug and everything ends in Barking Creek,' he repeated and laughed again. James was rather dourly silent. That sort of humour seemed to him silly and middle class.

Pat sat down and filled a pipe. Through the half-open window floated the sound of dance music from a radio. *My head is aching*, a tenor was singing, *my heart is breaking*, and the faint, blue, melancholy song seemed strangely affecting. They were silent for a moment, breathing, their hearts beating, their thoughts reaching forth and eddying in the air with the pipe smoke they blew out. Somehow the softness of the night had penetrated into the room.

Pat's room was long, with a sloping ceiling at one end; warm, yellowish, distempered walls; bare, stained boards with faded rugs. There were three Van Gogh reproductions, also there were two large framed photographs of ships and a slightly old-fashioned photo of a beautiful girl with an aloof mask-face. There was a large plain deal table, two arm-chairs, a divan, a dartboard and an old black sideboard. Low bookshelves ran all around the walls, filled mostly with revo-lutionary literature, novels and Elizabethan plays and poetry. Under the sloping end of the roof was a small writing-table with a portable typewriter on it, also a picture of Lenin and a *Daily Worker* calender. Above was a big Soviet photographic poster of blast furnaces. The room was rather untidy and had a pleasant kind of workmanlike plainness about it. Knowing Pat, you would be certain he lived in such a place.

The night had penetrated into the room. 'Life is mean-ingless,' sang the jazz tenor. 'Life is meaningless,' hummed Pat.

'What a lot of boloney these songs are,' said James.

'But it's a good tune.'

'Yes, it's a good tune . . .' He sighed. 'This weather makes me want to get hold of a nice girl . . .'

'April is a randy month,' said Pat sympathetically.

'Did you ever see that girl of yours again?'

'No,' said Pat. 'That's her,' and he pointed to the picture on the wall that gravely smiled to itself. 'I don't know where she is now.' And in his mind was roused the faint, nagging ache for the lost and uncompleted love that was an unlaid ghost in his life. 'I hardly think of her any more,' he said . . . He remembered the sweltering tropic night, talking to James on the fo'c'sle-head and telling him about Greta and how he had left her. James was the only person who knew the story. He was glad to be able to talk about her now. 'I try not to think of her, and I don't for weeks sometimes, and then something suddenly reminds me of her, and it's like a kind of dull toothache inside me . . .'

'I've never really been in love, like that . . .' said James rather awkwardly. 'There's been girls . . .' his voice trailed away while dim images floated through his mind, vague impressions of mouths he had kissed, of girls with whom he had slept. 'I got worked up about some of them, but it never really mattered.'

'I know,' said Pat. 'That's how it had always been with me till I met Greta. I'd got myself into states from wanting to have some particular girl, and I've got sentimental with them too afterwards and fancied myself in love. I've liked making myself think I was in love, I've liked thinking about it. But when I met Greta it was quite different. And afterwards it was just a hopeless, nagging kind of feeling, a kind of pain at the back of my mind. I've got a girl now, a nice dumb blonde, and sometimes when I've said goodbye to her and started to walk home, I get that tender, randy feeling of wanting her and thinking how nice she is. I like that. It's an agreeable feeling. But the real thing is a kick in the guts. It happens without you having any choice in the matter . . .'

'When I was quite a kid,' said James, 'there was a girl that I got upset about. I can hardly remember her now, but I remember how I felt sometimes. I wanted to kiss her, and it took me weeks to get up the nerve to try it . . . but with me it's been mostly tarts: mostly I've had to pay for my women. I've always had an idea of a girl, a comrade, you know, someone you could talk things over with . . . But I never seem to meet them. And when I come ashore, like I am now, feeling randy and with money in my pocket, I seem to get hold of the first good-looking tart I meet, and she lasts me till my money's gone and I've got to get to sea again.'

James has a streak of cold-blooded lust, really, thinks Pat. But he's never had a chance of any other kind of relation with a woman.

He stood up and walked aimlessly around the room. 'I suppose you'll be ashore for quite a time. What're you going to do about Party work?'

'I've got a kind of unsettled feeling till I can find John.

I'll join in the demonstration from one of the waterside rallying points. D'you know the address of their sub-district office?'

'No. But you can get into touch with them at the demo.'

'Sure . . . I'm looking forward to be doing Party work again. I've done nothing since Spain . . .'

And he started telling Pat about his long voyage after he had escaped. They had been away too long, they had been too far.

Once James began to get talking he talked well. A vivid picture of that voyage began to form in Pat's mind, and he was full of the old nostalgic sea-lust, the lust that knew the weariness of its fulfilment and yet was insatiable, unescapable . . .

'More whiskey,' said Pat and refilled their glasses. They drank and were silent.

Pat felt a little chilly from sitting still so long. He got up to shut the window, but he leaned out for a moment first, breathing in the night air, his head full of sea-thoughts, while still the ache of having remembered his old love troubled him. Greta, Greta . . . where are you now? he thinks, imagining her leaning out of some other window now, looking up at the sky and seeing the single, lonely ice-green star that pricked the dark canopy of the night . . .

* * * * *

And John, coming out of the cinema with Martine, looked up too and saw the little star, while Martine slipped her arm into his. As they walked the pressure of her thigh against his conducted a current between them, a current of the thoughts of their flesh. Not in words had their minds formulated the decision that tonight, soon, they would make love. But their bodies knew. They were silent. John breathed deeply, clearing the stale cinema air from his lungs, while he looked up at the little star; Martine faintly hummed the tune she had sung to herself when she had been shopping that morning. The thoughts that anticipated their delight held them silent.

When they arrived at the house John went upstairs first and lit the gas. Then he came down with Mick to let him out. He stood on the doorstep and lit the dregs of his pipe, while Mick sniffed around cheerfully. A few windows cut squares and oblongs of light in the dark silhouettes of houses. The air was soft, was quiet. Faint straggling noises that trickled from under the cracks of doors and out of windows did not intrude into the silence.

John puffed slowly at his pipe and waited for Mick. His mind was almost blank, serene yet urgent. A wordless, shapeless desire threw a heavy shadow across his thoughts. Inchoate images of warmth and softness and contacts of bare flesh moved before his inner eye.

Suddenly his pipe began to taste really nasty. He put it in his pocket, whistled for Mick and went upstairs. Martine was in bed. He took off his clothes very quickly and turned out the gas.

They slept naked now. Martine's sensual innocence had quite dispersed all John's sexual shames and fears. He had slept with a fair number of women before he had met her, but she taught him all he knew of lovemaking again. Through her he had become far better mentally balanced in every way.

He slipped into bed beside her.

Their flesh was no longer strange to one another. The period of their lovemaking when each night they learned new secrets of each other was over. Now they came together with the certainty and precision of a ballet. In the act of love these two achieved a perfect mutual adjustment, a complete mental and physical absorption and balance that was as beautiful as it was rare.

Clasped in each other's arms, their mouths and bodies locked, they sighed into consciousness of their separate selves.

* * * * *

And their sighs were echoed far and wide. From thousands
of beds into the enclosed air of thousands of rooms were
uttered the sighs of gratification, the faint, piercing cries of
love and lust. Now the ever-fleeting moment of delight
eternally renews itself, eternally is lost. With love, with lust,
with tender affection, with angry passion, with joy and with
despair men and women unite their bodies and draw apart
again. The wave mounts and breaks, the tide of delight rises
and recedes again into the sighing air, and thoughts of cares
and troubles, the preoccupations with everyday living, rise
up again, another lapping tide. In many minds the first of
these thoughts is concerned with the fear of having con-
ceived a child, the fear that can unknowingly poison even
the moment of delight. Some think of the morning, of how
in a few hours they will have to creep from their warm beds
and go out to work, while some reflect that they have yet to
go home, that the delights of this bed must soon be
exchanged for the chastity of their own couch after a walk
through the chill, night-empty streets; some think of growing
old, some of money troubles, some of schemes and ambitions; some begin to look forward to fresh pleasure, some
turn from their partners with weariness or disgust, some
meditate upon their happiness in a newfound love . . . Molly,
the red-haired girl who works in Langfier's machine shop,
still gasps, her desire not satisfied, the mounting wave sub-
siding before it has reached its peak, while still she is
pierced with a sharp pang of tenderness for the sake of her
lover's pleasure. And the thoughts come back, the voice of the
machines sounds again in her head, like the suddenly remembered ticking of a clock to one tortured with insomnia. After
sleep, after any moment of absorption or forgetfulness, there
always returns the endless song of the machines and the sense
of strain and hurry that haunts her working hours. These are

ghosts that walk in the minds of the factory girls and from which they are never quite free. Jenny Hardy, emancipated from their slavery, thinks of them now for a moment, as, still breathless from Dartry's ardours, she relapses into a drowsy wakefulness. To her he is irrevocably associated with the factory; he is also the one who has set her free, and to this thought she clings while she submits herself to his embraces. She can never prevent herself from being a little disgusted with his body every time, but she reminds herself that this brief slavery of the flesh is better than the long slavery of body and mind to the factory. And she remembers the noise, the particular note of her machine sounding amongst the others; her flesh remembers the smooth, cold, slightly greasy feeling of the controls, the sense of strain and fatigue, the workshop smells . . . While Dartry, lying beside her in the darkness, breathes hard and shudders to the insistent hammer blows of his beating heart. I'm getting old, he thinks, and the spectre of senility and impotence rises again in his mind, that spectre which he can only dispel by physical excess. There will come a time, he thinks, when this flesh will no longer be able to answer to the dictates of its desires. The fear, the burning shame of fading virility, overcomes him. He lies beside his mistress in the darkness and tortures himself with visions of impotent desire.

* * * * *

Now John and Martine are asleep, now Molly's lover has gone home and she drowses into oblivion. Vaster and vaster numbers are sinking into the mists of sleep; a tide of uneasy oblivion is lapping, is rising and submerging London's population. A suspirating rhythm of slumbering bodies rises into the air. Time is moving towards the hour before dawn, the hour when life sinks to its lowest ebb. Now the tide is running out down the river. The barges and ships are going east, their sirens' cries have faded down the streets, have been lost in the land noises, and now they are heading out to sea.

Now the personalities of houses are breathed out. Rooms are deserted by their owners; in tiny creaks, in little whispering sounds and smells they give back a metamorphosed version of the day's life that has passed within their walls. The slum rooms breathe a sourness of poverty: greasy walls exude ghostly echoes of old, poor meals, while the smells of cigars and women's perfumes leak from curtains and fabrics back into the stale, deserted air of wealthy drawing-rooms. William Harkness, moving with infinite care across the warm darkness of the library of Lord Plumer's Belgrave Square house, suddenly freezes to stillness as his mind's fixed vision of a diamond necklace glittering to itself behind safe doors is disturbed by the exhalations of the room. The personality of the house impinges itself upon his danger-sharpened senses, and he is aware of a tingling sensation down his back, as if someone was watching him from behind. At more or less the same time, Samuel Cohen, aged seven, sneaking downstairs behind his brother, intent upon burgling biscuits from the larder of their house in Finsbury Park, stiffens into a tense heart-shuddering panic at the sound of a creaking stair.

In these three seconds 7,283 more souls are asleep.

Life is sinking downwards to its lowest ebb in the hours before dawn.

THE HOURS BEFORE DAWN

To those who have been working all night, the dawn will show in a discolouration of the sky, a surprise that teaches them of their fatigue. The yellow radiance of artificial light will suddenly seem tawdry, as they run their hands over their chins and feel the night's growth of bristles. Cool and restful thoughts will tantalize them.

But there is no moment which is the moment of the dawn of a new day. The old day dies, the new is reborn each instant. Work, leisure, sleep, waking – these are always beginning or ending for some. But in the intermediate time of the hours before dawn there is the greatest neutralness. It is the interim in the greatest number of lives. Also, this is the time when the most suicides take place, the time when the vitality is at its lowest ebb, when melancholy, heartbroken spirits, people for whom life has proved too much, who have become saturated with pain or misery, are overthrown by the spinning silence of this hour's loneliness when the ticking of clocks is loud and menacing. Even the machines in the night shifts of factories seem to sing a different tune, and the endless electric whine of the powerhouses ebbs to its lowest note.

An ocean of bodies tossing beneath bedclothes gives off an enormous mist of unquiet dreams, for most dreams are thus, the flowing back of a tide held off during the day, a tide of shames and insults and miseries that strive to be forgotten. And when hungry men dream of food, poor men of riches, sex-starved creatures of lust, these pathetic fulfilments are bitter with a foretaste of awakening.

The last drunks lurching home down empty echoing streets are pierced with the sudden cold remorseful thoughts of soberness. A great load of wrongs and miseries seems to press unbearably upon miles of streets that stretch like graveyards of brick and stone where once trees grew and wild animals roamed. A large number of people stricken with disease or old age die around this time, while still the passionate outbursts of amorous cats fade down dark alleys. Sick children whimper in their sleep. But the dawn-haloed rim of the earth's shadow is chasing eastwards across the Atlantic.

The sun will rise soon.

PART TWO
APRIL 30TH

MORNING

The alarm clock sprays a jet of noise into the eardrums of Percy Faulkner, milk-roundsman, aged twenty-three. His eyes open to darkness; his day has started. Tuesday, he murmurs to himself, not even Wednesday, not even halfway through the week . . .

An immense avenue of waiting doorsteps stretching in a straight ever-lengthening perspective presents itself to his mental eye. The Chinese coolies work all the week round without ever a Sunday, he remembers having heard. That's what I am, he tells himself, a bloody coolie.

The bed is warm, is kind. Its irregularities, the bumps in the mattress, the places where the springs are broken, the place where the sheet has rucked itself into a little lump under the small of his back, have become adjusted to the comfort of his body. The warmth and darkness of the womb weight his drowsing flesh. A cold world of everlasting milk-rounds and innumerable doorsteps waits for him outside his bed.

Then, also, there is the world of hotels where human beings lie sleeping behind numbered doors. In the corridors soft lights glow unaudienced; the air is dry with the parching stuffiness of steam-heating. Only the numbers on the doors tell you where you are. Day or night, winter or summer, it's always the same here. There are no echoes of the lives, the hopes and ambitions and passions that slumber behind those numbered doors. The sediment of thoughts, the condensed exhalations of lives that deposit themselves on the walls and surfaces of human habitations do not form easily in this hotel world.

Outside the sun is rising into a sky strewn with ship-wrecked clouds. The eastern horizon bleeds like an open wound. A wind has come up in the night, its watery breath urging a slow avalanche of dark vapours to drift across the sky and drown the sun.

A forest of factory chimneys leans up against the troubled horizon like batteries of artillery trained at the sky, waiting for a signal. Then suddenly they jet forth the awakening cry of the sirens. Their music is fierce and mournful, strange and familiar, harsh and nostalgic, full of hope and despair. Steam plumes into the air like fountain jets in a garden where great events are saluted by some tremendous formal cannonade. But this fanfare only marks the beginning of another working day, its sounds cracking whips in the workers' ears.

The hurrying, straggling procession of men and girls dwindles as it is sucked in through the factory gates. The clocking-in machines stutter a diminuendo. Discarded May Day leaflets – yellow, green and orange – turn over in the breeze as they slide into the gutters. The Communists walk away from the gates, some looking over their shoulders for a moment to reassure themselves of a slogan that they had chalked the night before.

Doors have slid open. Machines that gleamed in oily gloom are washed with daylight. Starting levers are put over and power leaps from overhead shaftings. Everywhere the machines are waking up; the earth trembles a little under the gathering avalanche of noise that rolls onwards as the working day gets into its stride.

* * * * *

Now Martine is bathing the baby.

She didn't usually do it first thing in the morning, but an unfortunate accident had taken place during the night and nothing but total immersion could make David presentable to the eye and nose.

David was feeling cheerful. He lashed out with his hands and feet all round him in the tin bath. Mick, leaning over the edge and trying to lick David's ear, got an eyeful of water. He retreated, somewhat discomposed. David shouted ferociously and began to splash all the more. But then Martine began to soap his face with the flannel and he started to howl. 'Silly David,' she said. 'Silly David,' and she rinsed out the cloth and wiped the soap off. 'Isn't he a silly David,' she murmured to Mick who wagged his tail vaguely acknowledging that he was being spoken to. There was a little hole in the wainscoting in one corner of the room that had once smelled of mouse. He had sniffed and blown there for weeks until now only the faintest and most delicate trace of an odour lingered. But he always retained a hope that if he suddenly ran across the room he might be able to catch the smell out in some way. Sometimes he would sniff and grunt so much that John got annoyed and threw shoes at him. Now, as he tried to wipe the water out of his eye with his right paw, he was contemplating a sudden rush across the room at the hole.

David was being towelled. He gurgled a song about something that nobody could understand. The words were rather like 'Beeble beeble beeble . . .' This was his cheerful song. He had others for different moods and occasions.

Soon he was dry. He sat on Martine's knee, his straight fair hair all tousled and standing on end, his face a glowing red. Suddenly Martine pressed him to her breast and kissed him. She wasn't much given to demonstrations of affection; she loved David completely and unquestioningly. But sometimes she would be pierced with an instant conscious tenderness for him, for his laughing unprotectedness. To her the world seemed mostly made up of enemies. This helpless living flesh had passed out of her own body, but still her body and her thought were its only protection and safeguard. And she clutched him to her almost fiercely and angrily as she thought of the uncertain future whose security she always doubted now.

But also when she thought of the future, certain different ideas and images conjured themselves up: she saw, very small and distinct, as through the wrong end of a telescope, a little house with shining windows and very bright red-and-white check curtains, potted geraniums on the windowsills. There was a nice green carpet in the front room and a big armchair for John, a brown leathery comfortable armchair, like the one she saw every day in the window of the furniture shop in the Portobello Road. And she imagined the smell and the smooth texture of its covering. It's not real leather, she thought. It's some imitation stuff, I can't remember the name.

* * * * *

Probably quite a large, but certainly an incalculable number of people, were thinking about artificial leather at the moment in various parts of the world, including Mr Arthur Sloane, MP, who was coming downstairs to breakfast, lingering from step to step, trailing the long manicured fingers of his right hand over the smooth wood of the balustrade. His foxy face brooded under polished hair, and he chewed the ends of his little toothbrush moustache. The slight frown, the rather more than usually accentuated crinkle of forehead over the monocled right eye and the absent-minded moustache-munching, were the outward signs of Sloane's reflections upon artificial leather. It was a subject as near and dear to his heart as Martine's dreams of her armchair were to hers. Artificial Leather Products, a company that had a virtual monopoly in Britain, was more or less controlled by AIE. It was natural that Sloane should have an interest in the firm. But also he had acquired, very cautiously and privately through various nominees, the majority of the shares not actually held by AIE.

Sloane had thought of the armchairs in the shop windows, of the upholstery of motorcars and public conveyances, the Woolworthy tobacco pouches, the leather jackets of cyclists, the seats of perambulators, the almost general human necessity for backsides to rest upon leathery surfaces. And he had seen to it that this need should bring him profit.

This, however, does not account for the frown, for the abstracted air with which he descends the wide and well-proportioned staircase of his town house on the way to breakfast. Eichner's words at yesterday's conference had made him think. And he thought about unloading his private Leather Products holdings, a scheme that would swing it on his fellow directors of AIE, if he could get them to acquire more than simply a holding interest in Leather Products. And once they had started they would find it more expensive than they had imagined. But how secret were his private holdings, how well acquainted were his fellow directors with the ramifications of his influence? These were deciding questions whose answers he pondered.

At the door of the breakfast room he halted an instant, and swiftly, unconsciously, the habit become almost an instinct, smoothed his features, patted his tie and adjusted his whole attitude to face the light that came in through the large windows.

Everything in the room was very comfortable, but it was hard to the eye, with harsh lines everywhere and too much chromium glitter. Beside his place at the table were laid newspapers and his private secretary's selection of correspondence. On top there was a note saying that his brother had rung up and would be around to see him shortly.

'Good,' he said to himself aloud and rang for Roberts, the private secretary.

Roberts came into the room very silently, his sallow

compact face absolutely dead under a glistening helmet of thick black hair that was brushed straight back from the forehead. He wore a very dark-grey double-breasted flannel suit with a dark-red carnation in the buttonhole. Only the strong thin lines of his mouth prevented him from looking like a superior gigolo.

'Have you got those aero-engine cuttings I asked you about yesterday?' said Sloane.

He went to fetch them without saying anything.

Sloane stood at the window looking at the trees in the square and the overcast sky, while he clamped down a lid on the ideas he had just been considering. They were for later on, and now he must grapple with immediate matters, his brother's visit and the complications of the magnesium business. A government subsidy for the Staffordshire works was one of the matters he wanted put in hand. Already he had succeeded in getting a tariff on the imports of that metal, which had puzzled many people who thought they were in the know, since AIE had almost a world monopoly of magnesium anyway. 'We must make ourselves independent of the foreigner for supplies of this vital material. For vital it is today. We need it for our aero-engines. Are we to stand by and let ourselves be dependent upon the foreigner for the etc., etc. . . .' He was thinking of an article that would have to be written today.

Roberts re-entered stealthily, holding a very clean, new buff folder, as if there was something nasty in it.

'I obtained some figures that I thought might be relevant to the question,' he said in his nasal voice.

Sloane looked at him sharply. There was absolutely no expression on his face. 'Very bright of you, Roberts,' he said. 'Let's have a look at 'em.'

Roberts produced a typewritten slip from the folder. It contained, in a neat table, comparative figures of certain properties of magnesium and sodium. Sloane looked at them intently, but they didn't convey anything to him. He turned to the cutting that was mounted on a sheet of thin card. A sentence was underlined in blue pencil. 'The performance of these valves has been raised to a very high standard by stelliting the seats, nitriding the stems and partly filling them with sodium or some other material with the requisite heat cycle . . .'

Sloane looked back at the table and was about to ask Roberts a question but checked himself. The young man was too well informed it seemed. He would ask his brother. For the life of him he didn't see the point of using sodium in the stem of a valve.

Roberts went out with a ghost of a satisfied smile on his face. He knew that the figures would be meaningless to Sloane; the fact that he had hesitated to ask for an explanation proved what he had only guessed before. There was no immediate advantage to which he could put this knowledge, but it would come in handy for 'later on' along with many other little facts that he was accumulating.

'Despite the assurances of Mr Raggett, the secretary of the Transport Workers' Union, it seems almost certain that many Londoners will have to walk to work tomorrow morning,' Sloane read in *The Times*.

* * * * *

'"Despite the frenzied attempts of Raggett and his gang, backed up by every force of 'public opinion' that can be faked by the capitalist press and wireless, to smash the busmen's May Day strike, they are solid for coming out on Wednesday,"' Jock read out from the *Daily Worker*. 'There you are,' he said to John, in the manner of one making a point.

'What beats me,' said John, 'is what they say in the *Herald*. First it's only a few deluded people who are coming out, and then they make a fuss about the Communists try-ing to disrupt the unions. You can't 'ave it both ways.'

'Anyway,' said Jock, 'as I was saying about last night. Afterwards we all marched off to Brickling Street. It wasn't 'arf good, shouting and singing, we sounded like the bloody revolution. And when we got to the corner of the street – by where you useter live – there was a hell of a big meeting going on, hundreds of people and cops. There was a young feller speaking and he let 'em 'ave it all right. Only a young chap 'e was, but one of the best speakers I ever 'eard. He was talking about May Day in Russia and how different it was there 'cos it's the workers' own country and there's no bosses.'

'That's what I don't hold with about the Communists,' said John. 'They're always on about Russia – not that I'm against Russia; it's fine there and good luck to 'em. I'm not taken in by all the stuff in the papers, stands to reason the capitalists'd tell lies about it. But what I want to 'ear about is how we can get things better ourselves instead of how good they are somewhere else.'

'That's what this feller said, though. He said there's only one way of getting decent conditions for ourselves, to do same as they did in Russia – kick out the bloody bosses and it can't be done through voting either. 'E said it was different here to Russia. Course it is, it's much harder for us to win 'cos our bosses are so strong. Only once we've got power we'd be able to go ahead easily 'cos everything's organized already and there're so many factories and everything . . .'

'That's true . . . I'm on their side all right, always have been. I never took a' interest in politics. I always thought the Labour Party's no bloody good for us. It's nothing but talk with them, and soon as they get a good job to hell with the workers. Any of the leaders'd go the same way as Thomas and Ramsay if they 'ad the chance.'

'Sure. But the Communists say 's no good being on their side and not joining 'em.'

'I didn't know you went in for politics.'

'I wouldn't say I went in for 'em. One time I went to a lot of meetings and I've been up to the park with the unemployed, I go to most of the demonstrations. I get the *Worker* sometimes too. There's a lot of good stuff in it you don't see anywhere else.'

'But everyone's talking about politics now somehow . . . it's funny, the girls wanting to strike and the busmen and everything . . . there's a sort of feeling about, and everyone's talking about May Day – one time you never used to 'ear about it.'

'The busmen's what really got people talking.'

'You know,' said John confidentially dropping his voice, 'I think there's Communists working 'ere. Millman's one, I know, but there's more. All them stickers up in the bog didn't get there of their own accord.'

'Yeh . . . You seen that leaflet they gave out 's morning?'

'I got one, 's in my pocket. I'm going to 'ave a look at it at dinner time.'

'Well, I'll bet that was written by someone from inside, you read it and see. There's things said that no one outside could know . . . and they 'ad a bit about Langfier's in the *Worker* the other day too. A bloke I know showed it me.'

'I'd like to 'ave seen it. I'd get it at 'ome you know, only my wife wouldn't like it. She's against the Reds; she thinks they want to turn everything upside down, and it's no good arguing with 'er – *Blast!*' he said suddenly. 'I've cut me bloody self.'

He stood, still holding his chisel, looking at his left hand that was slowly dripping blood on to the sawdusty floor. 'Damn it,' he said. 'I haven't done that for years. Comes of talking politics when you're working . . .' He laughed ruefully. 'Don't stand there laughing and looking at it,' said Jock. 'Shove it under the tap.'

The water dripped an aching numbness on to the cut finger and blood-tinged rivulets coursed over the geography of his hand. He held it up awhile and he felt the icy rigour of the water ebb away as the little rivulets quickly dried up, leaving pallid ghosts of bloodstains at the edges of their courses. The sting of the cut pulsed forth strongly.

Jock peered at it interestedly. 'Deep, ain't it,' he said, with sympathy in his voice and also a certain pleasure, meaning that he was glad the cut was deep enough to merit a good portion of sympathy.

The pure blood welled out again quickly and dripped down and then John held the finger under the tap again and took it out quickly to peer into the clean gash that disclosed the perilous white and crimson inner world of the body that unconsciously reminded them both of death and mortality.

'You'd best go and get it dressed,' said Jock. 'You don't want to get no dirt in it.'

'Yeh, I s'pose I'd better,' said John, and twisting a dirty handkerchief tightly around the finger he went out.

He walked carefully, nursing the throbbing pain. He passed through different zones of sound. The fearful clangour of the machine tools was succeeded by the spinning music of dynamos. Then he went through a region of quietness, with only an echo of footfalls along empty passages and a sound like distant voices in empty rooms. The faint rattle of remote typewriters drifted down corridors and swelled out louder for a moment as someone, unseen, anonymous, in a place not thought of, opened and closed a door . . .

* * * * *

And now the morning's awakening machine-gun rattle of typewriters has risen and swelled into a barrage, a storm, a hurricane, a tornado of noise that sweeps out of office windows, through doors and down passages, rushing upwards and outwards and merging into the still growing and rising thunderous music of the working day.

Thousands of fingers – long, short, manicured, nail bitten, fat, slender, ringed, fresh, withered, stubby, tender or cruel – nicker and dance alphabet ballets over thousands of keyboards.

A million tapping keys beat out a tremendous rhythm, spattering a record of life – Dear Sir Madam Sir Dear Comrade Yours faithfully truly fraternally Thanking you in anticipation Requesting immediate settlement of your account Taking pleasure in enclosing Being instructed to inform you that unless The honour of your custom Hoping for your order in this matter – asking, demanding, threatening, cajoling, selling, buying, scheming, swindling, lying, making excuses, playing for time, hurrying up, wishing, hoping, requesting . . . the rained-down letters and figures, the fluttering, mounting sheaves of paper, thick, thin, flimsy, blue, yellow, white, make the raw material of tragedies, comedies, novels, biographies and autobiographies, histories, economic treatises, manuals of sociology, even poems and music and pictures, and carvings in wood, ivory, stone and metal . . .

From this record one half of contemporary life can be deduced and a material history and philosophy of the organization of society.

And behind the nerves and the dancing fingers that blindly and intently spell out this record, under the smooth, fluffy, waved, coiled, shingled, blonde, red, grey, black or mouse-coloured heads of hair function the lonely and incommunicable private lives and thoughts that make the other half of the record of society. Inwardly, under the taut sheet-lightning membrane of nervous discharge, each dreams desires, each hates and wants.

'I want' is the burden of these thoughts, and the hates and preoccupations are with the circumstances of their lives that give or deny them their desires. Love, happiness, lust, the bearing of children, the wearing of clothes, the ordering of comfortable homes, wealth and romance, travels – of these are the thoughts that dream, that vainly cry 'I want'.

* * * * *

. . . I want that coat and skirt in Ponting's window, the one that is dark blue, slim cut, eager to mould me, thinks Dartry's stenographer as she stands up, gathers her notebook and pencil and prepares to go. And she thinks how hard it will be to get, what self-denials she will have to suffer. Imaginatively anticipating, she savours delightful shudders of asceticism. And she closes the door softly behind her, seeing a picture of herself staying in in the evening while the others are out enjoying themselves; she has heard the front door bang, she has sighed and started to wash her underclothes. Also she can do without coffee after lunch. There are a thousand ways of saving . . .

The door closed after her as Dartry's gaze slid upwards from her ankles, caressed the back of her knees and thighs and leaned desiringly over the silk-stretched outline of her bottom. These little typists and these factory girls filled him with a hunting lust, filled him with a desire that the women of other classes could not arouse. The rays of his eyes explored the cheap finery of their clothing, fumbling for the curves beneath like blunt, sensual fingertips.

'It is essential that you should find out to whom these orders are going,' his thoughts were also repeating to themselves, functioning at a different level of his mind's activity, quoting from the letter he had just dictated.

His work was a hurrying strain, the amusements of his ordinary life faint anodynes: he had a home and a wife and children but his thoughts of these held no delight. There is an urge that reacts from the womb and sleep, that compensates for failures and disappointments, that makes men strive to equilibrate themselves with the world outside them.

And in Dartry it took the form of his hunting lust that an infinite number of women would never be able to satisfy. Also his strength would give out long before his desires faded. Of this he was too bitterly and continually aware, this was the serpent he carried within him.

Only three times, he said to himself, thinking of Jenny and last night; only three times, and the last was a failure . . . The upper part of his body became rigid with shame; he closed his eyes and rocked to and fro imperceptibly. He saw himself without money, stripped of the mask of power, a nasty, ridiculous, middle-aged lecher, his desires having to consummate themselves in glances.

'It is essential that you should find out to whom these orders are going,' he was repeating again to himself, and the sound of these inwardly enunciated words penetrated into the consciousness of his morbid reflections. I must pull myself together, he said to himself half aloud, and rang for his secretary.

* * * * *

Everywhere people press buttons and release electricity that manifests itself in the shrill metal utterances of bells. A lover at the door, a creditor, a surprise, a summons, something expected, perhaps a friend casually essaying if you are in, the milkman, news of death or birth, someone returned from a foreign country, a parcel with home-made jam and a primrose root from the country. Bells punctuate our days, divide them between the beginnings of events.

* * * * *

Sloane heard the bell and knew it was his brother Eric.

Eric was like Arthur to look at in the same way that imitations are like originals.

(Arthur had dared Eric to throw the stone at the window and it was Eric who had been beaten for doing it. But Arthur had thrown the first stone all the same. And thus it always was with them.)

Look at Arthur's eyes, then Eric's. They are alike, but Eric's are watered down, a little swollen, mild, globular, protruding. His chin receded slightly, but not his front teeth. He tried to dress like his brother but failed. He was in the Air Ministry and important. Arthur had driven him to it.

'Look here, Eric,' he said, 'this won't do, you know.'

'If it gets out too soon they'll know it's me,' said Eric weakly.

'But it's got to leak out.'

'It's not even definite yet.'

'We're going to have Diesel planes.'

'Yes, yes, I know all that. We've got two experimental ones.'

'And in the meantime America's manufacturing a hundred and fifty. The whole damned Air Force construction plan will have to be scrapped.'

'Now, Arthur, you're not dictating an article for the *Evening Mail*, you know. Things aren't done quite as simply as that in this country, you know.'

'One of the things *you* don't realize, my dear Eric, is just how things *are* done. You've got into that blasted permanent government-official way of thinking. You will imagine that your footling departments are able to make plans and issue orders out of their own sweet wills. You run the country – but not as you please. You forget that you are as dependent on us as the government is on you.'

'For Heaven's sake, Arthur, I didn't come to see you to discuss our respective roles in the maintenance of the State. I'm busy.'

'All right. Do you know anything about Diesel planes?'

'Dammit, I'm not a schoolboy –'

'Wait a moment before you get excited. I want to know

something – about this magnesium business. What's it used for in Diesel engines?'

'Well . . . it's not easy to explain non-technically. You see . . . well, the valves get too hot, and you can't have ordinary cooling arrangements on aero-engines. So they make the stems hollow nowadays and fill them with some material with a special sort of heat cycle – that absorbs a lot of heat in alternate boilings and coolings – of course, that's only a very rough idea of how –'

'Never mind. I understand. And you use magnesium?'

'They've tried various things. I believe sodium is best.'

'Look at these figures.' He handed him the table that Roberts had got out. 'Do they mean anything to you?'

Eric glanced at them, pursed his lips and sucked his teeth. 'They show, as far as my knowledge goes, that the sodium heat cycle is far better for the job.'

'What are they using on the experimental planes?'

'I don't know, but –'

'Of course, the one thing I really wanted you wouldn't know.'

'Dammit, I'm not an engineer. It's only a detail.'

'But it's an important one, isn't it.'

'Every detail of aeroplane manufacture is important.'

'Don't be pedantic. I mean if we are to develop Diesel planes it's vital that we should have our own magnesium supplies.'

'But I've told you, sodium is better, and anyway it's premature to talk of developing Diesel planes. We're only experimenting with them now, and I don't see the point of them except for large bombers and troop transports.'

'Leaving your theories aside, there's no reason why you can't fix it that magnesium is used on the experimental planes and that more are built pretty quick.'

'Honestly, Arthur, I don't see what you're driving at. First there was this damned tariff, and what's the good of it to you

I can't see, when you've got practically a world monopoly of the stuff. And now all this fuss about our using it for the Air Force. Don't you realize that if we had a couple of thousand Diesel planes *and* if we did use magnesium for the valve cooling the amount required would be negligible.'

'Listen. They've got an alloy in Russia that's going to alter the whole basis of aeroplane construction, and one of our chaps thinks he can get hold of it. They haven't started building yet. We know that magnesium is used, and if we can find out the formula and we control magnesium supplies we'll be sitting very pretty. We've got to develop our factory in advance. But it doesn't even pay now, and we may not get hold of the formula or it may be no good. We want a government subsidy for the factory. And it's got to leak out about the Diesel planes, so we can start putting out feelers . . .'

Eric rubbed his chin and sucked his teeth again. 'Soon as it gets out,' he said, 'the French and the Germans will start building them fast as they can. And then your damned paper and all the rest will be yapping about us not having as many as them – while we've got to get another ten millions supplementary estimate already, and it's going to give the Communists a chance to raise merry hell.'

'Good lord, you're not worrying about *them*, are you?'

'Your rag worries about them enough,' he said maliciously. 'Trouble is that even when you do tell the truth you don't believe it. As a matter of fact they're gaining ground no end. Look at this business about the busmen, it's a scandal . . .'

Outside, sudden gushes of wind were beginning to spatter raindrops on the window glass. Arthur looked up a moment and said, 'It's raining.' 'Fine,' said Eric. 'It's needed badly in the country.'

The barometer was falling slightly, the sky had filled with cirrostratus clouds. Irregular gusts of wind from the southeast sprang up, and now it began to drizzle.

In thousands of rooms people looked up from newspapers or conversations and saw the little drops splashing down the windowpanes and murmured 'It's raining,' some thinking of the country as did Eric Sloane, some of the projects threatened, some hoping it would stop before they went out, some of the delicious smell that would rise from the rain-quenched dust in the parks and the quiet streets.

And too, just as the Sloanes were interrupted momentarily from thoughts of the bus strike, so were others, including Mr Albert Raggett, secretary of the United Transport Worker's Union, as he sat in his study composing an anti-Communist encyclical to be issued as a last-minute appeal to the busmen.

He was writing 'Paid Agents of Moscow are trying to disrupt our trade-union movement, that has been built up by so many years of –' And he looked up from his paper, trying to think of a good juicy expression comprehending 'patient endeavour', 'selfless sacrifice', 'loyalty', 'devoted leadership' and all that, and then he saw the rain.

Rain, he said to himself. Rain, oh good! Maybe it meant the end of this month's fine weather and that the rain would come pouring down all tomorrow, and he thought of a straggling miserable little procession of Communists with drenched banners huddling into Hyde Park . . . If only the rain would stay . . .

And he got up and went to the window to look at the weather. The wind was getting gustier and the clouds darker. If the wind came up the rain wouldn't last, he admitted to himself.

Unconsciously he was impelled to survey the warm comfort of his study, the soft carpet, the book-lined walls, the electric heater, the comfortable armchairs upholstered by Leather Products Ltd, the fine mahogany desk, the presentation oil painting of himself hanging over the mantelpiece in the orderly recess of its large gilt frame – Raggett At His Best, Raggett The Leader with his arm outstretched, making a speech, his hair falling over one eye, his brow a bit ennobled . . . His thoughts dwelt with particular satisfaction on that picture, as he lovingly surveyed the comfort and tastefulness of the room, contrasting it with the wind and the rain outside, with the crowded, noisy, shabby North-country cottage of his boyhood.

But somehow the survey of his domains did not fill him with the reassuring feeling that it usually did. There was a kind of uneasy gloom at the back of his mind: perhaps it was his digestion, he should not have eaten so much fat bacon at breakfast.

The more he thought of the comfortable circumstances of his life the less was he able to summon up the warm and lovely glow of self-satisfaction that he desired. Instead he thought of the Communists, whose dark forces were undermining him. He tried only to think of them in a fury, in a gust of indignant rhetoric. He enjoyed thinking of them like that. But to consider them calmly, quietly, in private, without an audience, filled him with a squirming discomfort. Their existence and their growing strength was a threat to all the hardly-struggled-for and dearly bought things of his life, to his pleasant surroundings, to those comfortable round-table talks with the employers, those talks where he sat puffing a directorial cigar and speaking of 'the men', building up for himself and the others a picture of Raggett The Leader, the beloved of the workers, whose wise and temporizing sagacity led them safely away from strikes and violence and class hatred. How he loved to feel that he held the balance between the workers and those smooth rich men masked with power, knowing he was the vital link between them, the oil between the cogs of the machine.

He could sit at the polished tables, smoke the rich men's cigars and speak with them of 'the men', and he was more than their equal. And those Red fanatics, those agitators, those disgruntled misfits, came and talked of class struggle and how there could be no collaboration between worker and boss, only warfare. Where was the need for bitterness and struggle while he could sit at the polished tables and talk calmly of arbitration and impartial tribunals.

But something was happening; nowadays he began to get uneasy twinges that the situation was eluding him. He had an unerring instinct, a genius for divining the moods and feelings of masses of workers before they themselves were conscious of them. And it was the capacity of being able to turn those feelings to his own advantage that had lifted him out of his squalid boyhood, away from his class, until he had become the leader of the largest trade union in the country, the owner of a fine house and car, a man of weight, with a large income and twelve-thousand-pounds' worth of securities. But something was eluding him now. He sensed the feeling of the masses, but he could no longer control it. Lord Pitcairn, Chairman of the London Transport Combine, had looked a little oddly at him last week when they had discussed this May Day strike, a look that chilled his self-esteem and reminded him of a thousand forgotten shames.

A year or two ago he would have been able to break this strike easily.

'Paid agitators from Moscow are trying to disrupt our trade-union movement that has been built up by . . .'

He walked up and down the room, beginning to make a speech to himself. His feet were noiseless on the thick carpet.

He stopped in front of a mirror and examined his face. It looked back at him, a heavy moustached oval of flesh masked with a bluff geniality. There was a large blackhead at the corner of his nose. He squeezed it with a fierce and melancholy joy.

Then he suddenly thought of that look on Lord Pitcairn's face again, and he felt depressed.

* * * * *

The wind veered to the south-west, and the rain slackened a moment and stopped. The men in the Labour Exchange queue who had been huddling under the shelter of the wall scattered out on the pavement again. An oldish man with a melancholy walrus moustache, wearing blue overalls, was talking to a fat chap with a cheerful face.

'So 'e comes back and says, "I want a bit o' oak to screw the 'andle to." "Oak," says 'Arry, "No, no you ain't goin' to 'ave no bit o' oak. 'Tain't allowed for in the price." "'Ow the bloody 'ell d'you expec' me to fix it then," 'e says. And in the end they never done the job at all.'

''E's always like that,' said the fat man. 'Fair gives me the sick 'e does . . .'

They both sighed.

When the rain started again the shabby old gent with the white whiskers dressed in a courtly out-of-date suit, bent down and picked up a little flossy matted Skye terrier who was trotting timidly by his side. The gentleman had a square bit of cloth all ready to wrap his bloody dog up with. And bundling up the little brute and putting it under his arm from where it peered with beady currant eyes, he tottered across the road pretty majestically.

Miss Pamela Fosdyke, sheltering in the doorway of a decayed gentlewoman's art-and-craft shop, saw him and giggled. 'Reminds me of George Moore,' said her gentleman friend in a public-school voice.

In front, the traffic-lights blinked from green to amber and then red. Two taxis drew up side by side.

'Wotcher, 'Arry!' shouted one driver to the other.

'Wotcher, George!'

'Comin' up the park tomorrow?'

'Course . . . 'ope the bleedin' rain 'olds orf.'

The traffic-lights blinked, amber, green. The little knot of halted cars and cycles broke up and scattered.

Here are some more things happening now:

Peter Langfier was waking up with a headache.

Captain Ginnery, late master of the *Arundale*, was sitting in a train and thinking, as it drew out of Euston station, that this was the last time he would be coming home from a voyage.

James Seton was talking politics with two firemen off the *Corinthia* in the reading-room of the Sailors' Home.

The Earl of Dunbourne was being shampooed.

Bill Riley's mother was having her temperature taken.

Jean, the Langfier's maid, was repelling the advances of Henry McGinnis, the chauffeur.

A boat train was arriving at Victoria, bearing Jacques Duval, traveller in wines, who was actually Rene Vauclair, fraternal delegate from the French Communist Party to the May Day demonstration.

Also in the train was a bishop, three Rotarians playing poker, some journalists, some tourists and twenty-four chorus girls, a bestseller novelist, lots of businessmen in connection with drainpipe factories, gelatine, combs and brushes, chinaware, printable machines, vacuum cleaners, soap, etc. The train drew into Victoria, and they all tensed themselves, waiting to open the carriage doors. The three Rotarians were scrabbling on their knees picking up cards from the floor.

* * * * *

Newsbills, yellow or white, with black or red letters, damply flaunted themselves in the drizzle at street corners, proclaiming WORLD FLIERS OVER PACIFIC. FERNANDEZ CATCHING UP. PRIME MINISTER DEMANDS BIGGER AIR FORCE. CAPT. COE'S FINALS. FILM STAR SEEKS DIVORCE.

The newspaper offices were stirring and humming with activity. Thousands of telephone bells were ringing in rooms and offices, lifts were going up and down, queues filing in and out of Labour Exchanges, people running up and down stairs.

Film tradeshows were going on, also rehearsals of plays and musical comedies.

* * * * *

At the Pool Theatre, where the preliminary dress rehearsal of *Backwards And Forwards* was starting, all was confusion. The stage was littered with half-dressed, half-costumed chorus girls, half-finished scenery, stagehands and electricians. The stage manager was having a row with the foreman. Miss Rosita Flanders, the blonde bitchy leading lady, Mr Ralph Ginsberg, the producer, Freddie McSween, the musical director, Messrs Aubrey Falcon, Reggie Perceval and Isadore Levenstein, the lyricists, Cohen and Goldberg, the authors of the book, Hans Schnupf, foreign lighting expert, as well as Connie Deans, the ballet master, and old Mr Finkel and young Mr Finkel, the backers and a whole lot of female secretaries, young men in suede shoes and light-grey suits, odd lesbians, costumiers and sopranos, were all talking and arguing and bellyaching about in the front of the house, while on the stage the chorus girls were kicking up hell about the bitchiness of Rosita Flanders. Adela Smith stood amongst them, weeping, half with misery, half with anger, because she had been sacked, and the girls all knew that it was because she had kicked higher than the old sow Flanders in the Roseleaf number. Flanders couldn't dance for nuts, and there had been all that row in her last show where she had had a number dancing with the chorus and had got several girls sacked, the cow . . . The stage foreman was saying in a surly tone, 'Well, Mr Green, I'll put it to the men, but I don't think they'll stand for it.' And he walked away, while Henry Porter and George MacAlister looked down at the stage from over the edge of the fly gallery and said that they weren't going to stand any more all-night shifts. The foreman called them down, and the other flymen and all the stage hands went down under the stage in the dim catacomb light with the sound of the girls' feet tap-tapping above, and everyone was arguing and talking angrily.

'Let 'em put the bloody show off,' a chap said, and others said, 'They've got to take on another shift.' Everyone was saying 'We've had enough,' and then young Andy, the flaxen-haired electrics, came down to them from the other electricians and said, 'Look here, we're not going to come on tonight, and we're taking it up with our union. What about you chaps?' Then everyone started chipping in again, 'It's all very well for you –' 'If we strike and the show doesn't come on, what the hell's the good – ?'

Then Andy started to talk to them about the position in the show business and how the bosses had thought they'd broken the union in 1928 and how they'd got away with more and more and everyone was fed up and it was up to someone to give a lead. Some of the fellows said it was all very well for him, he was in the ETU and it was a proper union and anyway it was easier for them to get jobs.

And Bill Green, the stage manager, pushed and shoved his way in the babbling group around the younger and the elder Finkel and said 'For Heavensake lissen to me a minute. The stagehands won't work all night again, and they want double pay for last night, and they're talking about walking out.'

'Cheesus Christ,' shouted the elder Finkel. 'Lissen to vot the man is saying. O just lissen to him. As if I had not got some other things to worry about.' And Bill was going to chip in, but the younger Finkel said 'Tell them they should think themselves lucky for a chanst of the extra work with new cinemas opening all the time.'

* * * * *

'Harry 'phoned the union, and they said wait till they sent someone down.'

'Yeah, and when 'e comes 'e'll tell us about the pictures ruining the show business and we've got to accept –'

'It's OK for you electricians, you can easy get jobs, and anyway your union'll stick by you.'

'His union's full of Communists.'

'Don't that prove what I've been saying –'

'Now wait a minute, chaps, wait a minute. You've all had your say now. No one with any sense'll deny our position's easier than yours. But don't you see, it's not just *this* bloody theatre, it's all the workers in the show business. They're all as fed up as we are, and they're all standing back and waiting for someone or something to give 'em a lead. Now the NATE *never* will and we know it. If we come out it'll get 'em all going to fight for better conditions all round . . .'

'Why pick on us?'

'That's what everyone says, don't you see, Dick?'

''E's right, you know –'

'I'll tell you why it should be us – we've got a better chance here of winning concessions than you could get anywhere. Finkels'll do everything to get this show on to time – they've got a winner, and they're going to back out. And a blackleg stage crew brought in at the last minute won't be able to handle the stuff either.'

Then the stage foreman came back looking furious and they all clustered around him, and he said, 'Finkel says we're damned lucky to get the overtime these days at all, and wiv 'is bleeding compliments.'

Bill Green leaned up against the proscenium arch and lit a cigarette and folded his arms, thinking, let 'em get on with it. He was fed up.

* * * * *

'– So ole Finkel shouted, "Get on the 'phone and take on a fresh crew," and Bill Green says, "Shall I tell them they'll find the place picketed outside, just to encourage them a bit?"'

'D'you 'ear that, 'Arry, Bill Green tole old Finkel 'e could get a new staff 'is bleedin' self.'

Andy the electrician nipped across to the 'phone-box on the other side of the road and rang up the *Daily Worker* and told them about the strike and asked them to get on to the District Industrial Bureau to send a chap down. Then he ran back and said, 'We've got to elect a strike committee.'

There were twenty-four stagehands and ten electrics, one of the call-boys and some of the front-of-house staff standing around the stage door and a crowd gathering, and Andy got up on the big dustbin and made a bit of a speech about their rotten conditions and calling on the front-of-house staff to join in with them.

'He'll never get a job again,' some fellow said, but the others said his union'd see he wasn't victimized.

It was the twenty-third strike now on in London.

* * * * *

In front of the theatre a little knot of people was continually forming and continually drifting away, their idly curious eyes scanning the advance glorifications of the Finkel brothers' forthcoming outburst of glittering splendour in the shape of *Backwards And Forwards*, the musical comedy that is going to be DIFFERENT. Eyes slid over mist-haloed photographs of Rosita Flanders posturing draped in camera fuzz, over chorus girls' smiles and curves impaled under glass, as well as the noble vacuity of tenors and incredible disguises of character actors . . .

The little knot of people was always the same and always in a state of flux.

A man in brown loose tweeds, who looked like an

intellectual, stopped and shared in the weak life of the group, and then he went on, ambling down Charing Cross Road along the drizzle-slimed pavement. PRIME MINISTER DEMANDS BIGGER AIR FORCE he read from the newsbills, and, full of a sudden horror, he thought of war.

It's inevitable, he said to himself. You can't say just when and how, but it's got to come . . . and he thought of the early summer of 1914, the wonderful feeling of smartness and gaiety, the feeling of the people on top that everything was grand, while the secret treaties were being drawn up and strikes and labour unrest was brewing. There was poison sediment at the bottom of the champagne glasses. He was only a schoolboy at the time, but he remembered the hot summer so well and the smiling lovely women riding in the Row. Then it was August, war, the gala of the lice. And it was going to happen again, there was the 1914 feeling in the air.

He looked at the faces of the people passing and saw neither strength nor awareness in them. The buses thundered by, and he clutched at the thought of the busmen, the transport workers . . . they were striking tomorrow. Neither their leaders nor the press-faked forces of public opinion had fooled them, and maybe they would refuse when the time for war came. These men, the transport and munition workers, might prove with a stubborn mighty No to be the only salvation of humanity. The proletariat, the real proletariat, were his only hope, the only factor in the situation that he didn't regard with a damning hopeless certainty. Their faces and their speech were a little different to his, strangely alien to his class; he felt he would never be able to get close to their lives and their ways of living, but he had a kind of respect and admiration for them.

Yet also they were of the millions that were sucked in through the doors of the cinemas, who bought the newspapers, who listened to the wireless, the millions whom he alternately pitied and despised for accepting and believing the dope by which they were ruled, exploited, cheated and swindled and for which they would soon be asked to sacrifice their lives.

When he thought of the people sitting in the warm darkness of the picture houses, lapped with the sickly disgusting tide of drugging, lying thoughts and ideas that helped to enslave them, his mind grew ice-hard and contemptuous. Yet his only hope lay in the stubborn No of these millions.

He looked up at the sky and wondered if it was going to start raining again, and then he tried to ward off his gloomy thoughts by studying the bookshop windows, whose glass-fronted stages exhibited a show – 'culture of the day' – detective stories, highbrow novels about soul-sick intelligentsia, criticism of criticism, bits about Art, Great Men, Nudism, etc., verse concerned with typography and punctuation, and everywhere the symptoms of social decay – systems of world panaceas, cloudy debunkings of Socialism, Communism, Fascism, Religion, Social Credit, so-and-so unmasked, such-and-such exposed. Cover designs abounded with romantic photomontage and abstract representations of the Workers, red flags, hammers and sickles, fasces, swastikas, pound-dollar signs, Union Jacks, clenched fists and whips, a chaotic jumble of baggage dropped in the great retreat of bourgeois thought. There were popular unscientific essays about science and god, solemn pornography in artistic or psychological disguise. Ten novels were published every week. Literary critics subsidized by publishers acclaimed new geniuses every Sunday. Art and literature were a racket without the saving grace of gunmen.

He went into a pub and had a whisky, his first drink of the morning, and as he felt its familiar delicious sting at the back of his throat he wondered if there was anything left for him in life but temporary anaesthetics.

* * * * *

Mr Twitchett, MP, was sitting in the House of Commons in the place where he always did sit. He was a very old man. He had been a miner once, but it was a long time ago; it was a story that he told himself about a poor boy who had risen. He was quite stupid, an opinionated old man who got four hundred a year to help to rule the country. He had been in Parliament for years now; he would have been terribly unhappy if he was not returned; he wouldn't have known what to do with himself. He went to all the debates like a dull and dutiful student attending lectures. Sometimes he would get up and say something in a loud and agricultural sort of voice, something rather dull and not to the point that nobody took any notice of.

It was question time now. The newly appointed Minister for Tariffs was having a rough time. Old George Twitchett leaned forwards, his hand cupped to his ear listening attentively: he was a bit deaf.

'Is the Minister for Tariffs aware of the importance of magnesium in connection with new developments in aircraft construction, and if so, has he any proposals to make to the government for the development of the production of magnesium in this country?'

'Is the Minister aware . . . ?'

The Minister of Tariffs was apparently aware of very little; it seemed that he was practically in a dazed condition.

I haven't asked a question for years, thought old Twitchett. I'd like to ask a question one day. And he thought of himself standing up, rather shakily and slowly and booming out in his fine old-fashioned orator's voice, 'Is the Minister aware . . .' It would be nice to ask a question one day, show them up. They'd like it in the trade union too, not nonsense about magnesium duties or about some commercial traveller being arrested by foreigners, but a real smacking question about the mines . . . He ruminated . . .

Assuming that Mr Twitchett attended Parliament for

six hours a day for two hundred days of the year (a very generous estimate) he was getting about six bob an hour for sitting here.

* * * * *

Sometimes she grabbed hold of the radiator as hard as she could, so tightly that when she let go the palms of her hands felt bruised. Sometimes she bit the corner of her handkerchief and tore at it until in the end it was just a mass of shreds. Her pains were coming nearly every twenty minutes now; they lasted for about thirty seconds, but it seemed hours. She had asked the nurse if it wasn't time for her to go into the delivery ward and the nurse had smiled brightly and said, 'Not for a long time yet.' She felt she couldn't stand it much longer after that. She knew it would be worse in the delivery ward, but she couldn't really imagine anything worse than this, and once she was there she would feel it was *for* something, that she really would be having the baby and it was just a question of holding on until it happened.

The nurses made her keep walking about. She whimpered a little when they stopped her lying down, but she pulled herself together, stuck out her lower lip and started walking again.

She hated this ward, with the other women in their hideous, depressing dressing-gowns; she hated when one of them got a spasm of pain and would sit down on the edge of the bed just grunting a little. The three other women had all had babies already, it was easier for them. They were very nice to her and reassuring, but she would have rather been alone and not seeing their haggard faces and the pinched, wan look under their eyes and knowing that she looked like them too in her miserable grey-flannel dressing-gown.

She couldn't understand how they took it so calmly and easily. Perhaps their pains were much less than hers. There was that woman in the next ward: you could hear her moaning and screaming all the time, a long, horrible, hopeless wailing that never seemed to stop. She had asked what was wrong with her and they said she had been in labour for nearly a week now and she was bound to die, nothing could be done for her, she was getting weaker and weaker from the pain, they couldn't operate, and the baby couldn't get born.

Outside, through the window, she could see the road and the cars passing up and down and the rain. This was her comfort, the thought of the world outside going on just as usual: it made this seem less of a nightmare.

She supposed she ought to be feeling all those noble thoughts that people said you experienced when you were becoming a mother, but she couldn't, she couldn't somehow connect all this with the baby that she had thought about so much and made plans for.

She tried to think of Tom working in the factory: he would be worrying so, but it made her glad to think of it and that she could be sorry for him. He worked a hydraulic press in a dark, hot underground sort of place at Langfier's. She wished she had seen it, she wished she knew exactly what it was like so she could imagine him quite clearly, working there and worrying about her.

Then she had another spasm of pain; she felt as if her backbone was being split open, as if she was being torn apart.

And the pretty, dark young nurse came up and said she would have to go for an examination now. Her heart gave a flutter of fear and joy.

The nurse held the door open, and she went out into the white shining corridor.

* * * * *

The sounds of clocks striking dissolved outwards into the air, mingling with the dying, speeding cries of the factory sirens.

And the girls at Langfier's rushed into the mess room, jostling and shoving each other and trying to reserve places for their friends.

In a few moments they had all sat down on long forms in front of the trestle tables. The mess room had been built about twenty years ago. It hadn't been bad then, with its shiny white-painted matchboard walls and the bright oil-cloth on the tables, but now it was far too small, the paint was yellowed and chipped, the oilcloth cracked and worn. There was an old greasy smell, and everything glistened wetly with condensed steam. The girls were packed together so tightly that their elbows knocked and jostled together every time they raised their food to their mouths.

The tremendous clatter of knives and forks and plates was almost drowned in the din of conversations. A group of girls from the insulation-winding shop were letting off about Daisy Miller who had fainted this morning and hurt her head and arm on her machine. Everyone was saying that if there had been proper guards she would have been all right.

These little groups formed islands of serious talk in a sea of more frivolous conversations. Someone was drawing Mae West females on the table; some talked about boyfriends, some of film stars, some of bikes, some dancing, some clothes, some scandal.

And, like flickering marsh-fire, a rumour was darting about, springing up and dying away but almost always in being at some part of the room, that the main machine shop was going to be put entirely on piecework rates.

All these girls, packed close together and slightly sweating under their coarse grey overalls, some smelling of cheap scent or powder, gave off a powerful emanation of feminity that would have been stifling and oppressive to a man.

Between the ugly grey caps and the tops of the overalls the living flesh of faces blossomed like flowers. Like wind ripples across a lake, waves of laughter, of smiles or frowns, chased over the lines of intent mouths.

Taken individually they were just a lot of ordinary, silly, laughing girls, some noticeably prettier or uglier than most, a few who were sillier or more intelligent, a few more full of vitality, a few more lustful, a few harder or kinder than the rest. But also the whole lot of them together shared in a group consciousness: beyond their own individuality there was their individuality as a mass . . .

Molly Davis, the redheaded girl who worked a drilling-machine, was still holding forth about Daisy's accident. Daisy was a particular pal of hers. 'It's a bloody shame,' she kept saying, 'it's a bloody shame.' She was a splendid, vigorous creature, rather silly and impulsive, and she had the reputation of being a bit of a tart, but no one could help liking her; she carried people along in the current of her generous vitality. She wasn't exactly pretty or beautiful, but she dazzled with her splendid red hair and vivid white skin.

Ivy Cutford, who was a bit farther down the table on the opposite side, leaned forward trying to hear what she was saying: '. . . she's been that jumpy and nervous all last week. She used to have to go to bed as soon as she got home in the evening, she was so tired out.'

'We all get fits like that in our department . . .'

'It might be any of us next . . .'

And some of the girls were quiet and thoughtful, thinking of how their fingers shook in the last hour of their shift and how easy it was to have an accident.

Then they suddenly looked up and saw Daisy. She was standing in the door, just by the counter, her head bandaged up and her arm in a sling. She looked very pale and faint. She was looking around for Molly, and then she caught sight of her and began to walk slowly over to her.

There was a sudden oppressive lull in the storm of talk,

then Molly jumped up and shouted out, 'How much longer are we going to stand for this, girls!' and then everyone started talking again at once in an angry babble of voices.

Ivy Cutford gripped the edges of her seat tightly: her moment had come, and she didn't feel prepared to take it. She was trembling with excitement and nervousness. She knew so clearly what she had to do, it wasn't anything hard. She tried to think of Lenin, of Dimitrov in the Nazi court-room, of the heroes of her class who had not flinched before anything when their moment came. What she had to do was nothing . . . 'I must get up, I must get up,' she was saying to herself, and suddenly she sprang up and stood on the form. 'Girls,' she said, 'listen to me a minute.'

Her voice sounded loud in her ears, and she saw all the faces turning towards her, all the eyes looking into hers, and suddenly she felt calm, buoyed up by the rays of those glances, and she went on talking quite easily and clearly. 'You've heard what Molly said – "How much longer are we going to stand for this." That's what we've all been thinking, and Molly's had the guts to get up and say it. We're all fed up –' 'That's right,' the girls shouted back. 'That's right,' she said, her voice suddenly getting louder of its own accord. 'Sure, that's right, but it's time we did something about it. If we all stand together we *can* do something about it.'

Something was happening inside her: she could feel the girls' excitement and enthusiasm coming up at her in waves from which she drew strength. Unconsciously she began to shake her fist as she spoke, her pale cheeks were flushed and her eyes bright.

'There's Daisy,' she said. 'All cut and hurt, lucky she's not far worse. It might be any of us next, and we know. And we know it can be stopped. We want proper guards on the machines and no more bloody speed-up.'

'That's right,' they shouted. 'Good old Ivy.'

'Well, let's *do* something now we've talked about it.

There used to be a works committee here years ago. We can get one going now, and if we all stand together behind it we can tell Meek and Dartry and the rest of the bosses where they get off . . . How about some of us going on a deputation to the men now. They'll come in with us all right if they see we mean business. I'm ready to go, who'll come with me . . . ?'

She stopped and stood quite still, shaking a little. Someone giggled. She could feel a hesitation amongst the girls and with it she felt her strength and certainty deserting her. Then Molly burst out, 'I'll come with you, and we'll take Daisy too.' And the feeling of excitement and enthusiasm rose up to her again.

'What about you, Jean?' she said to a girl opposite, whom she knew to be serious and reliable and a bit of a fighter.

'Aye,' said Jean, 'I'll come wi' ye.' And she stood up to go quite composedly. Ivy jumped down and everyone was clapping, and the three of them walked over to the door and Molly took Daisy's arm and they went out.

As the door closed behind them there was a hush and everyone began to talk quickly in a whisper. The steak-and-kidney pudding was congealing on their plates.

Ivy didn't remember walking to the men's mess room. She seemed suddenly to find herself outside the door, and the four of them hesitated, hearing the deep undertone of voices within. They halted undecidedly. None of them had any idea of what they were going to say or what their reception would be, and then Molly said, 'Come on, they can't eat us,' and opened the door.

They stood awkwardly inside, aliens in this masculine atmosphere. Some of the chaps began to whistle and call out to them. 'Go on, Ivy,' Molly whispered, and Ivy stepped forward.

She felt awkward, deserted by her courage, and then she caught Millman's eye. He was grinning encouragingly at her. She saw he knew what had happened and she pulled herself together. She took a breath to begin. 'Pipe down,' Millman shouted. 'For Chrisake pipe down, and let's hear what they've got to say.'

'We've come on a deputation from the girls,' said Ivy. 'Look at her,' she pointed to Daisy. 'She was so dead beat she fainted at her job 's morning and hurt herself on the machine. If someone hadn't grabbed her she might've been killed. There weren't proper guards. We don't know who's going to be the next. We've had enough of these accidents but they'll go on getting worse until we all stand together and fight the management. We've come on this deputation to ask if you fellows will come in with us and help get up a works committee.'

There was an uncertain, approving murmur, and Millman jumped up quickly and said, very fast, 'Look 'ere, we've talked and talked about this works committee, and we've nearly all been for it, only lots of us've said it's no use without the girls and they'd never stand together with us. Well, they've shown us they've got more guts than wot we 'ave –'

'They've bloody well given us a lead and it's up to us to follow it,' Bill Riley chipped in.

One of the storemen, a middle-aged rather taciturn fellow said, 'I'm for the committee, but it won't be any good till we've got hundred per cent trade unionism 'ere.'

'I'm absolutely with you there, mate, and it's through the committee we'll get it.'

'Can't we pick two or three delegates from each shop temporary like and get them to meet the girls' delegates after the shift and talk it over –'

'That's right, 'sno good arguing the toss 'ere.'

The girls stood awkwardly at the end of the room while the men were arguing. Then the door of the foremen's mess room opened, and Harry Moss stuck his head round. 'Wot's up?' he said, his mouth full of suet pudding. 'Wot's them girls doing 'ere?'

'If you fellows are with us for a works committee,' said Millman, 'come in and listen. If you're with the bosses for accidents and speed-up you'd best stay out.'

'So *that's* the issue,' said Moss, tugging thoughtfully at his long moustache. 'I 'ave to talk it over with the others,' he said ponderously and shut the door.

* * * * *

Everywhere the accumulated bitterness of weeks and months and years, the dammed-up, painfully anaesthetized resentments of hardship and poverty, were bursting forth like this.

'Men make history – but not as they please.' This is what happens, a speech, an accident, an insult, a word that seems to initiate events, is like a switch releasing electric power.

* * * * *

London extends itself around the grey-silver curling worm of the river like some sprawling monster. The million sounds of machinery and voices and laughter, of traffic and typewriters and hammers and saws, of dogs barking and the cries of birth and death, the sounds of music and bicycle bells and pigeons cooing, blend together and rise into the air, varying in tone from hour to hour, the monster's breathing.

The rhythm is unchanged; the face of things is unaltered: the ferment works within.

Only in those invisible spider's-web lines in time and space that mesh lives with material objects is there a change.

It is the shape of these patterns that fashions and records history.

* * * * *

Smoothly, effortlessly, with only the faintest sigh of brakes, the Earl of Dunbourne's long cream-coloured Daimler drew up in front of Chantilly's Bond Street shop. A grave pug-nosed little pageboy opened the door of the car devotedly. The Hon. Pamela Allin extended a questing silk-sleek leg and stepped out, followed by her mother, who traversed the stretch of pavement between the car and the shop with an air of martyrdom.

Chantilly's crystal doors swung to after them, extinguishing the harshness of traffic noises and the crudities of the damp outer air. Within brooded a hushed luxuriousness. Polished, seal-smooth assistants materialized themselves when wanted.

How drowsy warm, how soft it is in here, thinks Pamela. In these shops one is wrapped up as in a cocoon, sheltered from the harsh outer air like a moth in its cocoon. There were beggars in the streets, suffering faces and cruel eyes; the sky was grey and smeared with dirt, the roads all drizzle-slimed . . . In London my thoughts are buffeted by the clangour of the lives of millions of people. I am reft from the slow assurance of the presence of my dogs and horses. I cannot think my own thoughts. And here, where this harsh and dangerous clangour of common life is shut out I am invaded and disturbed by other alien atmospheres. I am constrained to accept the values of existence in terms of shimmering silks and jewels; beauty becomes the line of a skirt from hip to ankle, morality the observance of harmony in the colours and shapes of fabrics. Of the rightness of these values my mother is convinced, while I am only momentarily hypnotized into their acceptance.

Silken dresses in the shapes and colours of halted waterfalls, a gown that would clothe her into a Hans Andersen snow-maiden, another that congealed her into the glittering aloofness of frozen fountain-jets, and then a little golden frock to wear for the laughing afternoons on lawns . . .

these were sheaths for her body, to mask her for evenings of pleasure, magnets for glances she did not desire and that yet could please her.

Holding that little golden frock out at arm's length she clothed herself in it and went sauntering down a country lane to meet Peter Langfier.

* * * * *

Outside it started to drizzle again.

A small cyclone, passing over London in a north-east-by-easterly direction, was the cause of today's muggy weather, cloudy sky, showers and drizzle.

The barometer stood around 29 and was falling slightly.

The approach of the cyclone centre had been heralded by small gusty winds from the south-east. In Deptford, Woolwich, East and West Ham, Dagenham and surrounding districts the wind flapped wet paper into gutters and blew rain into people's faces.

The wind backed and veered a little bringing a softer and more steady drizzle over Kensington, Hyde Park, St John's Wood, Hampstead and the West End, marking the front of the cyclone centre.

West of a line drawn from Golders Green to Wandsworth the barometer began to rise again slightly, and the wind came from west-north-west.

Further west, over Ealing, Hounslow, Acton and the Thames Valley, there was a steady downpour. A westerly wind was clearing the sky over Berkshire and Hampshire, though to the south there were still showers.

Over the West of England it was fine, with a blue sky and cool and invigorating air. By the evening it would have cleared over London, leaving patches of detached strato-cumulus cloud. There would be a splendid sunset.

Now the drizzle was heaviest in Central London around

Holborn and Theobalds Road. At first James pulled his cap over his forehead, turned up the collar of his jacket and walked faster. But he soon realized that he would be soaked if he stayed out, so he took shelter in a cafe.

It was a dingy little place, with marble-topped tables like slabs of old streaky bacon. The outstanding features were a tarnished tea urn surmounted by a great ecclesiastical-looking tin eagle, and a fly-blown bill of fare decorated with faded pink-and-blue watercolour scrolls. Behind the counter a billowing shapeless woman wrapped in a dirty white overall sat thinking about a film she had seen last night.

Two lorry drivers were talking about motor engines. A small cabinet-maker with a gingery waxed moustache and a bowler hat was reading the leading article in the *Daily Herald*. At the next table a young mechanic in a clean, faded-blue boiler suit was talking to two unemployed youths (in rakish peak caps, knotted white scarves, etc.) about dog racing.

James ordered a large tea, took the *Daily Worker* out of his pocket and began to look at it casually. A snuffly loud-speaker uttered waltz tunes. James began to feel a bit sleepy. His thoughts withdrew themselves into the warm slackness of his muscles. The mugginess of the air seemed to soak right into him, instilling a dreamy lassitude. What I need is a woman, he said to himself, putting down his paper and remembering Pat's description of what he called a 'tender, randy feeling'. I should like to be waiting to meet a woman, he thought, knowing that I'm going to have her, to be sitting here slackly letting that tender, randy feeling creep over me and knowing that soon I'll be going to bed with a nice girl, not any nice girl, but a certain one . . .

His thoughts were all scattered. Starting out from trying to picture to himself the 'certain girl' he would like to be waiting for, he found himself going over the argument he had had with the stokers that morning and thinking of better examples and replies than he had been able to give at the time.

Absently he spooned sugar into his tea and stirred it. He began to be aware of a changed atmosphere behind him. He turned around and looked. The cabinet-maker had put down his *Herald*, the unemployed and the mechanic had stopped their conversation and were leaning forward towards the lorry drivers, who were letting off. 'Course there'll be a war,' one of them was saying. 'Course there will,' his mate echoed.

'And it's no good blokes like you saying you won't fight . . . half of you'll fall for the dope when it comes –'

'– An' anyway,' his mate chipped in, 'we'll all be bloody well *made* to join up this time, they won't be taking any risks . . .'

'General Strike'll stop a war quick enough,' said the cabinet-maker in a squeaky voice.

'Yeah,' said the first lorry driver scornfully. 'An' you think the bleeding TUC'll call a general strike against war. Why, they've practically given up *saying* they will even now.'

'All they think about,' said his mate, 'is their soft jobs. They'll do what the bosses tell 'em, same as they did last time –'

'– Same as they're doin' all the time now.'

'They'll talk a lot about being against war all right, but we've been attacked and we've got to defend ourselves, we've got to defend democracy and all that –'

'Well, I'm damned if they'll get me to fight,' said the young mechanic in a hard, abrupt voice. 'Nor I,' said one of the unemployed chaps. His mate nodded his head in agreement.

James felt it was about time he chipped in. 'We can stop a war. But we won't do it by waiting for the TUC or something like that to give a lead when the time comes. Look at the busmen now . . .' The others shook their heads and made approving noises. 'Their union's no different to any other, their leaders're as much against a May Day strike or any militant action as any other TU leaders. But they've got a rank-and-file movement that's properly organized and *they* can get the line they want put over, and if the leaders don't like it they can do the other thing. It's up to the workers in this country to do the same about war. It's what we start doing *now* against war that counts, not what we think we'd like to do when a war comes . . .'

It's fine, he was thinking, it's grand the way everyone is arguing and talking about politics and war and everything now, so different to what it was when I was last home. The workers are waking up . . .

* * * * *

The glass window in the cafe door framed a procession of passing heads and shoulders against a shifting background of trams and buses. Every now and then there was a gap in the traffic and one could see across to the other side of the road where there was a Salvation Army place that bore a big poster over the door – WE INVITE U COME AND HEAR CAPT. WHENT AND BRIG. MRS BLOW 2-NITE ALL ARE WELCOME. A pimply young Salvationist was lolling up against the doorway, thinking about a girl he had seen walking in Oxford Street the other day, a lovely luxurious creature whose splendid body seemed to thrust itself forward through her half-open coat. Her movements, her lips, her laughing eyes, had awoken a fearful, tremulous perturbation in his mind . . .

The girl had been Jenny Hardy. His eyes would have popped out of his head had he seen her at the moment, slopping about the dishevelled pink intimacies of her bed-room, half-naked, a semi-Japanese kimono trailing around her, her hair all awry, her eyes drowsy and discontented.

This is what she was thinking:

. . . I'll put the bath on in a minute . . . I do look a sight . . . wish I had something to read . . . be all right if I had some of the girls up here now, they wouldn't half envy the flat and all my dresses. They must be just packing up dinner now, going back to work feeling slow and heavy and hating to begin. Glad I'm through with that, anything's better, day after day with nothing nice to look forward to, nothing nice to eat or wear . . . wonder if Molly's still there, wonder how she is . . . I'd like to see her again . . . she always was silly, throwing herself away with men . . . It must have stopped raining, I'll look . . . such a grey, dull day – wish the sun'd shine, I could go a walk. I do feel mouldy. Maybe I'll call up Jack . . . I don't know . . . don't feel in the mood now . . . it was rotten last night, he made a mess of it the last time, the old fool . . . I always feel mouldy like this after I've been with him, all nervy and fed up. If I see Jack now I'll have a row with him, I'd like to shout at someone . . . perhaps I'll go to the pictures . . . must put the bath on . . . the time drags so on days like this . . .

She switched on the wireless. A dance tune filled the room. 'Without a caress Life is meaningless,' crooned a gentlemanly young soprano. Soppy tune, she thought.

'Hell!' she said aloud suddenly and crushed out her cigarette with an abrupt gesture.

The sky seemed to be lightening a little. She crossed over to the window again and looked out.

She saw the woman who was always staring out of the window opposite.

The window glass was a shiny blackness: her face hovered out of nothing, intently bent head, smooth black hair drawn back hard over the hard dark line of the eyebrows, thin tight-closed lips, the sour middle-aged face of an unsatisfied woman who lived her life at the window in envy and malice, watching everything with intent stony eyes, while her husband sits in the basement kitchen reading newspapers and wheezing in front of the range.

She looked as if she might have been beautiful once. For a second their glances met across the street; the hard eyes of the woman at the window flickered, a sharp spasm of thwarted hate shook her. She knew all about Jenny, that whore . . .

Below, her husband hunched his skinny shoulders a bit more, shivered and gave the fire a poke. He had anaemia, he always felt cold nowadays. He was reading the leading article in the *Evening Mail* – Why We Must Have A Bigger And Better Air Force. PRIME MINISTER'S TIMELY WARNING. Diesel planes and plenty of them, Sloane's hack demanded.

* * * * *

'There's something fishy about it,' Pat Morgan said to Vernon in the *Evening Mail* subs' room.

'He wants a subsidy for the AIE Staffordshire works,' said Vernon.

'Yeh . . . but I've a feeling there's a lot more in it than that unless he's crackers . . . who cares about magnesium anyway.'

Someone slung a bunch of news-agency stuff over to Pat. 'Air race?' he asked, sighing. 'Hell, I'll have to run the Janet Millar divorce over to page two.'

'There's been a scrap down at that dock strike. Three arrests . . .'

* * * * *

The Black Maria was whizzing down Commercial Road. Perce Richards lay groaning on the floor, all bloody; the other two were doubled up and gasping from being kicked in the stomach. Everything was going by quickly, thoughts of their pain and the fight and what sentences they'd get. Perce was thinking of his wife and kids and hoping that the union'd look after them.

At the police station they were roughly bundled out and shoved into the charge room. They slumped down on the hard benches all dazed: the noise and confusion of the fight had hardly cleared from their heads.

A crowd had gathered outside, they cheered when Alf Hopkins, a local Communist Councillor went in to get bail. Assaulting the police, the charge was. Everyone said it was all rot, the cops had gone smack into the pickets hitting out with their batons without a word of warning. Several chaps had seen Perce Richards knocked down. He hadn't been doing anything; they'd beaten him up after they'd arrested him so as to make it look as if he had resisted the police.

Bail was refused.

Alf Hopkins 'phoned up the London District office and told them and asked them for a speaker for tonight. 'We've got to get as many street-corner meetings going as possible,' he said. 'George and I are speaking at the strikers' meeting. We must get someone else.' The comrade at the other end exploded, 'Jesus Christ, what the flaming hell's the use of coming to us for speakers *now*. Everyone's booked up for twice the number of meetings they can do. And it's the same with the Industrial Bureau too.'

* * * * *

The office was buzzing with activity. People were running up and down corridors and banging in and out of rooms, 'phones were ringing, typewriters going like mad and duplicators spewing out paper. Downstairs there was a continual coming and going of people fetching bundles of leaflets; the passage was choked with bicycles, and messengers kept on arriving. Meetings were going on all over the place, marshals' meetings, strike-committee factions, odd groups organizing things in corners. A retinue of splits lolled on the pavements or in the pub opposite, waiting for their various assignments to come out and gazing with lustreless eyes at a little red-headed chap who was stealing a bicycle.

In the back room of the bookshop they were doing up bundles of leaflets and handing them out as fast as they could. Outside in the corridor by the lavatories some Young Communist League chaps who were there to be helping with the leaflets were having a mike and gossiping. Bill Gunner was telling them about his experience, 'There was only three of us in the rooms when she comes in,' he was saying. '"'Ullo," she says, cool as anything. *We* didn't know 'er. Anyway, she sits down, takes out a packet o' fags and offers 'em all round and then, without saying a word, starts undoing 'er skirt. Down it comes and then she kicks orf 'er knickers. When young Alfie sees 'er doin' that 'e bolts out. I didn't know what to do, just stood there looking silly, but George – you know, George Sims – 'e gets 'old of 'er by 'er elbows and runs 'er out and chucks 'er skirt and knickers over the banisters after 'er. And when we went down to see if she'd cleared off there was a split and three coppers standin' outside looking sick . . .'

'All set to rush in and catch you on the job, eh . . .'

'Sure, and get the YCL nabbed for keeping a disorderly house.'

'The rotten bastards.'

'Wasn't a bad lookin' tart neither . . . you shoulda seen 'er, standin' there without saying a word, just in 'er blouse and stockings . . . coo . . .'

'Did George Sims know what she was up to when 'e shoved 'er out?'

'Course 'e did.'

'Smart feller, George . . .'

'Got a job at Hoopers now.'

'He's all right for tomorrow then.'

''E's a nice feller. I like ole George.'

* * * * *

Everyone liked George Sims. He was a sandy-haired young chap with a wide grin and a snub nose, very quick-witted and merry. He was fooling around cleaning a capstan lathe at the moment, passing the time. They were very slack at Hoopers now: the bosses didn't mind them coming out for May Day.

George looked at the clock and thought it was about time he started packing up in a leisurely manner. He began to wipe the grease off his hands with a bit of cotton waste, and he thought of his father, who was blind, sitting waiting for him to come home. He'd be glad when he came back early. It was dull for the old man: his wife was dead and there was no one to keep him company most afternoons until George got back.

He used to sit in the little stuffy front room in an armchair by the window, his blind gaze staring straight before him, while his hands played with the arms of the chair. The time went very slowly for him, hours and minutes passing to the accompaniment of the flowing discords of the traffic music that rose and fell senselessly. Sometimes it almost died away for a moment, falsely lulling the ear, so that he had the illusion of peace and solitude; sometimes he could even hear the faint mewing of the gulls on the river.

It was when the noise died down like this that he could most strongly visualize the outside world, achingly remembering the sky, the colours of the day, the shapes of people passing, the quicksilver patterns of light rippling on the river.

But the image never fully formed; it was always shattered by the swelling roar of some approaching lorry, and the traffic would begin to thunder by again, the rumbling lorries, the motorcycles, the speed-angry whir of sports cars.

Life flowed by him like this; only the jangling discords of invisible movements reached his perceptions from the outside world. He had been blind for seven years now. The image that he could most vividly recall and that troubled him most was the very last thing that he had seen – the blinding flash of the explosion lighting up the two towering chimneys that looked dazzling white against a fearful black sky, like something in a photographic negative. They seemed to reel down on him, and then he heard the roar of the explosion and everything was eclipsed into shattering darkness.

This image haunted his dreams. The sound of a car backfiring, a clap of thunder, any sudden loud noise would recall it with torturing vividness, and often it came unbidden into his mind when he was dreaming of pleasant scenes from his early life.

The clock struck, and he smiled, glad that another hour had passed and that George would soon be back.

Unconsciously his hands continually caressed the shiny worn arms of the chair. He faced the window, liking to sit as if he could see out over the river.

The house was at the corner of a little street that ran down to the Embankment. The door was in this street, but the Sims's front room faced on to the river.

Hardly any traffic went down the side street. Old Sims was able to take a little stroll there by himself on fine days, tap-tapping along the pavement with his stick.

* * * * *

Soiled, ragged children played in the road: they had nowhere else to go. At the moment young Edward Mulberry (aged four) was grovelling in the gutter, scraping with small dirt-crumpled fingers in the cracks between the cobblestones for bits of earth, which he solemnly deposited into a round cigarette tin.

He sings wordlessly a monotonous saga whose only inflection is an irregular rise and fall in volume. His tin is nearly filled. He half-stands up, squats, his pebble-blue eyes searching for some yet untapped, unprospected vein of dirt. But none can be seen.

So, very seriously, he pulls out his ridiculous dangling little penis, strains and piddles a few drops into the tin.

This done, he grovels again, rolls on his stomach like a ship in a heavy sea and stirs the mixture with a stubby forefinger until it attains a homogeneous plastic consistency.

His saga swells, grows louder, shriller, triumphant. His voice exults. Holding the tin firmly in both hands he suddenly inverts it with a bold, dexterous movement and sets it on the kerbstone. Then he taps the bottom smartly and cautiously lifts the tin. A rather crumpled and hesitant mud pie remains.

It was the very best anyone could have done in the circumstances.

A nasty flaxen-ringleted little girl in a grubby pale-blue dress sauntered around the corner, her hands behind her back, looking smug. She caught sight of a group of children playing cricket with a lamppost, a broom handle and a broken tennis ball. She stood still, rubbing her left foot against her right ankle and staring with a half scornful, half envious expression on her face.

Then she glanced stealthily around, picked up a stone and neatly and swiftly cast it at Ginger Watson who was batting. The stone caught him at the back of his ear. He yelled. The little girl looked more smug and demure than ever.

'I seen 'er,' bawled young Mulberry from the gutter from whence he had been an inconspicuous spectator of the crime. 'I seen 'er, Ginger. Winnie done it. I seen 'er.'

There was a moment's tense silence. Winnie stood still,

trying to look unconcerned. The cricketers gathered together into a little group and stared at her.

The voice from the gutter uplifted itself again. 'I seen 'er do it, give it 'er, Ginger . . .'

Winnie suddenly lost her nerve. 'I never done it,' she wailed. 'I never done it,' and she started a loud automatic blubber that she often found serviceable.

Ginger emitted a raucous yell, brandished his broomstick and ran at her. Winnie fled, still blubbering but keeping up a remarkably good turn of speed. The rest of the cricketers followed, shouting ferociously. Young Mulberry stood hopping delightedly from one leg to the other as the chase swept by him.

A shout came from an upper window, 'Let 'er be, Ginger, let 'er be, you naughty boy.' But they had gone by, and Ginger's mother withdrew her head from the window muttering, 'Wait till I get 'old of 'im, I'll wring 'is bleedin' neck, the little sod.'

The street relapsed into silence. Edward Mulberry returned to the contemplation of his mud pie.

A dustcart wearily turned up from the Embankment. The two dustmen were quarrelling with the horse, who had stopped still, standing droopingly between the shabby shafts. They smacked its hocks and swore gently at it.

'You're damn' near as tired as we are,' said one of the men.

The horse raised his head wearily, defiantly. He had a very long upper lip, which he twitched slightly, disclosing big yellow teeth. He looked at the men obstinately, with a strange, ancient, almost reptilian expression on his face, a rather awful timeless look of dumb obstinacy in revolt.

'Lo-ok at my mud pie,' shouted young Mulberry in a singsong voice.

'Gidap,' said the dustman and smacked the horse's hock again, heavily, yet with a caressing movement. The men and the horse were fond of one another. They were all tired and wanting to be done. They understood each other's feelings pretty well.

The horse leaned forward heavily and started to drag the cart. His head hung down again, his eyes were dull.

THE MOVEMENTS OF PEOPLE IN LONDON
ON APRIL 30TH

The sirens have sounded again, punctuating the day, marking a changed tempo of living, signalling a new phase in the movements of the human tides that flow, now fast, now slow, now full, now slack, through the channels of the streets.

Living torrents have poured out of the factory gates, drying themselves up into a dwindling stream . . .

The movements of the population of London take the form of an enormous seething confusion in which can be vaguely discerned, in certain districts, at certain times, inchoate driftings, gatherings and dispersals, streamings together in currents that run strongly for a while and disperse again into shapelessness.

In the morning the factories are magnetic points attracting vast converging streams that, taken over a large area at any given instant, will seem to be moving quite motivelessly. In the evening they are centres of dispersal, from which pour hundreds of thousands of men and women in great tides that are quickly scattered and whose identities as masses are lost.

Now, between five and seven, there is the greatest volume of movement. From the City and the West End there is a peripheral outflow to the suburbs. Along the river, East and West Ham, Dagenham, Barking, Silvertown, Canning Town, the Isle Of Dogs, around the docks and factories of south-east London, the volume of human movement is tremendous, but no order can be discerned in it, there is simply a recession, a surging back from the centres of industry and transport into the streets, into houses.

This flow consists of a daily tide between the centres of production and distribution and the places in which workers live. No description of it in purely geographical and statistical terms is adequate. It can only be understood and interpreted in the light of the economic structure of society.

Only the mathematics of class struggle can make order and design out of this seething chaos of matter in motion.

THE COMMUNIST LEAFLETS

Printing-presses have spun themselves dizzy.

The Communist cells have sprayed out leaflets like machine guns scattering bullets.

First, there were a hundred thousand yellow ones.

They were scattered, they passed from hand to hand, they were slipped into letterboxes and under doors. They were folded up and put in pockets, they were thrown into dustbins, the wind blew them into gutters.

The yellow paper ran out.

A hundred and fifty thousand more were printed, on orange, on green, on buff.

They fluttered into the air from the tops of buses, they were laid out on benches and lathes before the beginnings of shifts. They fell on to roads and pavements.

Like autumn leaves they gathered in the gutters beside Labour Exchanges and factory gates.

Also the cells printed and duplicated their own May Day leaflets, for streets, for boroughs, for factories, for dockers, for postal workers, for railwaymen, for meat porters, for printers, for busmen, for taxi drivers and shop assistants and window cleaners . . .

The printing-presses were spinning themselves dizzy. There had never been so many leaflets before. They fell like rain, they were scattered like machine-gun bullets.

On every one was written ALL OUT ON MAY DAY.

On every one was written WORKERS OF THE WORLD UNITE.

First,

 a hundred thousand times

  two hundred and fifty thousand times

and more

they repeated

FORWARD TO A SOVIET BRITAIN

FOR WORK AND PEACE.

Today is the last day, this evening the last chance of their distribution. After tomorrow they will be less than last week's newspapers.

Like autumn leaves falling into running rivers they were dropped into the living torrents of the homeward-hurrying workers.

They had thought about dog races and bicycles; they had spoken and pondered upon the forms of horses and boxers and film stars; they had brooded upon love, upon assignations, upon putting up a shelf in the front parlour when they came home from work, upon a game of darts in the pub in the evening; they had worried about illnesses and pregnancies; they had been preoccupied with debts, with instalments, with the rent, with losing jobs or finding them, on getting new clothes and wearing out old ones.

They had read the newspapers every day and seen the advertisements; they had been to the cinemas and the churches; they had listened to speeches about democracy, they had voted men into Parliament.

Not one leaflet was too many.

There should have been more.

* * * * *

John came upstairs slowly, his bicycle on his shoulder. It was an awkward job negotiating the turns at the landings, but he had done it so often that it presented no difficulties to him.

'You've cut yourself!' Martine exclaimed as he came in. 'Only a bit,' he said. 'I was talking and my chisel slipped . . . it's nothing.'

'How did you get it bandaged up so neatly?'

'They did it at the first-aid place . . . it's nothing,' said John rather shortly. He didn't want to talk about it: it made him think of the factory, of his conversation with Jock, and he felt tired, he wanted to sit down in peace and silence for a while. He had been looking forward to seeing Martine all the time he was riding back, thinking of her with a warm tenderness. They had both been very sleepy that morning, hardly speaking to each other as they dressed and break-fasted. They didn't think of their lovemaking of the night before. But now he remembered it tenderly, he wanted to put his arms around her and kiss her on the forehead, a kiss without desire. He was tired by the day's events. The news of the dinner-hour incidents had gone all around the factory, and everyone had been talking about them, and there, under the shadow of the chimneys, in hearing of the rhythm of the machines, he had taken his part eagerly in the discussions. Everything had seemed clear then during the excitement of talking, he felt he knew exactly where he stood, for the works committee, for striking . . .

But here it was different, it was quiet and familiar. Every sight, every sound and smell was bound up with memories of a whole different realm of his life. His fatigue made him wish to be enclosed by the islanded peace of this room that carried their own, their secret lives through the days and nights like a ship, alone under the sky. These buzzing thoughts of the outside world that teased him like a swarm of flies must be driven away and forgotten . . .

He took off his coat and began to fill a pipe. He had bought some tobacco on his way home. It was always a quiet pleasure for him to open a new packet of tobacco. 'How's old David?' he said. 'How's old David?' and he went over to the cot and prodded him in the ribs. David wriggled a bit, smiling seraphically, while John looked into his dark eyes and was pierced with an uneasy tenderness for this entirely helpless innocent creature that would grow up so soon, to become a man who would love and work and suffer. He could not tell what would happen to him, he could not help . . .

Martine was frying chops. An invisible cloud of cooking smells drifted into the room. John felt hungry suddenly. She had only just put the chops on, they'd be quite a while yet. 'I don't half feel hungry,' he said to Martine as she put the bread on the table. 'It won't be long,' she replied over her shoulder as she went back to the gas stove. He wanted to take her in his arms and kiss her. Somehow he wanted to apologize, to make amends for everything that he had thought and said today that would have distressed her had she known.

The smell of frying set up a strong, sensual feeling of appetite inside him. The smoke of his pipe interfered with these gastric anticipatory tremors. He didn't notice what was happening but felt vaguely that he didn't want to smoke, went on puffing for a little because he had just lit his pipe and it seemed a waste to put it away when it was drawing so well, and then he laid it on the table.

Suddenly he noticed a crumpled-up piece of yellow paper under the table. He saw it with a sense of recognition, he knew it was connected in his mind with a whole group of feelings, associations and events. But for a moment he was unable to summon up any of them . . .

(They had been slipped into letterboxes and under doors, they were thrown into dustbins, like autumn leaves they were gathered in the gutters outside factory gates . . .)

It's one of the May Day leaflets, he said to himself. How had Martine got hold of it?

He wouldn't ask her. It would mean an argument, it would mean an open conflict between all those ideas and feelings that he had experienced today and his tenderness for Martine.

But as he was thinking this he had unconsciously bent

forward, picked up the leaflet and straightened it out. He couldn't stop himself asking her about it.

'They put it in the pram while I was in the butcher's. Cheek!'

'It's not cheek,' he said slowly. 'It's as much for you as anyone, it's about your conditions . . .'

But he let his voice trail away. She hadn't replied. He didn't want to argue. She thought that if you were a worker you just had a rotten deal, it was luck, it couldn't be helped. You might be able to do well for yourself somehow, it was luck, but there were always the poor and the rich . . .

* * * * *

Two men were being lowered into the *Arundale*'s ballast-tanks to do oxy-acetylene welding.

Their burners roared and echoed in the hollow darkness. The edges of the iron plates glowed white hot where the flames burned through them. Then they slowly faded to a dull red, an angry glow like an inflamed scar.

The confined air grew heavy with fumes. Men often collapsed down here. The fumes were poisonous. In the end you died of them: the work was shortening the men's lives. But it was well paid, and there was never any difficulty in getting people for the job.

* * * * *

As the bus turned out of the Queen's Road by Kensington Gardens James was seized with an impulse to get out.

The lowering sun dazzled him. The air was still, tremulously sensitive to every sound. A few heavy clouds were sinking behind the western horizon, flushed by the setting sun from grape-purple to pink and orange, while others floated so high and far that the bright light of afternoon still lit them; some were strung out into miles of disintegrating smoke-writing; some were utter ruins, long ragged streaks, the shreds of emptied-out rain clouds. And at the highest point of the sky's dome were a few dazzling white fragments, the embryos of a future fine day's billowing clouds that would drift across a dazzling blue sky and cast racing shadows over down-land.

Houses, trees and people threw long shadows that leaned towards the horizon.

James thought of the glimmering, dusky evenings of early summer under the may trees in the park, the heavy coral blossoms of may shuddering in the soft air. Memories weighed him down and strengthened his mood of depression.

He was tired. He had wandered through endless streets until his walking muscles, grown slack from a long sea voyage, felt bruised and battered. He had visited estate agents, he had asked after John in pubs, he had accosted postmen and milkmen, and everywhere had been met with a blank, discouraging ignorance. John seemed to have vanished from Brickling Street without a trace. Then James fell back on his plan of trying to get hold of him through his trade-union branch. But no one seemed to know where and when the branch met. He would probably be able to find out from the head office, but now, in his weary and dispirited mood, grappling with this problem seemed an intolerable effort.

This search made itself into a symbol for him, the original impulse nearly forgotten. He felt it was a task imposed upon him and that he could do nothing else of importance until he had fulfilled it.

Now James strolled dejectedly, his hands in his pockets, his shoulders hunched, while his shadow lengthened behind him.

After a while he found that he was near Marble Arch. Wearily he lowered himself on to a bench. The sun had quite set now. The last stains of its light were being diluted and washed away by an ochreous electric glow that trembled around the horizons, the aurora borealis of the urban night.

James tapped his heels on the ground to relieve his aching feet. Soldiers in red coats, with brass buttons and shiny, vacant faces, passed in twos and threes. Some of them had girls fixed on to their arms. Randy youths prowled about in little groups, calling Hollywood wisecracks after girls, their cries like the yelping of hounds picking up a scent.

Every shadow had extended right to the horizon. Artificial light sprayed from arc lamps and irradiated the gathering dusk. The grass, already black with night, gave out a fragrant smell as it was crushed by the heavy boots of the Guardsmen. From all around rose a murmur of traffic like the sound of a distant sea.

Shop girls, telephone operators and waitresses fluttered by in little droves like wheeling antelopes. The randy youths lifted their heads and whistled after them. Every so often a biological change took place, portions of groups coming together for a while and disintegrating into male and female pairs.

James's downcast eyes dwelt upon silk ankles and the hems of skirts. Amongst this crowd there must be a girl for him. But it was no use going out of his way to look for her. He knew that if you wanted a girl you would get one sooner or later, wherever you were, whatever you did. You might as well sit still and wait for one to come along as get up and walk about. And if one didn't turn up tonight, he would meet her tomorrow, sooner or later . . .

But also the sight of these laughing coveys of young girls fluttering by engendered upon his melancholy that tender randy feeling, that empty yearning in the stomach that is responsible for more bastards than plain lust.

The darkness was loaded with the breath of spring. Incoherent tender thoughts, like the sentimental songs of jazz singers, floated in the dusk. People were sitting in rooms playing gramophones and radios, letting the bluish, smoke-dim dusk stream in through open windows, and their thoughts were carried away by the melancholy notes of oboes. The incense of different musics poured into the night, merging with the traffic songs and the motes of dust and soot that danced and swayed in the moving air.

Now the ten-o'clock pubs were shutting. Thousands of raucous voices were crying, 'Time, gentlemen, *please*,' repeating it again and again, italicized, accentuated, rising to an irritated crescendo. Last darts were thrown, last gulps of beer slid down throats, and the drinkers strolled out into the night, clustering in little knots on the pavements, unwilling to exchange the cheerful group life of the bar for their lonely thoughts, for the preoccupations of their daily lives. 'We toil only to live, live only to toil' – this was the burden of their minds that had been laid down for an hour or two and soon must be taken up again. At thousands of street corners these little groups clustered, held together by a strong and indescribable force. They would meet tomorrow, on the job, in the factory, at the garage . . . but now they hated to part. Their minds had been relaxed, they had been able to feel free human beings, forgetting for a moment that they lived only to toil, toiled only to live.

Now the lights in the pubs began to go out.

Beside a horse-trough two postmen and a lorry driver were arguing about the leadership of the trade unions. They said it was no good. The argument was: should one stay inside the unions, join them and recruit for them and fight for a change of leadership and policy, or was it a waste of time.

Leaning up against a public lavatory a group of dockers discussed Fascism.

Tomorrow we are coming out on to the streets, tomorrow we are marching, tomorrow we strike, tomorrow we're going to show them . . . this was the burden of ten thousand conversations.

Tomorrow is May Day.

People will come out of houses, will walk down streets, their steps directed to a rallying point, to a marching column, towards platforms from which will be proclaimed, 'Forward to a Soviet Britain'.

Now their thoughts are going ahead of time, their thoughts are streaming forward and converging around a flag, a banner, a platform from which their hopes and dreams will be enunciated.

Past the groups gathered at the street corners cars continually went by, anonymous, bound to no apparent destination; in their yellow-lit interiors they bore lives that did not touch these surroundings, thoughts that held no meaning for them.

Now people were going to sleep in the prisons. In stone cubicles, constructed with the depressing geometry of public lavatories, men and women closed their eyes, relaxed their bodies and patiently awaited the advent of a night's oblivion. Their lives were wasting away, rusting in the stream of time, corroding like the machines in the disused factories. Some were here only for weeks, some for years, for life. There was hardly one of them who had not the potentialities of a happy, human existence. But they rusted away, spoiling behind stone walls, like the machines in the factories closed down owing to over-production. They were criminals, now awaiting a night's oblivion.

George Potter (No. 1327, six months, petty larceny) thought of how he would like an egg for breakfast. He fought the empty, craving feeling in his belly. There were times when he couldn't stop himself thinking about food, however much he tried. Outside this prison world, he thought, nearly everyone could go to sleep with the confident expectation of an egg for breakfast. There were about forty million people in the country. At least half of them had an egg for breakfast (some had two, but that wouldn't bear

contemplating). Twenty million eggs a day went at breakfast
. . . Then there were the eggs used for cooking, for making
cakes and rich dishes, for omelettes and custards. More than
twenty million a day must be consumed. You could put it at
eight thousand million a year, at the very least. It was staggering. He was oppressed at the thought, at the vision of
earnest-eyed clucking hens, millions and millions of them,
battalions of Rhode Island Reds, regiments of Leghorns,
armies of Wyandottes, straining, contracting, dropping eggs,
a hail, a barrage of eggs. It was a humiliating thought to
remember how dependent the world was upon the vaginas
of hens. There must be nearly as many chickens in the world
as people . . . It would be awful if they went on strike.

* * * * *

James ordered another beer. Conversations, laughters and
the raucous hilarity of a mechanical piano beat upon his
hearing.

At his side he discovered a profile, hovering, cool, in a
lilac-scented aura, head delicately poised on a slender neck
stalk that rose from a low-cut blouse of heavy white silk. Her
eyes were large, slanting, a little depraved. She radiated a cool
bodily awareness, an unconscious challenge to ravishers. The
heavy silk of her blouse that faintly shuddered at the rise and
fall of her young breasts seemed an unsubstantial sheath, a
thin rind concealing a delicious flesh within.

James was stricken with a sinking, dissolving feeling inside
him when he looked at her. She was young, gay, unabashed
by the precariousness of her life, like a little antelope that has
never been hunted and knows no fear.

She directed her eyes obliquely away from him. The poise
of her head showed him that she was warming herself in the
rays of his glance.

In the delivery ward there was a dim light. Everything was hushed and unreal, like in a dream. There were two other women besides herself. They lay on their sides, their short nightgowns caught up under their armpits, their buttocks projecting over the sides of the beds.

She was at one end of the ward. She could neither see nor hear the third woman. The one next to her had a beautiful skin. It seemed to focus all the light in the room upon itself and glow with a pearly radiance. Sometimes she turned a little, moaning, and you could see one breast, distended with milk, the nipple eager and erect, the faint blue rivulets of veins showing plainly under the alabaster skin. The sight of that breast was somehow very beautiful and reassuring to her.

Even in here you could hear the woman in the other ward screaming. It went on and on, like a dog howling in the night, a hopeless wailing without beginning or end. But it was from far away and unreal, like something in a bad dream from which she knew she would wake up.

Her neighbour every now and then would call out for the nurse. 'Nurse, nurse,' she would cry, 'it's coming out, it's coming out, I know it is . . .' a sort of fearful gladness in her voice. But the nurse kept telling her 'Not yet, not for an hour or two yet.'

Three probationers kept coming and going. They were very nice to her, nice girls; one of them, who was very pretty, was quite a lady. She could hear them talking in the corner of a tennis match, of dances and going out with their young men. She liked hearing them, it told her of the reality of the outside world, and it reassured her to think that all this was simply routine to them, something that they saw happening to hundreds of women. She asked one of them, the pretty one, who had seemed to take a fancy to her, if she would ever want to have a baby after seeing so much of the pain and nastiness of childbearing. And the three of them all burst out saying how they loved babies and how much they wanted to have them. She couldn't understand it.

The intervals between her pains had become shorter and the pains worse. She had thought that it wouldn't be long now before the baby came. As each spasm welled up inside her she took a breath of anaesthetic and everything went muzzy and far away. But now the times between the pains grew longer again. They took the anaesthetic away from her. The doctor came and they put the screen around the bed and he examined her. He went away talking in a low tone to the Sister and looking troubled. She felt horribly frightened, with the lonely fear of a little child in the dark.

Suddenly, from the woman in the third bed came a strange muffled groan, terrible in its strangled intensity. She cried out in a bitter, suffering voice, a voice whose hardness was frightful to hear. 'I've had it, I've had it. I hope the little brat dies. I didn't want it, I didn't want it . . .'

She had borne her child in silence, in secret, without a sign, and she had let it hang by the navel cord. 'I didn't want it,' she cried. 'I didn't want it.'

The Sister came running to her. She understood everything immediately. 'You wicked, wicked woman,' she said in a cold, furious voice. 'For that I'm going to sew you up without an anaesthetic.'

The child was dead.

* * * * *

Now in the West End the cinemas and theatres were emptying. There was a swirling, streaming movement of humanity and traffic. People poured out into the channels of the streets, out of the clenched, artificial darkness of the auditoriums into the free night air, the petrol-laden air, that yet was soft and shadowed with a foretaste of the breathless summer nights to come. While the theatre smell was yet in their noses, while the images of curtains plunging downwards and splashing up applause were not yet dissolved from their minds, they halted an instant balancing at the edges of pavements and inhaled the night air that was warm and soft, a little moist, laden with the breath of growing things and shadowed with a delicious foretaste of summer.

The little territory of the theatre world seethed with movement like a disturbed ant hill.

The night quivered with the multicoloured explosions of advertising signs. Jewels of light strung themselves together out of blackness, proclaiming the virtues of kidney and liver pills. The red-hot worms of neon bulbs squirmed and wriggled, forming themselves into luminous exhortations to drink beer, take bile beans, travel by air and go on pleasure cruises. Searchlights, big guns bombarding the sky with rays of absinthe-green and rose-pink, projected the names of automobiles and film stars on to a moving screen of clouds. The whole sky glowed with a dull red heat from the violence of the electric blows that were showered upon it.

Ten thousand feet above, a flock of aeroplanes scattered themselves. This was a week of aerial night-manoeuvres, raids were staged to find the weak points in a barbed-wire fence of searchlights that laced the sky around London. These had got through.

Looking down the pilots saw this glow like the tarnished sparks of a distant, fading firework explosion. They followed the dull-gleaming silver worm of the Thames. The big powerhouses at Battersea and Lots Road were their objectives.

A defence squadron was coming up after them. They wheeled, lifted and dived.

Above Lots Road half a dozen tiny flashes in the sky showed the observers that several tons of theoretical bombs had been dropped.

The four great powerhouse chimneys lean up against the

immense blue darkness of the night; the long perspectives of the building, marked by regular flame-tawny rectangles of windows, sink towards the river. The whole dark mass juts forward, streaming into the night, four faint plumes of smoke from the chimneys endlessly slipping behind. A spider's-web network of cables, urgent with electricity, begins and ends here, from whence the crowded tube trains now nosing underground packed with homeward-bound theatregoers are driven.

Not loud, not shrill is the note of the dynamos, but a deep shaking of the air that drugs the hearing. The ugly little houses that stretch away under the shadow of the chimneys are endlessly bathed in this stream of sound; it has become part of the rhythm of living for hundreds of people, who have at once forgotten it and grown tremulously sensitive to every variation in its tone, like dwellers beside the sea, like those who live in hearing of a waterfall.

* * * * *

A ship was passing, going down the river to the sea, a battered old coal boat, riding high in the water, her engines panting asthmatically, her propellor threshing half out in the air.

Up on the fo'c'sle-head leaned the lookout man, heavy with sleep. He saw the four great chimneys sliding by on the port bow and then the lights of Chelsea Embankment, a long straight necklace of glowing beads. Ahead, the dark arches of Battersea Bridge barred their way. The thousand twinkling lights reflected in the water dazzled him through his half-shut eyes. His drowsing flesh was still weighted with the delicious languors of too much lovemaking. Only a couple of hours ago he had been lying in the arms of his girl. The pain of their parting was still far away, but he could sense it getting nearer, as if he was slowly coming out of a dream into a cold reality.

As they went down the river he would get more awake,

and the thought of leaving her and not seeing her again for so long would throb in his mind like the pain of a tooth-ache. He was very much in love.

* * * * *

Two artists were leaning on the Embankment wall, watching the quivering reflections on the water. When a tram passed over the bridge a glittering shoal of scattered light moved across the river with it. Each observer's eye was the centre of a thousand spokes of radiance that spread outwards to the opposite bank.

They listened to the water lapping against its stone bank, a mysterious, dangerous sound, then they heard the threshing of the old ship's rusty propeller and looked up as its dark silhouette slid into sight.

They were silent. They had been talking for a long time about their lives, the grandiose talk of young men who are full of hopes and dreams and who speak of the whole of life as a background for themselves. Now they were silent for a while, watching the ship go by, letting their thoughts drift idly with it in its lonely course.

* * * * *

At the bus garages they were holding late meetings. Everywhere the decision to strike was reaffirmed by overwhelming majorities. Raggett's last-minute appeal had been given a raspberry. The men came out from the meetings flushed with enthusiasm. They gathered around the *Daily Worker* sellers eagerly. Every garage door was the centre of a dozen discussion groups. They understood the significance of their strike, and they were proud of it.

* * * * *

One by one the lights in the windows of Langfier's house went out. The vanishing of each lit window square signified a human being's plunge into darkness, a dive towards sleep.

Tomorrow, thinks Jean the maid, tomorrow . . . we will be together again, we will be clasped in each other's arms under the tree shadows. The day will be too long until that moment . . . if only we had somewhere to go, somewhere of our own where we could be alone and private . . .

Tomorrow, thinks Langfier. Tomorrow will be another day . . . there is no sense in this procession of days once that I expect nothing from tomorrow that was not in yesterday.

Tomorrow, thinks Bertha the cook, tomorrow I will make a kedgeree.

Peter thought about Pamela. Her cheeks are like flower petals, he thinks. They have a bloom that I am frightened to touch, to spoil. Also I wish to possess her with the utmost shamelessness.

Lady Langfier dreamed the incoherent dreams of a child.

* * * * *

An old woman was grubbing in Soho dustbins for scraps of food. Clutched defiantly under her arm was a large, shabby bag made of squares of artificial leather. She wore a shapeless, trailing black coat; only her terrifyingly pathetic broken-down shoes gave away her utter destitution.

She raked amongst grapefruit peelings, broken bottles, twisted scraps of cotton wool, withered flowers, old tins, all the horrible intimacies of domestic refuse. Her fingers darted eagerly and quickly amongst the litter, like the tongues of snakes. Suddenly she pounced upon a piece of rotting banana, dropped it into her bag with a stealthy gesture and sidled off, quickly furtive.

* * * * *

An unemployed shop assistant was about to commit suicide in a little back room in Kennington. He took a quick look around the damp, shabby walls, turned out the gas, stood on a chair, adjusted a noose around his neck with trembling hands and kicked his support away from him.

He dangled, twitching.

For a fraction of a second every residue of vital force left in his starved, sickly frame welled up, so that for one convulsive jerk he was filled with a tremendous strength and intensity of living. He died in the midst of a brief orgasm.

* * * * *

James's eyes opened. He saw a window, framing a picture of night sky reddish with the reflection of city lights.

The atmosphere of his thoughts was like the clear, still air after a summer thunderstorm. The last, fading voluptuous images and sensations were dying down. The woman beside him, whose slant eyes and cool body had set a storm raging in his blood and moved him to tenderness, was now so much unengrossing flesh, the sensations of whose contact with his own nakedness were impersonal. He might remember her once, thinking of the moment of getting into bed with her he would say to himself, 'A nice girl.' He might forget the impulse that had made him seek the comfort of her slender breasts and cling so fiercely to her young body. But recollecting, at a later time, somewhere far away, he could be far closer to her in thought than he was at this moment.

* * * * *

The rising moon came out from behind a tarnished, silvery cloud. Pat's footsteps echoed emptily in front of him. He was a little chilly, he shivered from fatigue.

The streets were narrow, twisting and badly lit, the houses

blank and secret. By daylight the scene was only sordid, but now, in the darkness in which hung infrequent blots of dim yellowish radiance from windows, everything appeared faintly mysterious. Figures drifted quietly along the pavements, keeping close to walls. Then two drunk sailors, lurching wide gestures, passed down the middle of the road. The noise of sirens from the river trembled in the air. Fragmentary sounds floated from the houses, wind-borne clues of the lives that went on behind the bricks and mortar, the unguessed-at existences passionately and apathetically passing the time in little stuffy rooms.

Pat looked up at the silvery clouds straggling across the sky; the black shapes of chimney pots jutted irregularly against the luminous horizon.

A siren sounded, near and loud. He remembered another night, long ago, walking near these streets, drawn by the cry of a ship putting out to sea. That night had been a turning point in his life. It had set him on the course that led him to be walking here now.

Pat felt very tired. His mind became nearly blank. Tomorrow . . . tomorrow . . . repeated itself mechanically in his brain. He had come out of the stuffiness of the meeting, his head buzzing with thoughts, with arguments, ideas and words swirling around and around in a whirlpool.

But as he jogged along steadily walking home fatigue rose like a mist blotting out everything. A dim picture of red banners moved by the wind through a sea of caps floated behind his eyes.

'Tomorrow . . . tomorrow,' he repeated sleepily to himself.

It would be a good May Day.

* * * * *

The night was growing old, trickling away in a thousand little unimportant incidents . . .

SOME STATISTICS RELATING TO THE
MAY DAY DEMONSTRATION

At the end of April last year there were just under 250,000 unemployed in London; today there were 322,000: 178,000 on casual or poor-law relief and over 10,000 in workhouses or casual wards. The average rate of unemployment benefit per head had fallen by 13.5 per cent, while the cost of living had risen 5.3 per cent. (This figure is not inclusive of rents, which had gone up in many cases.)

Amongst the employed workers over 200,000 had received wage cuts in one form or another. Three hundred and sixty-eight thousand and twenty-six men and women were getting two pounds a week or less.

Notifiable industrial accidents had increased by 13 per cent. Large numbers of factories, particularly those employing masses of girl labour, had installed various forms of speed-up. Thousands of men and skilled workers had been replaced by youths and girls. Indeed, the increase in the numbers of unemployed represented a new class, mostly of skilled trade unionists accustomed to a good standard of living.

Ten thousand and forty-seven children under the age of one had died in the past twelve months, over a thousand more than for the corresponding period of last year. Maternal mortality increased 4.8 per cent; medical officers reported the increase as due largely to bad feeding during pregnancy, and also considered that this accounted in many instances for the increased infantile mortality. There were a large number of deaths due to attempts at abortion; it is impossible to trace the many illnesses arising from this.

Only 500 cases of malnutrition amongst schoolchildren

were reported, but to qualify for this a child had to be actually starving; tens of thousands of families were existing far below the most conservative estimates of a subsistence level.

Last year 895 cases of suicide were reported in the figures for the LCC area. In the corresponding twelve months 1,342 men and women had killed themselves.

There were 567 cases of theft with violence dealt with in the London courts, an increase of 68. Ordinary thefts without violence rose from 2,242 to 2,921.

Statistics as to the number of hours worked per week are valueless. While in certain trades there was an increase, in many others short-time was being worked, especially in heavy industry.

There are no separate figures relating to strikes for London. Taking the country as a whole there was a 30 per cent increase in the number of strikes reported, involving 39 per cent more workers, with 105 per cent more days lost.

Similarly, figures of incomes are only available for the whole country. During the last year the number of people with incomes of over £10,000 fell, but the total incomes of that number amounted to a 9 per cent increase over last year.

The above are a few facts, recording briefly an increase in unemployment, general worsened living and working conditions for the working class and a greater concentration of wealth in the hands of fewer people. From these figures can be deduced a vast load of wrongs and miseries, a piling up of woe and suffering, a decay and rottenness extending in the midst of the weltering confusion of a great city.

These facts produce their reaction that can be also recorded in a few figures.

Last year at the end of April there were 4,562 active dues-paying members of the Communist Party in London, organized in 183 factory cells and 237 other groups and cells, mostly on a street basis. Twelve months later the membership had risen to 7,084, organized in 342 factory, rail, workshop and transport cells and 386 other groups. But the Young Communist League, which last year only numbered 2,680, had more than trebled its membership, rising to over 8,000.

The London sales of the *Daily Worker* had increased from an average of 27,000 on weekdays and 41,000 on Saturdays, to an average of 51,000 on weekdays and 72,000 at weekends. However, the London District Committee had been severely criticized for these figures, which had been characterized as criminally lagging behind the situation, and a drive for a 100,000 London sale by the end of the year was being prepared.

The pamphlet *Red London* got out two months ago had sold over 100,000 to date. Literature sales generally showed a big increase.

The total number of leaflets distributed during the May Day campaign, including local- and factory-duplicated leaflets, was 310,000. Two thousand large posters had been put on the hoardings and 10,000 sticky-backs issued.

From reports delivered at the final marshals' meeting tonight it estimated that between 70,000 and 100,000 workers would march from the localities.

BETWEEN NIGHT AND MORNING

There is hardly a sound. The moon has sunk, the stars are very pale. At empty street-crossings traffic-lights blink stupidly to nothing; it is so quiet that you can hear the clicking of their com-mutators. A lorry loaded with milk churns devastates the silence like an earthquake.

Busy streets that are now quite empty have an unfamiliar shape, illustrated by rising and sinking perspectives of arc lamps, whose violet glow is growing pale.

The all-night trams on the Embankment carry the staleness of long night hours in their yellow-lit interiors. This night also remains in the antiseptic whiteness of hospital casualty-reception wards, whose cold geometries are lit so harshly that it seems no day can ever break through the violence of their artificial suns.

Telephones ring in the ears of sleepy night porters. 'Your wife has had a fine boy weighing eight pounds, they are both doing well.' Or she has not yet had her fine boy weighing eight pounds but is doing as well as can be expected.

The dream went on, but also she knew that there was something outside, that she had a body lying somewhere in another world. Like a heavy bubble rising from the oozy floor of a deep lake, bursting upwards through tangling weeds, coming out of darkness towards light, her consciousness was returning to the outside world.

She felt herself coming back into her body; slowly she began to be aware of her limbs, of flesh forming around her. These sensations came from far off, as through a heavy mist. At some unimaginable distance brilliant light existed.

Her eyes opened. She came from nothing out of nowhere

into a world that dazzled and confused her. She struggled to think back, to discover a point from where she could start remembering.

She was staring at whiteness, a white ceiling and walls that swam in floods of white radiance. She felt extraordinarily light, as if she was floating like a piece of thistledown borne up in a tide of ethereal, snowy brilliance.

In front of her was a big white tank that bubbled and hissed out jets of cotton-wool steam. What has happened, where am I? she thought, and then she heard the sound of a low laugh behind her, and as she turned to look around she remembered everything, the pain and the fear, the smell of the anaesthetic, the storm of blood beating in her ears and everything going far away . . . 'I'm a mother, I've got a baby,' she said to herself in words and was flooded with calm joy.

PART THREE

MAY DAY

'This waste of wealth and misery, this factory servitude, this bloody, murderous, constant struggle is, for the rich, the men masked with power, a senseless chaos incomprehensibly destroying their world; for the working class it is the birth pangs of a new life, of a new world painfully fighting to be born from the filth, the rottenness, the miserable decay of capitalist society. Every true story of today is the story of this struggle.'

The police of five continents have polished their buttons and made ready; behind them glitter the bayonets of soldiers. Rows of red, beefy faces, expressionless eyes, heavy boots, and uniforms are drawn up.

Today things are made plain: there is a line, on one side are the proletariat, organized into a militant class by life itself, on the other are the forces of the State.

The class struggle is not simple. A revolution is not a fight between those on one side of the line and those on the other. But today things are artificially simplified. This morning in every great city there are a number of empty police cells that will have tenants tonight.

But the spectators outnumber the participators, and they see a play whose subject they don't understand, it might almost be in a language unknown to them. The middle-class daughters, the refined young lady dancing-partners, the good-hearted fathers of families, the stamp collectors and bibliophiles as well as a host of prostitutes and pimps and bookmakers, see strikes, demonstrations, red banners and police charges and are mystified.

But listen, May Day isn't the same in England. Things are different here.

Things are different here. In 1926 there was a tremendous May Day demonstration. And a day or two later the bourgeoisie woke up to find themselves without newspapers. Everything had stopped. Such wonderful views hadn't been seen in London for a century, the sky had never had such a chance to get clear of the smoke of factory chimneys.

That was years ago; it was only a rehearsal, but a great deal was learned from it; many parts had been quite miscast.

They would have their newspapers all right today, even if they had to walk to their offices. They had seen the red banners filing into the park year after year, and they had forgotten 1926, while the revolutionary movement had been gathering its forces. Those who march today will be shouting new slogans, ones that are much more dangerous and threatening to the spectators. This would be another rehearsal, a trial of the strength of Communism in London. Soon a lot more people will be having to take sides.

* * * * *

Langfier's. The morning shift begins. A slack belt flaps complainingly. The machines sing, hum, growl, groan and rattle. The compressors hiss and the furnaces in the yard sigh to themselves. Flap . . . flap . . . flap . . . goes the loose belt in the big machine shop, and it gets on everyone's nerves.

Yesterday they had all been excited about the factory committee; they had broken up from work chattering eagerly. This morning there was the reaction: they came in to work with a bad-tempered sleepy sulkiness. The girls were nervous and irritable. Many of them had walked to work. This and the strikes were outstanding topics for conversation, but no one spoke much. It was as if they were deliberately holding back from reminding one another of these facts. They nearly all knew someone, had a brother, a relation, a pal, had some personal link with people who were striking today or marching in the demonstration. And, somehow, they felt, sulkily, like children not allowed out on a holiday, that they were being done out of something. It wasn't as if they had a political feeling of wanting to come out and demonstrate, but they just felt left out of it.

Sunrays slanted through the grimy windowpanes. The length of the shop was sliced into fifty-four sections of light and shade; shapes of people continually flickered from light into darkness, out of gloom into light. This was a familiar transitory phenomenon of the morning shift. The light dazzled the people who worked facing the windows; they had always to be dodging it with their heads.

The complaint of the loose belt went on, flap . . . flap . . . flap . . . Then a lathe began to chatter furiously.

* * * * *

The carpenter's shop. Jock planing, John marking out. John: 'I wish ole Peter was 'ere. I've thought of a better way to fix these drawers – look – if I make the front overlapping a bit at the sides and bottom like this it'll be a better job and simpler too . . . I dunno whether to get on with it or not . . .'

Jock: 'Go ahead, I would. He don't mind you doing things your own way like some fellers do.'

John says, 'Mmm . . .' and sits on the edge of his bench reflectively, staring at his working drawing.

John: 'It's funny they don't make a row about 'im not coming in on May Day.'

Jock: 'They don't notice it – I mean, they don't notice it's any special day . . . an' e's been 'ere years and years and 'e does 'is job all right. They don't bother about us 'slong as the work's done proper, that's what I like about this job . . . but I wish I was going up the park along with 'im.'

John (very meditatively): 'Ye-es . . . it ought to be a fine turn-out.'

Jock: 'Best for years. The busmen'd make a good demo by themselves.'

John (suddenly): 'I'll get on with making up the frame and leave marking out the drawers till I can ask 'im.'

* * * * *

The hydraulic-press room. A group standing around Bill Riley's machine.

Millman: 'The washers're leaking, that's what it is.'

The machine is gently hissing to itself. Bill Riley pulls the release lever over for a second, and there is a tremendous rushing, gurgling noise.

Perce Higgins: 'Working 'em day and night is running 'em to pieces. I 'eard old Langton saying they want a proper over'auling.'

Bill Riley: 'It's the same upstairs. They're running them to bloody pieces, never any time to give 'em a do-over. Ivy tole me they're gettin' no end of rejects now . . .'

Enter Tom Rundall hurriedly taking off his jacket and whistling very loudly and cheerfully.

Millman: 'You're bloody late, Tom. You didn't have to walk far, did you?'

Tom: 'I've bin up to the 'orspital.'

Riley: 'What – 'as your old woman 'ad 'er kid then?'

Tom: 'Sure. A boy. Weighs eight poun'.'

They all shake his hand and congratulate him.

Riley: 'On May Day too. That's a fine date for a birth-day . . .'

* * * * *

It's a fine day for a birthday. The sky is cloudless, pale blue, scoured clean for the morning. A mist trembles over every distant view; already the horizons are smeared with the dirty thumb marks of factory grime.

It's going to be really warm later on.

This is a day when 'London' means the parks, the purplish clods of earth tumbled up under the hoofs of silk-sleek horses in the Row; you think also of those quiet little streets in Kensington and Chelsea and around Regent's Park, those streets of creamy stuccoed houses with green doors and windows, whose decorousness has a faintly romantic tinge; at night the trees and flowers and earth in the little gardens breathe out such poignant smells, somehow more intense than country smells of soil and vegetation. The windowpanes are diamond-bright, glittering in the sun. Within, people live harmonious, well-ordered days. Though they are usually dull and prejudiced, cruel out of stupidity, there is a certain beauty in the pattern of their lives that nothing can argue away. These backwater streets whose quietness is even a little stagnant represent something rather fine that will pass away, that is passing away. Also, the price of this minor harmony is the vast, harsh discord of the rest of London.

The houses are knocked down, the streets are invaded and devastated, and then luxury flats spring up like some quick-growing unhealthy tropical weed. Or sometimes a creeping decay sets in, the stucco cracks, the paint peels off the walls and blisters on the doors and windows, the bourgeoisie leave the neighbourhood; its very name becomes synonymous with bugs, broken-down perambulators and snotty-nosed children shrieking in gutters; Georgian elegancies become covered with grime and six layers of flowered wallpaper.

'London in May' . . . barrel organs romantically tinkling worn-out tunes in green squares where pretty children are playing under the shadow of some grey, undistinguished church spire, while hosepipes fountain the lawns. In parenthesis between taxi doors and the entrances of well-to-do houses strawberry and cream blondes appear rustling across the pavements in summery frocks. A luxurious hothouse breath from expensive flower shops mingles with the musky odours wafted from tube stations. There are green salads, promises of summer delights, the opera season and holidays by the sea. Young girls swaying at the edges of shining ballroom floors feel their lives are about to burst open and unfold like the flowering of budding roses.

* * * * *

There was a funeral today. Some old man, a retired pepperbroker, had died. The ceremony takes place at ten-thirty promptly, Golders Green Crematorium. The coffin, shaped like a ship, is covered with flowers that fill the little chapel with an overpowering smell. A young clergyman reads the service mechanically from a very smooth pink face with sensual lips and rounded features; his eyes are masked with horn-rimmed spectacles. He reads clearly, as if he knew it by heart and was thinking of something quite different, of his career most probably, for stamped all over him is a worldly determination to succeed.

At the other end of the chapel a door is open, framing blue sky, growing trees and flowers. This interferes with the organ music.

The mourners stand up, coughing and rustling. They are old or middle aged, sober, obscure people, wearing drab clothes.

A door like a serving-hatch opens, and the coffin slides forward down a slipway, tactfully and unobtrusively steadied by an official old man with a shining bald head; it moves very slowly with a movement like a ship being launched.

Then it has gone, and with it the shape and form of death.

A loud organ-sobbing drowns the snivelling of the female relatives. It's all over. There are no material remains. Only in the minds of a handful of friends and relations is there anything to show that this human being ever existed. And they will be dead and gone without trace quite soon. They're already dispersing and thinking about luncheon engagements or wanting to go to the lavatory.

* * * * *

The corner of Brickling Street. A crowd is gathered. Furled banners lean against a wall. Twelve policemen, an inspector and two mounted police loiter in the background. A very tall thin young man is speaking from the platform. His voice is quick and excited.

'Have you ever seen a dog that's got worms?' he says, leaning forward. 'At first you can't make out what's wrong. He eats plenty, his appetite's fine, and you give him lots of good food, but he begins to get thin, he begins to act as if he was starving. You go on feeding him, but he goes on getting worse. You've got to get rid of the worms: they'll never go away of their own accord; they won't just die off. You've got to dose the dog with a whacking strong worm powder. Well, comrades, that's a comparison with how things are in this country today. We can make plenty of everything that's needed, there's plenty of everything about, plenty of houses, plenty to eat, plenty of work waiting to be done. *But we aren't getting it.* We're starving for lack of all kinds of things that we've got, we're like the dog with the worms. And the worms are the capitalist class. Imagine someone trying to tell you that the only way to keep your dog alive is to give the worms as much to eat as possible, that the dog'd die if you got rid of the worms – but that's what they're trying to persuade us. We've got to get rid of them. And we know the recipe now – Soviet Power, workers' power. And that's what we're demonstrating for today.'

He steps quickly down from the platform while the crowd, that has been steadily growing, claps vigorously.

The chairman jumps up. 'The next speaker,' he announces, 'will be Alf Skinner of the Amalgamated Engineering Union. I dare say he's well known to many of you as speaking from this platform for the Communist Party, but he's 'ere today officially from 'is branch.'

Alf Skinner gets up ponderously, a big middle-aged chap, with a ginger moustache and a fiery complexion. 'Comrades,' he says in a booming voice that fairly rattles the windowpanes, 'as our chairman stated, I'm speaking today as a representative from my branch. And I'm very glad to be able to so do. This demonstration's not a Party demonstration but a class one. We may march under our different party or trade-union banners, but we're all marching as members of one class demonstrating for working-class power. Now I don't want to make a long speech, comrades, we've had enough meetings this week. The demonstration's already started, they're already on the march from the outlying districts. We've just had a report from Dagenham and West Ham. It's the biggest turn-out they've ever had. Everything shows that today's going to be the finest May Day we've ever seen in London –'

* * * * *

Dagenham and West Ham were already on the march. A thousand feet above the contingents hovered a police gyroplane, its windmill sails flickering lazily in the blue air. The observer, looking down, saw the marchers, a long black snake, a slow-moving black river winding along the channels of the streets.

The plane dropped lower momentarily, so low that they

could even see the banners, little spots of red glittering in the blackness. 'There's a good few there,' grunted the observer. Then they rose again and circled across the sky, towards the north-west. The living map of London smoked and glittered under them, a wilderness of streets, a forest of chimneys, a vast maze of houses. East and west, north and south, through the streets, in and out of houses and shops and offices, of libraries and schools and hotels, of hospitals and factories and railway stations, swarmed a million moving dots of blackness, clustering together, breaking apart, drifting through the streets like wind-driven autumn leaves rustling along the dried-up ruts of woodland cart-tracks.

The dark mass flows through the streets, meanders like some caterpillar crawling across a map of London, its head a mile away from its tail, its red spots the colours of banners, its solidity the cohesiveness of men and women marching in fours.

Drumbeats mark the time of their marching feet and make a rhythm for the slogans that rush echoing down the narrow chasms between the sides of houses.

Dagenham and West Ham are marching. They have picked up other contingents on the way; they grow in strength all the time; the side streets become tributaries whose streams mingle into the main river and swell its volume. The slogans rattle like thunder against the sides of houses, and when the demonstration has gone by, when the circles of sound have rippled outwards into calmness, the street does not simply relapse back into its everyday tempo of living. They have passed like a wind that strips the dying leaves from autumn trees, they have gone by like a spring shower fertilizing the thirsty earth: it is not quite the same when they have marched by. There are new thoughts in people's minds, the thought of them all marching on through the morning and how, after an hour has passed, they will still be going on through other streets, like a gust of wind, like a shower of rain, the sound of drums and shouts preceding them and fading away behind.

A contingent of cyclists rides in front of the demonstration. A word is passed forward to them, and a couple spurt ahead with a movement like the sudden darting flight of two dragonflies, their wheels glittering in the sun.

The riders are glad to stretch their muscles. They bend forward over the handlebars, stamp on their pedals and lean steeply as they race each other around corners. The sounds of the demonstration fade away from their ears like the sound of the sea becoming faint as one rides inland.

One of them, a young unemployed metalworker, thinks soberly of his pleasure in going fast, of the fineness of the morning and the liveliness of his bicycle under him, while his partner dramatizes their ride to himself, seeing them as revolutionary dispatch riders, bringing news to a waiting crowd of workers who will thrill with excitement when they see them riding in . . .

In a moment, too soon for both of them, they arrive at the next rallying point, where a huge crowd stands waiting quietly, full of expectation. Between them and the advancing marchers the air is charged with an electric tension.

Dozens of people are selling *Daily Workers* and literature. The Communist Party members form little groups in the crowd talking animatedly together, but the mass of the workers are quiet, standing silently or speaking in undertones. The scene is quite without animation, but the quietness and expectancy is tense; they might all be waiting to get a job, but equally they might be a crowd ready to fight for their lives.

Leaning against a lamppost James meditates to himself. A year ago today, he thinks, a year ago today we were waiting like this in Barcelona, we were thinking of barricades then, of fighting and death and revolution . . . Here, now, we are only waiting for a peaceful May Day demonstration, yet I am more strongly and deeply moved by this moment than I was then. There, I tingled with an excitement, I tingled at the thought of the shooting and the danger. I was moved too with pride at the thought of sharing in those moments . . . but mostly it was the excitement of watching a scene in a theatre, mostly I felt as a spectator. Here, now, I am conscious of my own people (the workers are my own people everywhere, but that fact does not contradict this), I am conscious of the dear familiarity of these surroundings and the deep meaning for my own life in this scene. I know too that we are setting out on a road whose inevitable end will be a moment when we stand with guns in our hands and thinking the thoughts of death and revolution.

Now I am quiet, I am serene. I sink my identity into the calm quietness of this waiting crowd, I am part of it, sharer in its strength . . . and the solution of my conflicts is bound up with the fate of this mass.

He leaned against the lamppost, rolling a cigarette, meditating, quiet and inconspicuous in the crowd.

The word went around that the demonstration was coming. There was a slight stirring movement, a subtle change came over everybody. There was hardly any outward alteration, the men still stood waiting, hands in pockets, faces considering under caps. The buzz of talk hardly altered its note. But there was a change, a tightening of tension.

Then the air bore to them the faint and distant sound of the 'International', a few wind-tattered fragmentary notes, and this was the signal for the discharge of the strain between the two masses: a current of excitement suddenly leaped between the marchers and the waiting crowd like an electric spark snapping between two highly charged terminals. There was a sudden, confused swirling movement, in which no one was conscious of the part they played but all found themselves being swept forward towards the road.

The sound of the singing grew louder; they could hear the

hollow echo of the voices booming down the street. Then the cycle detachment rode in and dismounted, and behind them came the head of the demonstration and a waving confusion of banners. The rising clamour of thousands of voices resolved itself into cheering. The two masses merged together, all singing the 'International'.

The marchers broke their ranks to rest. Banners were leaned against walls. The road was suddenly clear. A mounted policeman's horse deposited a small neat pile of dung on the smooth, empty tar surface.

* * * * *

At Langfier's, in the big machine shop, the loose belt went on with its interminable flap . . . flap . . . flap . . . setting an irritating, despondent rhythm to whose beat the girls continually found their thoughts going.

The morning shift was half through. This was the time when everyone settled down to their work like runners in a cross-country race who had got their second wind and adapted themselves to a steady, easy pace. This was the time when everyone worked best, when they shared most in the life of the factory. Early morning thoughts that yearned back to the dishevelled warmth of beds, thoughts of hastily gulped last cups of tea, of the bright early-morning streets and the sense of weariness and oppression that dwelt amongst the gloomy aisles of the clocking-in machines, had gradually been dissolved away by the reiterated movements of their work. Now it was yet too early to start looking forward to the dinner hour, while release from work and the evening's occupations were altogether too far away to seem real. It was at this time that the work went best, fitting together harmoniously. Sometimes it was even possible to get a sense of pleasure from the most monotonous of their operations, when the whole work of the department seemed to fall into a steady swing and each was conscious of a task, hated and senseless in itself, being part of a process, so that there was a kind of strange numbing beauty in the rhythm of the work.

But that was before the time of the speed-up. Now it was almost impossible for the department to function as a whole. Sometimes, for a second, it nearly happened, but the moment faded before it had quite materialized. On the very best of days there was too much rush and hurry.

Also, even before, when things had been better, there were the times when everything went wrong, when instead of all the different parts of the work coming together like the instruments of an orchestra, a positive anarchy reigned, when everyone's nerves got on edge, when quarrels and accidents easily happened, and everything went at different speeds so that one part of the work was struggling to catch up with the other, one process tripping over the heels of its successor.

This morning was notable. Everything went wrong – lathes chattered and spoiled work, people were kept waiting for supplies, drills broke, machines got out of adjustment . . . and all the time the loose belt went on with its dismal complaint, setting a note for everyone's irritation.

A row of drilling machines that prepared the carbon brush blocks for the contact screws stood idle: a breakdown yesterday had slowed down the previous process and there was a temporary shortage of blocks. The girls hung about, most of them talking irritably about their lost time for which they would not be paid. But a couple were laughing together, setting up a prolonged, high-pitched cachinnation, a shrill, noisy duet for which the two of them had achieved a notoriety.

A mechanic was going by burdened with tools, his face greasy and sweating, looking bad tempered. 'You at it again?' he said to them. 'Can't you laugh like human beings?'

'When I say worm, crawl in,' Ruby Hoskins called after him and giggled. She was a dark, sprightly little girl with remarkably well-developed breasts. She wasn't bad looking, though she spoiled her appearance by a thick crust of cheap make-up. Mabel, her mate, a willowy fresh-complexioned blonde, with a tender, sensual mouth, admired Ruby immensely for her wit and worldly wisdom. They were both very young, irresponsible and rowdy. Ruby was a naturally vicious little creature and a bad influence on Mabel, whose sensual innocence was rapidly becoming corrupted by her really filthy talk.

At the moment they were apart from the others, who were letting off about their lost time. Their heads came together and whispered, then they separated with a mutual shriek of laughter. 'Cut it out, you two, can't you?' someone shouted at them. 'Gets on my nerves that bloody row of yours does.'

'All right,' said Ruby coolly. 'Don't get out of your pram.'

That was a brilliant reply. Mabel was convulsed. She rocked helplessly to and fro. The floor was greasy with oil and graphite dust and she slipped over backwards.

Her head struck a piece of shafting that wasn't properly guarded. Her cap was snatched off and whirled along a belt, her hair and scalp following it, winding around the pulley.

In the startled silence after her piercing scream the noise of the machines seemed tremendous.

The loose belt flapped steadily, then stopped. All the machines stopped, and there was only a loud, angry, horror-stricken babble of voices.

* * * * *

In the hydraulic-press room they were suddenly aware that the machines above had stopped, and they all unconsciously looked up. 'What's happened?' they said.

Then their machines went dead: the power had been cut off; everything stopped.

The silence was strange, dangerous. The men looked at each other, their glances full of unformulated thoughts.

'Something's up,' said Bill Riley.

There was an urgent sound of running feet. Eyes looked towards the door. They waited while the sound came nearer.

Then George Haines, who had been put forward for the works committee as the electrician's representative, burst in.

'A girl's been killed up in the big shop,' he shouted. 'She was scalped. I cut off the power.'

He suddenly stopped, his excitement cut short. He looked at Millman in an embarrassed way, while the men all gathered around.

They were looking expectantly at Millman. He knew that they were waiting for him to tell them what to do, and he hesitated. For an instant he was stricken with uncertainty. 'We ought to call a meeting of the committee,' he said slowly. 'Course, they're not properly elected yet . . .'

He was crushingly aware that he was being weak; the thought of his responsibility overwhelmed him. He saw the chaps looking at him, waiting, and he thought of the mass of the workers in the factory, all looking at him, all demanding with their eyes that he should give them a lead. And there was only a moment in which to decide, a moment in which to weigh up everything and give an irrevocable decision that might lead to disaster. In a second those eyes would be looking elsewhere. He could not afford that he, the Communist, should not lead this mass.

'Never mind waiting for a bloody meeting,' said Bill Riley suddenly stepping forward. 'Call 'em all out into the yard and we'll 'ave a meeting of the 'ole blasted factory.'

Millman suddenly let out a deep breath as if he had been relieved of a heavy burden, of the weight of all those glances resting on him. It was not of himself he had been thinking so much, but of the Party. If Bill or Ivy gave the right lead it was as good as if he had done it. He saw them all look at Bill. Bill was strong, cool, determined. They all looked at him and shared in his strength and determination.

'Come on!' he shouted. 'We'll call 'em all out into the yard.'

And he turned and ran upstairs, the rest following him. Meek, the works manager, stood at his office window watching them streaming out into the yard, hearing their voices coming up to him in an angry babble.

I ought to go down, he told himself, but he hesitated.

He felt frightened and tried to persuade himself that it was best for him to keep out of the way for a while. There was an ugly sound in those voices; it wasn't any particular threat of violence that frightened him but the strength of them all together. He stepped back from the window out of sight from below and stood tugging at his straggling moustache.

This moment was bound to come, he thought. He had shrunk away from imagining it for years, but he had always known that it would come. For years he had heard the angry sound in their voices, for years he had known their hate of him, but it had never happened before like this, with them all together in a mass. He felt a childish weak anger at his helplessness.

'Get me Sir Edwin Langfier immediately,' Dartry shouted into the 'phone. He had a fantastic idea that someone might cut the wires before he got through. 'And get on to the police directly. Put the call through to Mr Meek.'

He bit his nails furiously while he waited, shaken with anger, his heart beating heavily as he tried to keep a tight hold upon himself. He swore to himself, saying every filthy word he could think of over and over again. Suddenly he was conscious of his pounding heart. One day I'll get a stroke, he

said to himself. He had never thought of it before. It upset
him terribly.

* * * * *

Peter answered the 'phone. 'I'll get my father,' he said. He
heard Dartry's voice buzzing angrily in the receiver. 'No,
don't wait to fetch him. Ask him to come down here as
quickly as possible, it's very urgent. There's been an accident,
and the hands have stopped work. They're in a nasty mood.'

He heard the angry click of the receiver being banged
down, and he went to fetch his father.

When he told him, he said, 'I expected this,' and shut his
mouth tightly. Peter could see the end of his beard trembling
a little. He was shocked to notice how old and ill he was looking, and a warm unreasoning wave of sympathy swept over
him. 'I'll come with you,' he said. Langfier said 'Thanks,'
very shortly, his voice rather unsteady. 'Go and get Henry,'
he said. 'Tell him to hurry, I'll wait at the front door.'

* * * * *

By now over twenty thousand workers were on the march.
Six of the main contingents had started. From the east,
north, north-west, west, south-west and south-east they con-
verged towards Hyde Park, six rivers fed by innumerable
tributaries.

All the normal police beats and traffic-control posts
were taken over by the specials. Two big marquees had
been put up in the park for the police to have tea in. A wireless station was working at the top of the Marble Arch in
communication with the gyroplanes and the motor police.
A number of Guards companies were standing by on duty
at the barracks. Every available St John Ambulance man
was mobilized.

The workers had provided their own first-aid corps, including six cars, one with each contingent, and a lorry fitted up by a group of Communist doctors and students with an operating table, anaesthetics and a flashlight photographic apparatus. Workers taken up by official ambulances after any trouble usually found themselves handed over to the police. Everyone had been warned of this.

The police were not expecting any disorder, except in connection with scab buses, of which a few were running. They were instructed that they were to take every step to prevent any demonstrators from coming into contact with them and that the contingents should be kept strictly to their prearranged routes.

* * * * *

Pat put his pipe down and began to read. As he went on a warm flush spread over his face. He was angry, but it wasn't only anger that moved him, he experienced a feeling of shame, almost of embarrassment. Certain phrases, certain sentences repeated themselves in his mind and gave him a baffled, shamed sensation because he couldn't immediately do something to refute them.

He handed the typescript to Vernon. 'Sloane's May Day leader,' he said. 'It's just a little bit too thick.'

He watched Vernon's face while he was reading it, searching in the lines of its features for a reflection of his own feelings.

The refusal of the *Daily Mail* men to print a similar article had been the vanguard action of the General Strike. Things were different now, he thought, but not so very different . . .

'Sounds 's if Sloane'd written it himself,' said Pat as Vernon put it down.

'Remember the *Mail* article in 1926?'

'Sure . . . I was thinking about it.'

'What d'you think . . . ?'

Pat looked around quickly and unobtrusively to see if anyone was in hearing. 'Old Jackson's a good chap.' (Jackson was Father of the Printers' Chapel.) 'I've had a few talks with him.'

'The chaps like you, don't they?'

'I s'pose so.'

'What would happen if you went and showed it to Jackson and asked him what he thought?'

'Can't say. I don't mind trying though.'

'It's worth it. I can have a talk with some of the fellows here.'

'OK,' said Pat and walked away.

Vernon looked at his watch and then at Pat's retreating back. Good old Pat, he said to himself.

The noise of typewriters, tape machines and telephone bells fell unnoticed on Pat's ears as he walked down the long corridor. He was thinking of the workers marching. Already the main contingents will have started, he thought. All over the world today they have started marching through the streets, our slogans echoing in every language. It had been fine walking to the office and seeing no buses running, seeing the procession of office workers filing along the pavements. It's being a good May Day, he said to himself. But how he hated having to go in to work while they were marching through the streets . . .

Then his mind went back to Sloane's article, and anger stirred in him again. He thought of what he would have to say to Jackson. He'd have to be careful, take his cue from him as much as possible.

Now he was out of hearing of the typewriters and the telephones, the sound of the printing-machines grew louder, and he could smell the warm oiliness of their breath. The midday sports edition was being run off. Only a few of the machines were working yet, the men were slack, standing around chatting. They smiled at him, they all liked him, and now he was warmed and encouraged by their looks.

He found Jackson gloomily regarding a pile of stereos. 'Morning, Mr Morgan,' he said. 'And what can I do for you?'

'Can you spare a moment,' Pat said, and Jackson knew that something was up from his tone. 'Take a look at that,' said Pat. 'Sloane's May Day effort.' He handed the article to him and stood fidgeting with impatience.

Jackson got out a pair of old silver-rimmed spectacles, wiped them deliberately on a clean handkerchief and put them on his nose. He was a stout, oldish man, with a rugged face and big white whiskers under a bulbous reddish nose; he had the sort of face, with such pronounced features and a strong expression of its own, that it was impossible to tell what he was thinking.

'Well,' said Pat. 'How d'you like it?'

They looked at each other searchingly, a sudden penetrating look. They were men who knew each other well by routine, who were hardly acquaintances yet who had been in contact every day for a long time and were thoroughly familiar with one another's appearance and superficial habits. They looked into each other's eyes, and the moment suddenly transformed their relationship as each tried deeply to pierce into the other's inmost thoughts.

'It's a bloody provocation,' said Pat.

'Mmm,' said Jackson slowly, 'we know what Sloane stands for.'

'Yes, we know what he stands for. But it's not often that he says it so plainly. And it's workers, trade unionists, who've got to print it.'

There was a pause. Jackson took off his spectacles and began to put them into a worn aluminium case very deliberately. Then he suddenly snapped it shut and said, 'You and I needn't beat about the bush, Mr Morgan. We understand each other. I know your views and though they're not quite the same as mine I sympathize with 'em . . . You remember the *Mail* article before the General Strike.'

'Yes,' said Pat very quickly. 'I was thinking about it.'

'Well, I was one of the men there . . . this article's just the same sort of thing. It would be a grand thing for the trade-union movement if we could refuse to print it. But this isn't May Day 1926.'

'No, no. I understand that all right. But the situation isn't so very different – and things are moving pretty quickly –'

'There's more 'n an hour before your leader-page make-up's got to be in. I'll talk to the men about it. And we'll all forget that you came down here.'

He put his spectacle case into his breast pocket with an air of finality. There was a certain dignity and power about him. It was quite plain that there was no use trying to carry on the discussion. There were a lot more things that Pat wanted to say, but he realized it was no use; whatever happened depended on Jackson, and the old chap would act honestly according to his views.

Pat walked away quickly.

* * * * *

Langfier's car went fast through the half-empty streets.

'I knew something like this would happen,' said Langfier. 'They've turned the factory into an absolute death trap. I knew something like this would happen . . .' He repeated it with almost a querulous note in his voice.

Peter looked searchingly at his father, studying him as if he was a stranger. He's suddenly got old, he thought, and he's looking so ill. The usually neat beard was ruffled, and there were dark purplish pouches under his eyes. He had a kind of dry, withered air about him, something a little repulsive. Peter felt his sympathy turning into a disinterested feeling, the sympathy of a stranger for some poor old man.

'It's funny seeing no buses,' said Peter, trying to make conversation.

'Mmm . . . the May Day strike . . . You know, I can understand why they do it. I like the working class . . . but when they are together in a mass something gets into them, they become quite different, frightening somehow. Don't you ever feel that?' he asked abruptly in a different tone.

'I'm just repelled by *any* large mass of people,' said Peter. 'It's a kind of agoraphobia with me.'

'Well, you'll see today. You'll learn something. If that swine Dartry thinks he can get me to try and pacify them, he's mistaken,' Langfier suddenly burst out. 'He can get himself out of his own mess!'

He really is behaving oddly, thought Peter, regarding the impassive back of Henry, the chauffeur. I wonder what old Henry will feel about all this, he thought, and he tried to picture for himself what was going on at the factory now.

'What are you going to do eventually?' his father said.

'How d'you mean – eventually?'

'Have you decided on a career for yourself?'

'Well – I've always wanted to write – critical stuff, you know.' There wasn't much conviction in his voice.

'Our money hasn't done us much good. The factory's a millstone round my neck now. And you – you really haven't any idea what to do with your life –'

'Well, I wouldn't say that –'

'If you'd had to earn a living, if you had known all along that you'd have to go out into the world and fight to keep yourself you would probably be much happier and more certain now. And you would be able to have an illusion – everything that interfered with your desires, all the dreams you couldn't fulfil you would be able to put down to a lack

224

of money. Life is disappointing, and it's best if we can fool ourselves that the reason isn't the nature of life itself but it's due to something we haven't attained and that is yet possible. But you'll have to get yourself some other illusion to keep your sanity. Even if we are ruined you won't be able to believe that it's only lack of means that prevents you being happy.'

How could Peter reply. He didn't really understand what his father was talking about. He would have liked to be able to say something that showed he was speaking from his heart, as his father was speaking, but some inhibition prevented him and made him dislike himself for his lack of sympathy. He wanted to show him that he was ready to give him sympathy and also to accept it from him, and he couldn't.

Now they were at the factory. A long blank wall, covered with chalked slogans, hid the river, along whose banks were drawn up a regiment of smokestacks that fountained dark, rolling smokes into the air. The scene was strange and repulsive to Peter. They went straight into Dartry's office.

'This is my son,' said Langfier in a cold voice.

'Terrible business this,' said Dartry briskly. 'The situation is rather difficult. They seem to have elected some sort of committee. They're all out in the yard having a meeting. I have made no move yet beyond calling in the police.'

'What exactly has happened?'

'A girl slipped and was injured on some shafting. It caught her hair and scalped her. Some fool cut off the power, and they all stopped work and trooped out into the yard –'

'How is the girl?'

'They've taken her off to hospital. It's likely that she will recover. I'm not sure what action the hands are contemplating. The trouble is that some Communist elements have been busy here lately, and they will probably try and use this accident as an excuse for stirring up a strike.'

'And you want me to speak to the workers – is that it?' Langfier's voice was hard and contained. He had become a different person since they had entered the factory.

'Yes,' said Dartry. 'To be frank with you they wouldn't listen to me or any of the staff here. We're not exactly popular. But you . . .'

'I should like you to understand that I consider your policy here to be responsible for the whole of this situation, and I haven't the least intention of helping you out of it.'

Dartry flushed angrily. 'That's an extraordinary attitude to take up. Whatever my policy may or may not be responsible for, your interests are concerned now, and –'

'My only interest in the factory now is how quickly I can get it off my hands.'

'In that case I will not trouble you. But I must say, your choice of a moment in which to rid yourself of your responsibilities –'

'I am not interested in your personal opinions, Mr Dartry.'

Langfier turned to go. Peter was thinking of the girl, of the accident. It filled him with an acute sense of nausea, of physical discomfort. He shut his ears to the argument, despising it. Automatically he followed his father out of the room.

Dartry strode heavily across to the other door, that opened into the boardroom, where the departmental heads were gathered, standing about or sitting in awkward attitudes.

'Well, gentlemen,' Dartry began. 'I have just been interviewing Sir Edwin Langfier. He is of my opinion that we should leave the first steps to the workers. The longer they wait for something definite from us the more likely it is that they will come to their senses. You all understand the importance of averting any trouble at the moment when we have so much on hand, and I have every reason to believe that you will stand by the management loyally in any crisis that may arise.'

There were mutters of 'hear, hear'.

'I must say,' began Meek, caressing his thin moustache, 'I can't see what else they can do but come to their senses if we leave them. They will probably be sending in some kind of deputation sooner or later. But there's no issue upon which they can strike. Of course, the unfortunate girl will be compensated, although I do not consider we have any legal responsibility. But this seems to be the only cause of this – upset.'

'I am afraid,' Dartry replied, 'that there have been Communist elements at work here. I have definite information to that effect. There is no doubt that they will use every effort to make this accident an excuse to stir up trouble. These people must be removed. I should like all you gentlemen to be very alert for the least sign of them. And now I think that the best thing is for you all to return to your departments and carry on with what work you can. I have no doubt that this matter will be settled shortly. Will you stay behind, Mr Meek.'

When the others had gone out Dartry turned to Meek. 'I think Langfier is out of his mind. He has taken up the most extraordinary attitude, refuses to do anything. We are going to be in a mess.'

'You think that they'll strike?'

'I'm afraid so . . . I knew this was coming. It wouldn't have mattered in ten days' time when we'd got these blasted Vickers' orders out of the way. But this damned accident has set them off too soon. You know, they had a meeting to elect a works committee yesterday.'

They walked over to the window and looked out. They both stood to one side, Dartry chewing his nails, not wanting to be seen from the yard. Each was conscious of a baffled, humiliating feeling of impotence and anger, that the only thing they could do was to stand here helplessly peering from the shade of the curtains and waiting the will of the workers.

* * * * *

Down in the yard they were standing about talking animatedly, waiting for the committee who were meeting in the foremen's mess room.

Someone saw Langfier hesitating at the entrance of the main machine shop and began to hiss. It was taken up by everyone. There was no sort of outburst of indignation or anger, the hostility was cold and controlled and very deadly. Langfier turned blindly and stumbled back through the door.

'He looks all broken up,' Tom Rundall said.

'Yeh,' said his mate. 'Cuts 'im to the 'eart, I dare say, it does to fink of the money 'e's losin' while we're out 'ere.'

They blame me for it, Langfier said to himself. They see me behind all the accidents, the cause of all their hardships.

Without noticing where he was going he walked on automatically, Peter following him. They passed through the worn swing doors of the big shop and stood inside, looking down the long rows of the stilled machines. Everything had a dead, deserted appearance.

There were pools of blood on the floor. In places it was mixed into the oil and graphite dust, trodden into a brownish mud.

Langfier understood the impulse that had directed his unconscious footsteps here, the desire to experience the full range of his suffering.

The shafting was wound with long blonde hairs. A tangle of blood and hair was wedged between the belt and the pulley-wheel. Thin slanting rays of sunshine caught some of the hairs and made them glisten.

Peter thought of her. Perhaps she had been beautiful, a young girl who may have been looking forward to seeing a lover that evening . . . He went deadly pale. 'I think I'm going to be sick,' he said in a subdued voice.

* * * * *

In the yard there was a sudden excited stir. The committee emerged, walking close together in a little group. When they stopped everyone crowded around them. The loose, drifting mass clotted, shrank and became a dense crowd.

Millman got up on to a packing-case and began to speak. His voice was clear, not very loud but distinct. He talked without any mannerisms.

'Fellow workers,' he began. 'The committee have come to some decisions. There's no time nor no need to make speeches. I'm just going to read out the decisions and ask for you to vote on them.'

He fished a notebook from his pocket and began to read.

'One. The management should recognize the works committee as the accredited representatives of the workers and conduct all future negotiations in regard to working conditions and rates of pay with them.

'Two. That an agreement between the committee and the management should be drawn up, covering working conditions, safety precautions and a unified wage scale with definite minimum weekly rates. That this agreement should be ratified by mass meetings of all the shifts.

'Three. The management must recognize the right of the workers in all departments to belong to their respective trade unions, and the works committee should include union representatives. Also, a clause must go into the agreement making victimization impossible.

'In order to make these demands effective we suggest that there should be no return to work today, that we come in tomorrow, but in the event of no agreement being reached by the end of the week a vote should be taken for strike action. The committee pledges itself to do its utmost to recruit for the unions in the next few days and to prepare the necessary machinery for possible strike action.

'I'm going to submit these proposals right away, I don't think there can be any argument about them. All in favour.'

Almost simultaneously, like a salute, a forest of hands shot up.

'Any against?'

The crowd stirred a little, standing on tiptoe and looking around them. No one voted.

'Carried unanimously. That's fine,' he said, suddenly dropping his official tone. 'Now there's a further proposal that we've decided to put separately, as we're not certain what you'll think about it. I'm going to ask Ivy Cutford to put it to the meeting.'

There was a burst of cheering as Ivy got up.

Millman's proposals had been greeted with applause, the excitement was growing all the time. It was quite a while before Ivy could speak; she stood waiting, a little awkwardly, not knowing when to begin.

'Fellow workers,' she said, her voice rather shrill and unsteady at first but gathering strength and confidence as she went on. 'Today is May Day. It's a day when our class demonstrates against the bosses all over the world. We know about the busmen and the other strikes, in some places there's a general strike and everything's stopped for today while the workers are marching in the streets. Well, we've come out today too, against our rotten conditions and to revenge poor Mabel. And now we're out I think our place is along with the others in the demonstration. I know the papers say it's all a stunt of the Communists to stir up trouble. But I know too that the men and women who are marching to the park now are the same as us – workers, workers protesting against their bad conditions, just as we are, and marching to demand that things should be better, that there should be a change. There *is* a big change needed and it's only our class that'll make it. I'd like to say a lot more, but time's short, and I'm not used to speaking. I'm going to ask Alf Millman to put it to the vote for us to join in with the others and march to the park.'

Millman got up again. 'You've heard what Ivy said. The demonstration's on the way now. If we look sharp we can join up with the East London marchers as they come near here. Who's for coming out into the streets and showing the bosses that we can fight them?'

There was a great shout. The anger and excitement of the workers suddenly gathered together and exploded into an outburst of enthusiasm. Millman tried to say something, but he couldn't make himself heard. He bent down to Bill Riley and said, 'Get a bike and go like hell. Tell Wilson what's happened, and get him to make a turn off down Lancaster Street – they can come right past the gates and we can fall in behind them.'

* * * * *

While they were cheering and shouting Tom Rundall was thinking about his wife, how he had left her in the hospital, pale and weak, with a strange proud look on her face. The baby somehow wasn't quite real to him yet. But to think that there was a new living creature in the world . . . it was amazing. Yet also it was quite ordinary, it was something that went on all the time. But everything today was extraordinary. Here he was, suddenly a father, full of pride and tenderness. And he had come along to the works in an exalted frame of mind, struggling to fit himself to the ordinary tempo of his life and job, and then the machines had stopped, everything had stopped, and they all streamed out into the yard.

He had listened to the speeches and shouted with the others, he had thrust up his hand and voted passionately, he had shouted for them to come out and march, he was altogether caught up in their fighting mood, while at the same time the other, the tender, wondering thoughts were going on inside him, as if he was two different people, as if his mind was thinking for two separate lives.

Soon they'd be marching out through the factory gates, soon they'd be demonstrating through the streets. Theirs was a fighting mood, an angry fighting spirit that made them strong and conscious of their strength all together.

For a moment Tom's mind dwelt on that poor girl who had been so full of life, who had been charged with hope and eagerness an hour ago, and now lay mangled and perhaps dying in hospital. It wasn't so long ago since she had been a little squirming bundle of just living flesh, an odd little semi-human creature like his son, and then quite quickly, terribly quickly, she had grown up and been immolated in the factory, suddenly torn and mangled in the machines that also had slowly been eating up her youth.

It was right that they had stopped the machines, it was right that they had come out on strike.

And then he suddenly thought about the money. He had a son now, he had responsibilities. He was for fighting against the bosses, he was ready to suffer and go short in order to fight. But there were two other lives altogether dependent on him now . . . what would happen to them if he were to lose his job . . . but also, it was for their sake that he had to fight for better conditions. He didn't want to see his son grow up and wear away his youth in factory servitude without a chance in life, he wanted something better for him, and he would have to fight the bosses to get it. His enthusiasm was chilled, he was unhappy, he didn't know what to think . . .

* * * * *

The ranks of the marchers conducted the news of the strike like wire conducting an electric message. 'D'you hear?' said the chap next to James. 'Langfier's 'ave come out, and they're going to march with us.'

'Yes,' said another, 'they're going to fall in behind. They've only just come out.'

Another strike, thought James excitedly, imagining rows of stilled machines, factories stricken dead. 'Bloody fine, isn't it,' he said.

'See here,' said Wilson, the Chief Marshal, to Bill Riley. 'You nip back on your bike and tell 'em to get ready, fix up some marshals and everything, so that they can march straight out after us. We may have a bit of trouble turning off the route, and if we do we'll break up and re-form by the gates. The important thing is to get 'em ready to come straight out.'

Wilson was a huge redheaded chap, with a strong, rather brutal face. He watched Bill riding off and thought hard. He had about ten minutes in which to fix things up. It would take some time passing the word right down the ranks.

He stopped casually and let one of the Dagenham marshals catch him up. 'Look here,' he said. 'The best thing we can do to get to Langfier's is to turn off sharp at Lancaster Road. They may try and stop us, and we don't want a scrap now if we can avoid it, so if anything develops I'll blow the whistle three times to break up. We'll get down to the gates as fast as we can, and I'll give two blasts as the signal to form up. Pass it along and see that the Party members know so they can rally the others.'

James was in one of the rear sections. He saw the marshals

stopping and talking to each other, passing a message back, and then the comrade in charge of their section walked beside some of the Party members for a while talking earnestly to them. There's something up, he thought. I suppose it's arrangements for picking up the strikers.

The demonstration was over a mile long. When the head suddenly turned sharply around into Lancaster Road the police were taken by surprise. They had strict orders to keep them to the prearranged route, and they were flustered. The mounteds in front found themselves going on alone. They wheeled their horses around and galloped back, cutting through the column that was turning the corner. The band in front suddenly stopped in the middle of a phrase. Then a whistle blew three times and was repeated all down the different sections. 'That's for us to break up, comrades,' shouted a chap behind James. 'Stick with me and keep tight together. We're to form up again when the whistle blows.' And they all began to run forward, holding close together.

The police couldn't do anything directly, so they got down side streets and tried to form a cordon across the end of Lancaster Road, by the factory gates. There wasn't time for many of them to get there before the first lot of demonstrators arrived. The mounteds were going hard down the side streets and hundreds of cops were running along the pavements. About fifty or sixty managed to string themselves across the end of the road before the marchers arrived and then the first lot came, going fast, the banner-bearers amongst them, their jogging poles sloped forward like spears. They smashed straight into the cordon and broke through, driven by the impetus of the mass behind them. Two fellows shot forward ahead towards the gates, which the police were shutting. One got knocked down but the other got through inside.

Then the mounteds arrived from a side street, their horses trotting, the long batons swinging from their wrists.

In front, where they had broken through the cordon,

the crowd was loose and spaced out. The mounteds rode amongst them and strung themselves out across the road, and immediately a lot more police reinforced them. Another cordon was formed in front of the gates. About five hundred demonstrators were cut off between the two cordons. The front of the main section halted.

There was a moment's pause. The horses reared, the marchers stood panting and wiping sweat from their faces. As more people arrived they packed tightly together in front of an open space facing the mounted police.

Where James was they were just turning the corner into Lancaster Road. They were still more or less in a loose formation. As the vanguard halted the mass began to shrink together, spreading over on to the pavements and right across the road, so that while the front stood still the rear was still running forward and gradually slowing and spreading outwards.

In a few moments the whole demonstration was in Lancaster Road, those right at the rear still going at the double. Then they had to slow to a walk, it began to be difficult to move. The space between the cordon and the front ranks gradually lessened as they found themselves irresistibly being pushed forward right under the horses' heads.

The movement of the crowd was like a breaking ice floe with a strong current running underneath.

As yet they were irresolute, no one quite knew what was happening except those in the very front.

Then they heard the workers banging on the factory gates, trying to get out. There were screams from some of the girls as they were swept forward in a rush to the gates.

'Let 'em out!' someone shouted. 'Let 'em out.' The shout was taken up. A dull angry roar spread outwards through the crowd, inarticulate and unindividual, like a wave, breaking out into hoots and hisses. The workers inside heard them and shouted back, banging harder at the gates.

'This is no bloody good,' said Millman. 'We want a battering-ram.'

'Get something for a battering-ram,' they shouted. 'We'll smash the bloody gate down.'

John and Jock ran off to their workshop. 'We've got some old flooring joists somewhere,' panted John. 'And there's some new four-by-four that'll do fine,' yelled Jock after him excitedly. 'Won't ole Peter be fed up 'e's missed this.' Jock was all worked up.

They grabbed some long pieces of thick timber and rushed back with them, forcing a way through the crowd to the gates.

Outside they suddenly heard a much louder banging and could see the big door shivering under the blows. They began to cheer and push forward more.

The police didn't know quite what to do, the mass was too tightly jammed together for them to clear it now. About seven thousand of them were packed into the lower end of Lancaster Road. Only at the front, behind the cordon of three hundred police who were strung across the road in files of fifty with arms linked, was there any open space to be seen.

At the back they had taken up the shouting, though they didn't know what it was about. Somehow James managed to worm his way right forward. He was trembling with a cold joyous fighting anger.

Suddenly the situation began to develop very quickly. With a tremendous crash the gates burst open, and John and Jock, holding on to their battering-ram, with half a dozen chaps hanging on at the back, staggered forward, borne along by the force of their own blow and the rush of the workers behind them. They broke through the cordon around the gate and a general fight developed. The crowd at the other side surged forward, and at the same moment a regiment of mounteds galloped out of a side street, their batons swinging. They rode straight into the crowd, who couldn't get out of their way. They tried to scatter, and the other police were amongst them, hitting out furiously and dragging people away. James stumbled, fell and got up. There was a little space around him. He could hear the horses' hoofs clattering hard on the pavements. There was blood on his face, he didn't know how it had got there.

For the moment the police were having it their own way. The space around James grew larger. The workers were struggling to open out in front of the horses. Then they burst forward around them, through the cordon, overflowing along the pavements like water in a torrent parting around a great rock.

James heard a tremendous shout as the factory workers burst through the gates. He looked around and saw John staggering through a fighting mass of police and workers, clearing a way with his battering-ram. 'John! John!' he yelled frantically and began to run towards him.

Two cops tried to stop him. He tripped one and the other came down over him. He felt something give under his foot, an arm breaking or something, as he dashed forward.

John saw him. 'Jimmy,' he shouted. 'Look out!'

James half-turned, saw right above him the red beefy face of a mounted policeman, his mouth open in a fierce grin, his baton raised, the horse's head so near that he smelled its breath as he tried to duck.

The baton came down on the side of his head. In the split second in which he knew it was going to hit him he thought of the girl of last night, a laughing mouth fluttering to tenderness under his lips, and then something huge and hard seemed to collide with him, and he felt himself falling, very slowly, the image of the horse's teeth and spread nostrils before his eyes, and the ground swinging up to meet him and frenzied hoofs kicking against the sky and everything fading and dwindling away, and then the hoof came down smash on the back of his head and the world exploded into a scarlet oblivion. Warm blood ran from his nose, and his brains littered the road.

* * * * *

The top of the Marble Arch is a nerve centre for electric messages. Here sound voices from police cars and aeroplanes and 'phone boxes. The police chiefs stand like officers on the bridge of a battleship going into action. From this spot they can shake a tangled skein of copper wire strung underground and overhead netting all London together.

General Fitzroy, Chief of Police, impatiently struts his cavalryman's walk up and down. From under a cap (like some superfine chauffeur's headdress – how he hates the livery of his job) his clear grey eyes stare at nothing. His face is lean, wrinkled with thousands of fine sundried creases like the surface of a scorched-up riverbed. His long narrow jaw munches the air under delicate rusty grey moustaches that support a hawk nose like wings. His appearance breathes an aristocratic militarism made fine and fragile by old age.

When the message came through from Lancaster Road he smiled for an instant, a cold smile, as he thought of ordering out a company of Guards with fixed bayonets. If only he was back in India . . . Then his lips compressed themselves. 'Get me the Home Office,' he said irritatedly to the 'phone operator. They won't let me use the Guards, he thought. There'll be nothing for it but to call off my men and let the marchers get on with it.

* * * * *

The ambulances speed through the streets bearing away the casualties from the scene of the fight. Some are brought to the hospital where Mabel is lying transfixed to the

238

chromium-and-steel pedestal of an operating table, breathing long snoring chloroform breaths while doctors and nurses clean and probe her wounds.

* * * * *

Out of the confusion of jostling bodies and hard blows the East London contingent and the Langfier strikers have organized themselves into fours and marched off behind the torn banners, their ranks held tight together with a fighting anger.

The police have been withdrawn. The marchers have won the streets.

The blood is still running fast in their veins, they feel heroes, still filled with the sharp joy and anger of fighting. They feel something strong within them, something huge and strong, an emotion that transcends their separate individualities and joins them into a single conscious mass.

Men and women who have never marched in a demonstration before are becoming revolutionaries in the course of a few hours.

Outside the factory the blood is drying on the road; the gates lie splintered on the ground. Within it is silent, the furnaces drawn, the machines dead. The sound of typewriters in the office echoes emptily, like the noise of rats gnawing the boards in an empty house.

* * * * *

The tape machines spell out their story: 'EAST END DEMONSTRATORS INVOLVED WITH THE POLICE.' There has been an accident, some poor fellow has fallen and fractured his skull under a horse's hoofs.

But soon after Pat has read this and wondered at the truth he is standing at the office window and seeing the broken banners, the body borne at their head, seeing the ranks of marching workers filing through the narrow channel of Fleet Street and hearing their shouts ringing out.

Later he will know more, he will rejoice at a victory and mourn for the death of a friend. But now as he stands and watches he is caught up with the rhythm of the marching feet, he is filled with their strength and with gladness at the consciousness that he has thrown in his lot with their class and their party. For a long time he watches the faces going by, the thousands of faces, no two the same, yet each stamped with something indefinable that is common to them all and different from those who stand and watch them from behind windows.

And from the room above, Sloane sees them filing by and smiles, a twisted smile. 'I'm waiting for the tumbrils,' he says to Matheison, his editor.

'Not this time,' says Matheison. 'But I don't like it.'

'Let them have their shout,' says Sloane. 'Put 'em in khaki and have a different sort of band at their head and they'll go off singing "It's a long way to Tipperary" with equal zest and discordance. It's easy enough to put a stop to *this* kind of thing when it gets dangerous. This business of the printers is much more serious. They need another lesson like they had in 1926.'

* * * * *

The Marble Arch is islanded in a dark sea of caps in whose midst slowly move forward the red sails of banners. For two hours the contingents have been marching in.

Last of all come the East London marchers, the band playing slowly, a revolutionary song to a funeral beat. The workers seethe around the base of the Arch like an angry sea, and the noise comes up to the men at the top like the sound of a storm as James's flag-draped body is held up and saluted by a hundred thousand clenched fists raised in the air, a hundred thousand shouts of 'Red Front'.

General Fitzroy turns to the Assistant Commissioner by his side. 'Well,' he says bitterly. 'How much longer will we have to stand by and watch this sort of thing going on? After today I don't think there'll be so much damned squeamish argument against arming the police.'

Everyone has agreed on the need for a big change.

POSTSCRIPT:
AUTHOR'S NOTE FOR THE 1984 EDITION

Novels written in early youth, however they may have seemed to the writer at the time, are best not looked at again in later life.

May Day was, in fact, written about half a century ago. But, when a new edition was suggested, I had to re-read it – I'd forgotten so much of the story and the people and the scenery.

It turned out to be not the sort of book I'd vaguely remembered it to be; and definitely not the book I'd intended it to be at the time of writing.

You don't have to be a social historian to realize how much the world has changed in the last fifty years – probably more than in any other comparable period. Of course, a lot of things have stayed the same. Not quite the same but nearly so. We still live in a class-structured society, but the divisions are less obvious and less extreme now; the under-privileged majority are not so under-privileged as they were and less resigned to the facts of their social inequality; also, most of the professional and middle classes don't have so much of what they used to have – in terms of social status as well as money. Only the truly rich and powerful can still carry on more or less as if nothing had really changed at all except for electronic improvements in the means of selling goods and bending minds.

When I wrote it I'd have probably said that *May Day* was socialist realism. Now I'd call it early '30s Communist romanticism. I'm not in any way apologizing for the book's enthusiastic, simple-minded political idealism. Because it was a genuine idealism. There was a lot of it about then. And there still is now, not in the same forms as before, but still alive and hopeful.

The material circumstances and social climate of every-day life in this country now would have seemed unbelievable to the people depicted in *May Day*. And whatever the book was *then* it has become an historical novel – worth reading *now*, I hope, in relation to our own times.

John Sommerfield
May 1984

LONDON BOOKS

FLYING THE FLAG FOR
FREE-THINKING LITERATURE

www.london-books.co.uk

PLEASE VISIT OUR WEBSITE FOR

- Current and forthcoming books
  - Author and title profiles
- A lively, interactive message board
  - Events and news
  - Secure on-line bookshop
  - Recommendations and links
- An alternative view of London literature

ON SALE NOW
All titles hardback / £11.99

THE GILT KID – JAMES CURTIS
Introduction by Paul Willetts
ISBN 978-0-9551851-2-0

NIGHT AND THE CITY – GERALD KERSH
Introduction by John King
ISBN 978-0-9551851-3-7

A START IN LIFE – ALAN SILLITOE
Introduction by DJ Taylor
ISBN 978-0-9551851-1-3

THEY DRIVE BY NIGHT – JAMES CURTIS
Introduction by Jonathan Meades
ISBN 978-0-9551851-4-4

WIDE BOYS NEVER WORK – ROBERT WESTERBY
Introduction by Iain Sinclair
ISBN 978-0-9551851-5-1

LONDON CLASSICS

THE GILT KID

JAMES CURTIS

The Gilt Kid is fresh out of prison, a burglar with communist sympathies who isn't thinking about rehabilitation. Society is unfair and he wants some cash in his pocket and a place to live, and he quickly lines up a couple of burglaries in the London suburbs. But complications arise, and he finds himself dodging the police, checking the newspapers and looking over his shoulder, fearing the ultimate punishment for a crime he hasn't committed. He remains defiant throughout, right up until the book's final, ironic conclusion.

James Curtis recreates the excitement of 1930s London as he delves into the sleazy glamour of the underworld mindset; a world of low-level criminals and prostitutes. His vibrant use of slang is as snappy as anything around today, his dialogue cosh-like as the Gilt Kid moves through the pubs and clubs and caffs of Soho. Curtis knew his subject matter, and this cult novel doubles as a powerful social observation.

This new edition comes with an introduction by Paul Willetts, author of *Fear And Loathing In Fitzrovia*, the best-selling biography of author Julian Maclaren-Ross, and an interview with Curtis's daughter, Nicolette Edwards.

London Books
£11.99 hardback
ISBN 978-0-9551851-2-0
www.london-books.co.uk

NIGHT AND THE CITY

GERALD KERSH

Harry Fabian is a cockney wide boy who will do anything for
a pound note; a storyteller who craves recognition, his endless
lies hiding a deeper, inner weakness. He is also a ponce, and
one who is walking on the edge. It is only a matter of time
before he topples over the side.

Set in 1930s London, against a fluorescent West End backdrop,
Night And The City brings the Soho of legend to life, the streets
a tangle of drinking dens and night-clubs, author Gerald Kersh's
characters flamboyant creations who add a cosmopolitan edge to
the book's journey into the darker shades of human nature.

Twice filmed, *Night And The City* remains a 'lowlife' classic,
and comes with an introduction by John King, author of
The Football Factory and *Human Punk*.

London Books
£11.99 hardback
ISBN 978-0-9551851-3-7
www.london-books.co.uk

WIDE BOYS NEVER WORK

ROBERT WESTERBY

Young Jim Bankley yearns to leave behind the production line
in a provincial town when he chances on a London razor-gang
at a local dog track. Seduced by the opportunity to live life on the
edge, he follows them back to London. He is thrown into a milieu
of bruisers, brasses, car dealers and con-merchants. Drenched
in sleaze and brutality, he begins to wonder if the simple
life is so bad after all.

Robert Westerby's 1937 novel provoked a stir at the time,
authentically lifting the lid on an underworld metropolis that
many pretended did not exist. It has lost none of its punch in the
ensuing 70 years – and slang historians generally credit Westerby
with coining the term wide boy. The book was filmed in 1956
under the name *Soho Incident*.

This new edition boasts a penetrative introduction from leading
London author and broadcaster Iain Sinclair, whose work
includes *London Orbital* and *London, City of Disappearances*. He
is a long-time champion of often overlooked vintage London
writers such as Westerby, James Curtis and Gerald Kersh.

London Books
£11.99 hardback
ISBN 978-0-9551851-5-1
www.london-books.co.uk